THAT WILL SHUT 'EM UP!

"I've heard the stories." Rick wagged his chin at the man in gray. "How many is it they say you've done in? Forty or fifty or some nonsense?"

"Saloon talk," Rondo James said.

Rick tilted his head and put a hand to his ear. "I don't hear you sayin' you're sorry."

"And you never will."

Rick eased his hand down to his revolver. "Last chance, Reb, to walk out of here breathin'."

"Rick, don't," Dorsey said.

"Shut the hell up!" Rick glanced at his pards for support.

"Any of you want to try him on for size?"

"It's your fight," a rough-looking cowhand said, "but we'll back your play."

"Did you hear that?" Rick said to the man in gray. "When you ride for the Bar H, you ride for the brand."

"A man can die for a brand, too."

"Enough of this," Rick spat. He went for his six-gun.

Dorsey saw it all. He saw Rondo James's hands flash and heard the boom of a pearl-handled Navy and Arn Richter was sent tumbling as if he had been kicked by a mule, a hole in his forehead spurting scarlet.

With a loud oath, the puncher on Rick's right clawed for his smoke wagon.

Rondo James shot him in the face.

THUNDER VALLEY

DAVID ROBBINS

A SIGNET BOOK

SIGNET
Published by New American Library, a division of
Penguin Group (USA) Inc., 375 Hudson Street,
New York, New York 10014, USA
Penguin Group (Canada), 90 Eglinton Avenue East, Suite 700, Toronto,
Ontario M4P 2Y3, Canada (a division of Pearson Penguin Canada Inc.)
Penguin Books Ltd., 80 Strand, London WC2R 0RL, England
Penguin Ireland, 25 St. Stephen's Green, Dublin 2,
Ireland (a division of Penguin Books Ltd.)
Penguin Group (Australia), 250 Camberwell Road, Camberwell, Victoria 3124,
Australia (a division of Pearson Australia Group Pty. Ltd.)
Penguin Books India Pvt. Ltd., 11 Community Centre, Panchsheel Park,
New Delhi - 110 017, India
Penguin Group (NZ), 67 Apollo Drive, Rosedale, Auckland 0632,
New Zealand (a division of Pearson New Zealand Ltd.)
Penguin Books (South Africa) (Pty.) Ltd., 24 Sturdee Avenue,
Rosebank, Johannesburg 2196, South Africa

Penguin Books Ltd., Registered Offices:
80 Strand, London WC2R 0RL, England

First published by Signet, an imprint of New American Library,
a division of Penguin Group (USA) Inc.

First Printing, April 2012
10 9 8 7 6 5 4 3 2 1

ALWAYS LEARNING   PEARSON

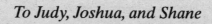

To Judy, Joshua, and Shane

1

The armpit of creation, some called it. There was a plank saloon with a room in the back for the owner to sleep in, an outhouse that on a windy day could spread stink a mile, and a chicken coop.

Three horses were dozing at the hitch rail when the rider trotted up and drew rein.

He was astride a grulla, his saddle as weatherworn as he was. Of middling height, he wore a brown shirt, brown pants and a brown coat with sleeves that were too short. His hat was frayed, his boots scuffed. Nothing about him was remarkable except his face. Long and narrow, it was marred by a deep scar that split his left cheek, and by an eye patch over his left eye.

Dismounting, he tied the reins off and strode into the saloon. He didn't push the batwings lightly. He slammed them open and marched to the bar and pounded it. "Tonsil varnish, and make it quick."

The bartender was a rake handle with a lower lip that

drooped. He took his time stepping to the shelf lined with bottles and he took his time finding a glass and he took his time pouring. "I don't take to being bossed around," he said as he set the glass down.

"Do I look like I give a good damn what you take to?" the man with the patch said. He swallowed the Monongahela in a gulp and barked, "Give me another, you turtle."

The bartender bristled. "I'll have you know my name is Hanks. I own this place. It's the only whiskey mill in a hundred miles so you'd better stop growlin' at me or you'll go thirsty."

The man with the patch moved his coat aside. High on his right hip was a holster and in the holster a Remington revolver with walnut grips. "You have any notion who I am, you peckerwood?"

"How the hell would I—" the bartender began, and stopped. He stared at the man's scarred face and his own blanched. "Wait a minute. That patch. That scar. You're him, ain't you? You're One Eye Smith."

"I only go by One Eye," the man with the patch said. "Don't ever call me by my name."

The bartender couldn't move fast enough. He refilled the glass and offered a sickly smile. "It's on the house for the grief I gave you."

"Ain't that downright sociable," One Eye said, and laughed a cold laugh.

"I didn't know who you were when you were poundin' the bar."

"How many people in these parts or anywhere else have a patch like me and a scar like me?" One Eye said. "When it comes to brains you're a lump of mud."

"Whatever you say, Mr. Smith, sir."

"I just got done tellin' you I don't like the Smith part," One Eye said, glowering with his good eye. "I'm commencin' to think you're too dumb to live."

The bartender's throat bobbed. "How about all your drinks are on the house? How would that be?"

"Tryin' to bribe me, huh?"

"Why, no sir. I'm only bein' sociable, like you pointed out."

One Eye's right hand flicked and in less than the blink of the barman's eye, the Remington was leveled at him. "Now I'm pointin' this."

"Please, no."

One Eye snorted and the Remington returned to its holster.

"Give me the bottle and shut your cornhole. I am tired of your stupid."

The barman went to say something but shut his mouth and placed the bottle next to the glass.

Gripping it by the neck, One Eye turned and walked to a corner table where three men were playing cards. They had seen the whole thing.

"You shouldn't ought to pick on Hanks," said the tallest. He wore black. Black everything: black hat, black shirt, black pants, black boots. Which made the ivory-handled Colt on his hip and the silver conchos on his black gun belt stand out that much more.

One Eye pulled out a chair. "Are you tellin' me what to do now, Ritlin?"

Ritlin looked up from his cards. He was uncommonly handsome. He had the kind of face that made women look at him twice. Then they noticed his eyes. There was no emotion in them. They were as flat and empty as the eyes of a rattler.

"Be very careful," he said quietly.

One Eye Smith colored slightly at the cheeks but he didn't say anything.

"This is a fine start," said another cardplayer. He had an ample belly and thick arms and a great moon of a face that was nearly always smiling. Except for the Smith & Wesson on his left hip and the bone-handled knife on his right hip, he had an air of perpetual friendliness. "I didn't ask all of you here to bicker."

The last of them now raised his head. He was compact and wore clothes typical of a cowhand. But there was nothing typical about the nickel-plated Merwin Hulbert revolver in a cross-draw rig to the left of his belt buckle. "Why did you send for us, Brule?"

"Because we're all the best of pards, Axel," Brule said cheerfully.

One Eye snickered. "The hell we are. We've worked some jobs together. Doesn't mean I'll lick your boots."

Ritlin sat up straighter in his chair and set down his cards. "The problem with you is that you were born with a lemon in your mouth."

"What the hell does that mean?"

"You have a sour disposition," Ritlin said in his quiet way. "You go around miserable and do your best to make everyone else the same."

"Strange thing for you to say," One Eye declared. "You're hardly a daisy."

Brule let out a sigh. "You two are always clawin' at each other. I, for one, am tired of it. And to answer Axel's question, I sent for you because I thought you might be interested in a job."

"Now that I like," One Eye said.

"Tell us," Ritlin said.

Brule filled his glass and settled back in his chair. "To

start, the man we work for wants us to keep it quiet. No one is to know."

"What else is new?" Axel said. "Most of the work we do, we can't hardly crow about it or the law would have us doin' strangulation jigs."

"True," Brule said. "But this time our employer doesn't even want us talkin' about it among ourselves."

"That's just stupid," One Eye said.

"We have to talk it over to do it right," Ritlin said.

"Who is this lunkhead?" One Eye asked.

"In a minute." Brule made a tepee of his hands. "As another precaution, we'll meet with him once, and after that, I'm the only one who will have any contact with him."

"What if somethin' happens to you?" One Eye interrupted.

"Then any of you can go see him," Brule said.

"I want to know about the money," Axel broke his silence. "How much are they offering?"

"You're always only interested in the money," Brule said. "And for this job it's five thousand dollars."

One Eye whistled. "Not bad. Makes for a nice split."

"Each," Brule said.

Ritlin, One Eye and Axel sat straighter, and One Eye said, "Did we hear that right?"

Brule nodded. "Five thousand dollars for each and every one of us."

"Why, that's—" One Eye started ticking off the fingers of his left hand with his right as he counted.

"Twenty thousand, altogether," Axel did the addition for him.

One Eye whistled.

"That's more than we've ever made for all our jobs put together," Ritlin said.

Brule chuckled. "When he told me, I about wet my-self, I was so happy."

"That much money," Axel said, "the job is either big or there's extra risk of the law."

"Yes and no," Brule said. "All we have to do is per-suade a bunch of hayseeds and some ranchers to move off their land."

"That's it?" One Eye said.

"How many is a bunch?" Axel asked.

"Eleven families," Brule answered. "Nine farmers and two ranchers. The ranches are small outfits and neither is a gun crowd."

"Hold on," Ritlin said. "There are women involved then."

"There are."

"And kids."

"A lot of kids, yes."

"I am goin' to like this job." Ritlin smiled, and a flicker of pleasure came into his dead eyes.

Brule stabbed a finger at him. "You do any of that, you do it so no one knows, you hear? The man we'll be workin' for doesn't want us attractin' attention."

"You haven't said about the law," Axel said.

"That's the beauty of it," Brule said. "There's a small town not far from the valley but it doesn't have a tin star. It's called Teton."

"I've been there," Axel said.

"Besides a few dozen townsfolk, there's mostly tim-bermen and a few old-timers from the trappin' days. Nothin' we have to worry about."

"The county sheriff?" Axel asked.

"He's a week to ten-day ride there and back. That leaves the federal law, and we know how thin those marshals are stretched. They send for one, it could be a month of Sundays before he shows up."

"God Almighty," One Eye said. "This job will be as easy as takin' puddin' from a baby."

"Don't jinx it," Axel said.

Ritlin asked, "How much in advance? My poke is about empty."

Brule laughed. "You're the one who has to pay the whores more for what you like to do to them."

"I don't do to them what I'll do to them in that valley."

A frown replaced Brule's smile. "I just got done tellin' you. You can't do that this time. Why you have to anyway is beyond me. It's—"

"What?"

"Nothin'," Brule said, and cleared his throat. "To answer your question, we each get a thousand, in advance. The rest will be paid when the job is done."

One Eye chortled. "That's more than I've had at one time in all my born days."

"Money always puts me in a good mood," Axel said.

One Eye was about to reply when he glanced toward the bar and his good eye narrowed. Lowering his voice, he said, "That Hanks is listenin'. Look at how he's got his head tilted our way."

Brule pushed his hat back and stretched and contrived to peer over his arm at the barman. "Could be he is. But so what? I haven't said where or who."

"I don't like it," One Eye said.

"Me either," Axel said. "He might gab and word will get around, and later someone with a tin star will link us to them."

"All right." Brule rose and walked over to the bar, smiling, as always. "Say there, Hanks," he said good-naturedly. "I've got a hankerin' for some of that brandy you sell. Got a bottle?"

"Sure do," the barman said. He turned to the shelf and selected the brandy and turned back and held the bottle out. "Here you go."

"I'm obliged."

"Want me to open it for you?"

"I want you to die." Brule's hand came up holding the bone-handled knife and he thrust the nine-inch blade into Hanks's chest. Hanks's mouth gaped and his eyes showed their whites and he melted to the floor without a sound. Just like that, he was dead. Brule picked up a cloth Hanks had used to wipe the bar and cleaned his blade of the blood. Sliding it into its sheath, he turned. "Happy now?"

"Pleased as punch," One Eye told him, and showed his yellow teeth. "I hope we get to spill a whole heap of blood before this is done."

"Just so we're paid," Axel said.

Ritlin was interested in something else. "This valley you mentioned. The one near Teton. What's it called?"

"Thunder Valley."

2

The sun was hot on Royden Sether's dusty face. He mopped his sweaty brow with his sleeve and said, "Get along, there, Samson."

The ox bent and the plow lurched. Powered by its massive muscles, the curved blade cut into the earth like a hot knife through wax, spewing dirt to either side.

Samson was in his prime. He'd cost Roy a pretty penny, as his wife liked to say, but Samson was worth every cent. Some of Roy's neighbors preferred horses for plowing. Not Roy. Oxen were slow but they were stronger than a horse and could go all day without tiring.

Roy was so intent on his plowing that he didn't realize someone had come out on the field until a hand plucked at his overalls. He glanced down into the freckled face of his youngest son. "What is it, Matthew?"

Matt was ten. He had Roy's shock of yellow hair and Roy's square chin but his mother's blue eyes. "Ma says she needs you to come to the house."

"Can't it wait?" Roy hated to break off in the middle of plowing; he liked to see a job through to the end.

"She says you have to come now."

Roy knew Matt was quoting her. He brought Samson to a stop and stepped out of the ribbons. "What can be so all-fired important?"

"Ma didn't say."

Roy hurried toward the distant white farmhouse. Their hundred and sixty acres might not seem like a lot but it was still a good quarter of a mile from the outer fields to the house.

Their plot was situated near the west end of Thunder Valley. An early settler bestowed the name on account of the frequent spring thunderstorms with their ear-shattering thunderclaps.

It was as beautiful and fertile a valley as Roy ever saw, and he'd known the moment he set eyes on it that here was where he'd live out the rest of his days.

"What's your hurry, Pa?" Matt was taking two strides for each of his. "Ma didn't say you had to run."

"If I was running, I'd have to pick you up and carry you. You couldn't keep up."

"I could so," Matt said. "Almost."

Roy grinned. The boy was forever trying to show he was as good as his older brother.

Separated by strips of trees, the other sections they passed had already been plowed. Roy was working on the last. Once he was done, he could set to planting.

"Sally was saying we're going to town next week," Matt brought up. "Is that true?"

"It is," Roy confirmed.

Now it was Matt who grinned. "I like going to town, Pa. Do you reckon I could have a piece of that hard candy from the general store?"

"We'll see."

"I've been good, haven't I?" Matt said. "It's only a penny. That's not much."

"Your penny or mine?"

"Pa?"

"Is it your penny or my penny we'd spend on the candy?"

"Well, yours," Matt said. "I spent the one I got for Christmas a good while ago."

"If you get into the habit of spending money you don't have," Roy said, "it'll cause all kinds of problems when you're older. A body has to learn to live within their means."

"In what way, Pa?"

"Never spend money you don't have. Once you start, before you know it you're in debt up to your chin. That can ruin you. Trust me. I've seen it happen."

Just then a snake slithered out of the grass onto the path, and stopped.

"Look, Pa!" Matt squealed. He glanced about, spied a rock, and scooped it up. "I'll kill it."

Roy gripped his son's wrist. "You'll do no such thing. It's not a rattler."

"But it's a snake."

Roy squatted and pulled his son down beside him. "Take a look and tell me what kind it is."

Matt tilted his head back and forth. "It's all green so it's a green snake."

"And what did I tell you green snakes eat?"

Matt scrunched his brow. "Bugs and such."

"And one thing we aren't short of is bugs," Roy said. "Why kill a snake that's doing us a favor?"

"I hadn't thought of it like that."

"Killing for killing's sake is wrong," Roy said. "I thought I taught you better."

Matt sheepishly dropped the rock. "I'm sorry, Pa. Sometimes I do stuff before I think about it."

"Don't feel bad, son," Roy said. "A lot of grown-ups do the same."

"Do you?"

Roy grinned. "I try not to but I do." He stood, and in doing so startled the green snake, which darted into the high grass.

"It sure is fast, Pa."

They walked on, Roy remembering back to when he was a boy in Ohio, and his dad, and the talks they'd had. He hoped he was as good a father to his son as his father had been to him.

"Where are your brother and sister?"

"Sally was in the house helping Ma bake cookies," Matt answered. "I haven't seen Andy since you sent him to clean out the manure."

Ahead the ground sloped toward the low rise the house sat on. Roy was surprised to see his wife on the front porch, waiting for them. He walked faster.

"Gosh, Pa, you have long legs," Matt puffed at his side. "I can't hardly keep up."

"Did your ma say what this is about?"

"She sure didn't. She just said to fetch you."

It troubled Roy even more when they got to the yard and he saw his wife pacing. She never paced unless she was upset. He also noticed a horse at the corner of the house, its reins dangling, nipping grass. "You didn't tell me someone is here, son."

"Oh," Matt said. "It's Mrs. Kline. Ma took her into the parlor and shooed me out."

Martha came to the top of the steps. "Thanks for coming so quickly."

As Roy always did, he drank in the sight of her. He

wasn't one of those men who barely tolerated their wives. He didn't just love her, he loved her with all he was. She had raven-black hair that hung past her shoulders and which she often tied into a tail, like now. Some would say her features were plain, but not him. He had every line, every dimple, every inch of her skin memorized. Many a night he lay awake while she slept and stared at her face and marveled that she cared for him.

"What's wrong?"

"It's Irene. She came over in a dither. She's worried about what Tom will do. Someone got to his hogs."

"Some*one*?" Roy said. He would have thought it would be a mountain lion or a bear or maybe even wolves.

Martha nodded. "You'd better come and talk to her."

Nodding, Roy followed Martha in. The screen door smacked behind them. They turned into the parlor and he saw their daughter by the window, looking nervous. Sally smiled and he smiled back.

On the settee sat Irene Kline. She and her husband owned the next farm over and had been to Roy's house many a time for social visits. Roy liked them. Irene was a bit humorless but Tom liked to toss back a beer and joke and was easy to get along with.

"Irene?"

She was sniffling, her head bowed, her hands clasped in her lap. Looking up, she dabbed at her thin nose with a handkerchief. "It's awful. Just awful."

"What is?"

"Didn't Martha tell you? They got into our hogs. You know how Tom is about them. They're his pride and joys."

Roy nodded. Tom Kline raised some of the biggest and best hogs anywhere, and sold them for top dollar.

"Whoever it was, they—" Irene stopped and glanced

at Sally and Matt. "Well, it's awful. You have to see for yourself."

"You keep saying 'they,'" Roy said.

Irene nodded. "There's footprints. There was more than one of them."

"Who would kill hogs," Martha asked, "and just leave them lying?"

"Maybe it was Injuns, Ma," Matt piped up.

"No, boy," Irene said, and sniffled. "They weren't wearing moccasins."

"I'd best ride over," Roy said. "Matt, go to the barn and tell Andy to saddle my horse and bring him around."

"Yes, sir, Pa."

Roy went upstairs to their bedroom. He opened the closet and moved some of the clothes so he could get at his rifle and box of cartridges. When he turned, Martha was in the doorway.

"What's that for?"

Roy shrugged. It bothered him a little that she was so against guns. He hadn't known that when he married her. Not that it would have made a difference if he did. He'd still have said, "I do."

He understood why. A favorite uncle of hers had blown part of his head off when he tripped over his shotgun as he was about to go off pheasant hunting. She'd been only seven at the time, and had seen it, and ever since she couldn't stand guns of any kind.

Roy sat on the edge of their bed and commenced to load his Whitney-Kennedy rifle. It was a .40-60 caliber. He'd bought it because he liked the S-shaped lever. That, and it cost less than a Winchester.

"Do you really need that? If it's not Indians?"

"Anyone who will kill a hog will kill a man just as easy," Roy replied without thinking.

"That's not so, Royden," Martha said. "A hog's not a person. It's an animal. Killing an animal isn't the same as killing a human being."

Inwardly, Roy winced. She used his full name only when she was annoyed. It was the rifle. "Maybe you're right," he tactfully acknowledged. "But why take chances?"

"Well, you be careful. You're no gunsman like that Chace Shannon the newspapers were talking about a while back."

Now it was Roy who was irritated. "I can take care of myself, thank you very much." It was true he'd never shot anyone. But he hunted a lot. And while he wasn't what you would call a marksman, he usually hit what he aimed at. He went on feeding the shells until the magazine was full. "I left Samson out on the back forty. He should be fine until I get back. If I'm delayed, have Andy bring him in."

"Be careful," Martha said again.

Roy nodded. She stepped aside and he started past but paused to kiss her on the cheek. "I'll be fine."

Irene and Sally were out front, Sally still looking nervous, Irene on her horse, waiting.

"I'm grateful for you coming over. I'm hoping you can calm my Tom. He's fit to ride into Teton and cause a ruckus."

"No one from town would do such a thing," Roy said.

"Not any of those who live there, no," Irene agreed. "But there's all sorts who pass through. You've seen some of them yourself."

Yes, Roy had. Teton was getting a reputation for wildness that he didn't much care for. It was the timbermen. They came in on the weekends and got drunk and rowdy. The worst that ever happened was fistfights, but still.

Sixteen-year-old Andy came out of the barn leading the saddled bay. Matt was at his side.

Roy moved to meet them.

"What's this about Mr. Kline's hogs being slaughtered?" Andy asked.

"You know as much as I do," Roy replied as he took the reins. He slid the rifle into the scabbard, gripped the saddle horn, and swung up. "Is that manure shoveled yet?"

Andy frowned. "Just about, Pa."

"You should have been done an hour ago." It bothered Roy that his oldest cared so little for farm work, or, for that matter, work of any kind. He worried the boy would turn out shiftless.

"Ten cows is a lot of shit," Andy said.

About to cluck to the bay, Roy gave him a stern look. "Don't use that kind of language where there are women who might hear."

"But that's what it is."

"A man doesn't use bad language in the presence of a lady. Ever."

"Sally's no lady. She's my sister," Andy said, and laughed.

Roy would have liked to take his son aside and have a talk but Irene was looking at him impatiently. "Keep an eye peeled while I'm gone."

"Are you expecting trouble, Pa?" Andy asked.

"You never know," Roy said.

3

The town was called Savage. It seemed a strange name for a town until you learned it was named after Lucian Sauvage, a French trapper. Sauvage built a trading post and the post drew others, and when there were a dozen or so buildings the settlers called a meeting and decided they were a town.

In its prime Savage boasted one hundred and seventy-six inhabitants. But it was so far north of anywhere, near up to Montana Territory, that once the fur trade dwindled, jobs became scarce. Now fifty-three people lived there. A lot of the buildings were boarded up. Others had simply been abandoned to the dust and the tumbleweeds.

In a few years Savage would wither and die and be just another of the many ghost towns that speckled the plains and the mountains.

Once, though, Savage lived up to its name. Once, it was a slab of raw meat dripping the red juice of human blood. Gun affrays and knife fights were common, and Boot Hill never lacked for fresh graves.

Those were the old days. There hadn't been a killing in Savage in nigh on seven years. There had been a few woundings, though, and plenty of fights.

The Hascomb outfit was to blame. Ike Hascomb prided himself on hiring the wildest and woolliest cowpunchers this side of Hades. With their monthly wages in their pockets, they liked to ride into Savage whooping and hollering and discharging their pistols.

That was when the three saloons did a thriving business. Liquor was chugged by the gallon. The doves wore out their backs and their bedsprings.

It was pure chance that the man with the white hair showed up when he did. If he'd come the day before the Bar H hands blew into town or the day after they took their empty pokes and pounding heads back to the Bar H, the newspaper wouldn't have had anything to write about.

It was the second day of the monthly cowboy spree when the white-haired man rode in from the north. His horse was as fine a Palomino as anyone in Savage ever saw. But it was the man, himself, who attracted the most attention. For starters there was that white hair—shoulder-length, and combed down so that the ends curled up over the collar of his gray slicker. His hat was gray, too, and reminded some who saw it of a wide-brimmed Confederate officer's hat, without the insignia and the braid. He drew rein at the Tempest Saloon and dismounted. Those near him noticed that his pants were gray and that his shirt, what they could see of it, was also gray. They couldn't see much else because the rider made it a point to keep his slicker close around him as he stepped under the overhang and paused at the batwings.

Sam Jolson, who happened to be walking by on his way to the blacksmith, would later say he saw the man better than anyone, and what struck him was that although the man's hair was as white as snow, his face wasn't that old. Sam guessed the man couldn't be more than forty. It was a handsome face, Sam said afterward, but a sort of sad face. The man looked at him, and Sam was startled to see that the man's eyes were the same gray as his hat and his clothes. Sam also noticed bulges on the man's hips under the slicker but didn't think much of it at the time.

The gray man entered the saloon. He paid no attention to the dozen or so cowhands playing cards and lounging about. He went straight to the bar and in a quiet voice asked for a whiskey.

Dorsey, the bartender, brought a bottle and a glass. Dorsey liked his job and he liked people and he was always friendly to everyone. He smiled and said, "You're not from around here."

"No," the gray man said. He watched as the whiskey filled the glass, then raised the glass to his lips and almost delicately sipped. A suggestion of a smile touched his lips.

"Goes down smooth, don't it? You won't get no watered-down red-eye here, mister," Dorsey boasted.

The gray man fished out a coin. He took another sip and closed his eyes as if savoring the taste. "Been a while," he said softly, with a Southern drawl.

"Since you had a drink? Where have you been? Off in the middle of nowhere?"

"More or less," the gray man said. "Stayed away as long as I could."

Dorsey didn't understand, and said so.

"It's personal," the gray man said.

"Ah." Dorsey had learned a long time ago not to pry. He was about to turn away when shadows fell across the bar and four Hascomb punchers bellied up, two on either side of the newcomer.

"What do we have here?" The speaker was a cowboy with close-set eyes and no chin to speak of. The reek of alcohol clung to him, and his dark eyes glittered as he appraised the man in gray.

"Don't you start, Rick," Dorsey said. "This gent is entitled to drink in peace."

"Did I ask you?" Rick said. He pushed his hat back on his tangle of hair and leaned on the bar. "I'm Arn Richter, mister. Most everybody calls me Rick."

"I don't want trouble," the man in gray said. He wasn't asking. There was no worry or fear in his voice. He was stating how it should be.

"Well, now," Rick said, grinning. "You hear him, boys? He don't want no trouble." Rick touched the gray slicker. "Nice fish you've got on. Don't see many gray ones. Most are yellow."

"It's army issue," the gray man said.

"Why, bless my soul," Rick said, pretending to sound surprised. "Do we have us a Reb here?"

"Rick," Dorsey said.

Rick jabbed a finger at him. "Stay out of this, bar-dog, or so help me."

Dorsey held his hands up, palms out, and took a step back. "I'm just sayin' you should leave him be."

"Is that right, mister?" Rick said. "You afraid we won't leave you be?"

The man in gray set down his glass, and sighed. "There won't ever come the day I'll be afeared of a puny gob of spit like you."

Rick blinked. "What did you just say?"

"He insulted you," another of the punchers said. "I heard him as clear as anything."

"Called you puny," declared a third, and snickered.

Rick took a step back and raised his voice. "Why, you miserable Reb son of a bitch."

Throughout the room, cowhands looked up from their cards or stopped their conversations and turned toward the bar.

"Oh, hell," Dorsey said.

The gray man raised his glass and took several swallows. He set the empty glass down and said to no one in particular, "Some things never change, I reckon."

"Mister," Rick said, his hand poised over his six-shooter, "you've got half a minute to eat crow and say you didn't mean that."

His hands flat on the bar, the gray man did a strange thing; he smiled. "That will be the day."

"You will, or else," Rick warned. "In case you ain't taken a tally, there's a lot more of us than there are of you."

"There are eleven of me," the gray man said.

"Hell," another puncher said, and snorted. "He's so roostered, he can't count."

"On one drink?" Dorsey said.

"There ain't no eleven of you," Rick said. "And I won't wait forever for that apology."

"Sure there are," the gray man drawled, and he opened his gray coat.

"Lord Almighty," Dorsey said.

An ordinary brown leather gun belt was strapped around the gray man's waist. But there was nothing ordinary about the way he wore his holsters, or the revolvers in them. The holsters were reversed so that the butts of the six-guns jutted out and up. The revolvers were a matched pair of Colt Navies with pearl handles and nickel-plating.

"Look at how he wears his artillery," a puncher remarked.

"The only hombre I ever heard of who wore them like that was Wild Bill Hickok," chimed in one other. "And he's long dead."

Rick sneered at the gray man. "Is that who you think you are? Wild Bill?"

"My handle is Rondo James."

A hush fell. The cowboys became statues. Dorsey, too, stood immobile with disbelief. Finally a puncher at a table blurted, "You can't be. He's been dead goin' on six or seven years."

"No," the white-haired man said. "I've been layin' low. I got tired of all the peckerwoods like Rick and wanted peace and quiet." He nodded at Dorsey and started toward the batwings.

"Hold on, mister," Rick called out more shrilly than was his wont. "You ain't apologized yet."

Rondo stopped. "Let it drop, for your own sake."

"Listen to you," Rick said. "Treatin' me as if I'm second-rate."

"You are."

Rick looked at his friends. "Did you hear him, boys? Sounds like he's full of himself, don't it?" He motioned and other punchers spread out.

"In God's name, stop," Dorsey intervened.

"Stay out of this," Rick warned.

"Now that I think about it," Dorsey said, "Rondo James was supposed to have white hair, just like this gent."

"So?" Rick said.

"So it's *Rondo James*, damn you."

"I've heard the stories." Rick wagged his chin at the man in gray. "How many is it they say you've done in? Forty or fifty or some nonsense?"

"Saloon talk," Rondo James said.

Rick tilted his head and put a hand to his ear. "I don't hear you sayin' you're sorry."

"And you never will."

Rick eased his hand down to his revolver. "Last chance, Reb, to walk out of here breathin'."

"Rick, don't," Dorsey said.

"Shut the hell up!" Rick glanced at his pards for support. "Any of you want to try him on for size?"

"It's your fight," a rough-looking cowhand said, "but we'll back your play."

"Did you hear that?" Rick said to the man in gray. "When you ride for the Bar H, you ride for the brand."

"A man can die for a brand, too."

"Enough of this," Rick spat. He went for his six-gun.

Dorsey saw it all. He saw Rondo James's hands flash and heard the boom of a pearl-handled Navy and Arn Richter was sent tumbling as if he had been kicked by a mule, a hole in his forehead spurting scarlet.

With a loud oath, the puncher on Rick's right clawed for his smoke wagon.

Rondo James shot him in the face.

A cowhand at a table cleared a Starr revolver from a holster.

Rondo James shot him in the face and backed toward the batwings.

Other Bar H hands stabbed for their six-shooters. A tall drink of water got off a shot and missed, and like lightning, Rondo James shot him in the face.

A puncher in a cowhide vest fumbled his revolver free and Rondo James shot him in the face.

Two Bar H hands who were playing poker heaved to their feet and grabbed for their hoglegs and Rondo James simultaneously shot both in the face. Then he was at the batwings and the batwings opened and swung shut and Rondo James was gone.

Dorsey gawked at the crumpled form of Richter and the other bodies and summed up the situation with "Sweet Jesus."

4

"Who would do such a thing?" Tom Kline asked in bitter sorrow.

Roy Sether didn't have an answer. He stared at the slaughter and was speechless.

Nine hogs lay sprawled in dark pools. Each had had its throat slit, and the pen reeked of blood. Flies crawled in black legions. None of the hogs had been carved on; no meat had been taken.

"It makes no damn sense," Tom said. He was thickset with curly brown hair and a small nose that looked as if it had been pushed in. "Explain it to me."

"Like you say," Roy found his voice. "It makes no damn sense." He glanced at Irene and said, "Sorry."

"That's all right," Irene said. "It makes no damn sense to me, either. Wanton killing, is what it is. Cold, sheer wanton killing."

Tom stepped to his prize boar and placed a hand on the lifeless bulk. "My babies. My wonderful babies."

Roy coughed. Tom and Irene didn't have kids. Once Tom had confided that it wasn't for a lack of trying. The doc said they couldn't, for some medical reason or other, and they'd have to live with it.

"Whoever it was must have snuck in last night," Tom said. "I was out here about six in the evening and the hogs were fine then."

"Your dog didn't bark?"

"That old hound of mine?" Tom said, and gestured at the wrinkled specimen snoozing in a pile of straw. "He can't hardly get around anymore. And he's half blind, to boot. He'd only bark if something walked right up on him."

"Or someone," Irene said.

"Did you look for sign?" Roy asked.

"I found a few prints but I ain't no tracker," Tom said. "Hell, I don't hardly ever hunt."

"I do." Roy went out and scoured the ground. It took a while but near the rear of the barn he found what he was looking for. "There was more than one horse." He sank to a knee and examined the ground. "The shoes were shod so they were white. Looks like they headed thataway." He pointed to the west, toward Teton.

"You'd have thought it would be Injuns," Irene said.

"How can white men do this to other white folks?" Tom lamented. "To kill a man's hogs like that, then just go?"

"Maybe they were liquored up," Irene speculated. "People do mighty strange things when they're liquored."

"We should go after them," Tom said. "I get my hands on them, I'll thrash them within an inch of their lives."

"You'll do no such thing," Irene said. "They cut our hogs, what's to keep them from cutting you? Besides, how would you tell who it was? It's not as if they'll be wearing signs that say 'hog killer.' "

"She's right," Roy agreed. "We have no way of knowing who to blame."

"It has to be strangers," Tom said. "No one who lives there would be this cruel."

"Listen to you," Irene said. "Half of the people in Teton on any given day are passing through."

To Roy it was clear she didn't want Tom to go because she was afraid, and he didn't blame her. Anyone who would massacre hogs wouldn't think twice about doing the same to the man who raised them.

Tom swore and kicked the ground. "I wish we had law in this country."

"We have a sheriff," Roy said.

"Hell, we'd have to go all the way to the county seat," Tom said. "Ten days there and back. Never knowing when hostiles might jump us. Or a griz might decide we're its supper. And then what could the sheriff do, anyhow?" Tom answered his own question. "Nothing, is what. Them that did it would be long gone."

"Get word to the federal marshal," Roy suggested.

"What good would that do?" Tom retorted. "There's no telling where he is. And do you honestly think he's going to ride all the way here over a bunch of hogs? He's got his hands full with people-killers." Tom bunched his fists. "I tell you, if I could find the vermin who did this, I'd take the law into my own hands."

"You would not," Irene said. "I wouldn't let you."

"There's only so much a man can abide," Tom said angrily. He came out of the pen. "I need a drink."

"At this time of day?" Irene said.

"Don't start on me, woman."

Roy followed them to the house. It was white like his and it was about the same size as his but theirs had a wider porch and a swing instead of rocking chairs.

Tom bid him sit and went inside with Irene.

Roy sat back and spread his arms. As hard as it was on the Klines, it was just hogs, after all. The Klines still had their crops and a few cows and a whole lot of chickens. So they'd get by.

It was the viciousness that troubled him. Never in a million years could he do such a thing. Yet there were people out there who could, men who thought no more of snuffing out a life, any life, than he did of sneezing.

Roy supposed that the reason he was so troubled was that it could have been his place they struck.

It'd been his idea to come west. Martha had been perfectly content in Ohio. He was the one who'd yearned for a new life, who'd listened to all the stories about the glories of the frontier and wanted to see them for himself.

Martha had objected at first. She'd mentioned Indians, and he'd assured her most of the hostiles were on reservations. She'd mentioned outlaws, and he'd pointed out that outlaws mostly went after banks and trains and left ordinary folks alone. She'd mentioned bears and cougars and other beasts and he'd promised they wouldn't settle anywhere that wild beasts ran rampant.

Eventually Martha gave in, and here they were.

The door opened and out came Tom, carrying glasses of beer.

He gave one to Roy and sat. "Irene is going to lie down. She's feeling poorly."

"How are you holding up?"

"I'm mad," Tom answered. "Mad as hell that there's not a blessed thing I can do about my poor babies."

"I heard tell that Mr. McCarthy, who runs the general store, has a hog," Roy recollected. "She had a litter a while back."

"Say, that's right," Tom said. "Could be he'd sell me a

few." He swallowed, and frowned. "'Course, it'll be years before I'm back up to where I was."

"If there's anything I can do," Roy offered, knowing full well there wasn't.

"That's decent of you," Tom said. "I've got to say, the best part of coming here is having you as a neighbor. You're as good a friend as a man can have."

Roy shrugged. "I just do as the Good Book says. Or try to, anyhow."

"How about going to town with me?" Tom said. "We'll take my buckboard. Maybe bring back some of McCarthy's litter."

"To Teton?" Roy hesitated. With a bunch of hog-killers on the loose, he didn't care to leave Martha and his kids alone.

"No, Cheyenne," Tom said, and snorted. "Of course to Teton. What's the matter? I'd go alone but it might not be wise if whoever killed my hogs is still around."

"How wise is it to leave your wife alone?" Roy asked.

Tom gnawed on his bottom lip. "You have a point. Could be that whoever killed them is still close by."

Roy stood and stepped to the edge of the porch and gazed the length and breadth of Thunder Valley. Here and there pockets of woodland broke the flat of the valley floor, and there were gullies and other places riders could hide.

"What are you looking at?" Tom asked, coming over.

"I think we should get word to all the farmers and the ranchers," Roy proposed.

"That's easy enough to do."

"And organize a search of the whole valley."

"From end to end? Why, Thunder Valley is ten miles long and five miles wide. That's, what . . . ?"

"Fifty square miles," Roy said.

"A hell of a lot of country to cover," Tom said.

"They were your hogs," Roy reminded him. "Don't you want whoever was to blame caught?"

"I'd like to see them strung up by their thumbs and gutted," Tom said.

"Well, then."

"But covering the whole valley would take a week or more. I have my planting to do."

Roy shrugged. "You're the one who thinks the hog-killers might be close by."

"Let's hope to God they're not," Tom said.

5

The Teton Range of the Rocky Mountains was a spectacular sight to behold. Ten of its peaks thrust more than two miles into the sky. Grand Teton thrust the highest, at over thirteen thousand feet. It was unusual to find so many high peaks so close together. It was unusual, too, that unlike the ranges to the south and the north, the Tetons had no foothills.

The range was broken by canyons that generally ran from west to east. And it was in one of those canyons, in the shadow of a broad six-thousand-foot mountain, that the town of Teton nestled.

Ninety-three souls lived there year-round. The owner of the general store and his wife and eleven kids made up more than a tenth of the population. Then there was the blacksmith and the hotel owner and the timber mill owner and the workers in his employ and a parson and many more.

There was a main street, either dusty or muddy depending

on the weather, lined by businesses with false fronts and boardwalks. The rest of the buildings were made of logs, as trees were plentiful and easy to cut and shape.

Situated as it was on one of the main trails between Colorado and the prairie states to the east, and Montana Territory and Oregon Country to the northwest, Teton was a stopping point for settlers and prospectors and other travelers.

The hotel was seldom empty, and the six saloons were seldom closed.

The four men who showed up early on a sunny morning rode down the middle of the main street, making way for no one. They drew rein at the Grand Lady, named after the highest peak, and dismounted.

"Ain't been to Teton in a coon's age," One Eye said as he wrapped his reins.

"Me either," Axel said. "Last time was in the dead of winter. The snow was piled eight feet deep."

"What in hell were you doing up here at that time of year?" Ritlin said.

"Huntin' a man."

Brule breathed deep of the pine-scented air, and smiled.

"I like it here. I like it a lot. Any of you care to guess why?"

"There's no law," One Eye said.

Brule nodded and rubbed his hands together. "It's enough to make a man drool, the things he can get away with."

"Like killin' hogs," Axel said.

Ritlin stepped onto the boardwalk and shook his head at Brule. "What the hell were you thinking? Hogs, of all things."

Brule patted the bone-handled knife on his left hip. "We had to start somewhere."

"But hogs?" Ritlin said. "Most farmers value their cows more. We should have killed cows."

"Whatever puts fear into them," Brule said. "We get them so scared that when they're given the choice between stayin' and leavin', they pick leavin'."

"But hogs?" Ritlin said again.

Brule shrugged. "I never could stand any critter that oinks. Pigs, hogs. When I heard that squeal as we were ridin' by, it gave me the idea to sneak on in and pay my respects."

One Eye laughed. "Don't ever pay your respects to me. I like my throat as it is."

They entered the Grand Lady. It was early yet and only a few men were drinking at the bar. At a couple of tables card games were under way.

"Lively little whiskey mill," One Eye said.

Brule bought a bottle and they adjourned to a corner table.

Ritlin, as always, sat with his back to the wall. So did Axel.

"Now, then," Brule said after he had filled their glasses, "suppose we get down to business. We have three months to clear the hayseeds out. I reckon that's more than enough time."

"Hold on," Axel said. "You told us we'd get a thousand in advance."

One Eye nodded. "And we ain't seen the money yet."

"We will," Brule told them. "The man who hired me, the man we're to have all our dealin's with, will be here in a few days to personally hand us the money."

"That's more like it," Axel said.

Brule looked about the room, then leaned forward on his elbows and said so only they would hear, "Now remember. We scare off as many as we can. Those that won't go, we buck out in gore."

"We should buck them all out," Ritlin said.

"Massacrin' all those families would stir up the whole countryside and bring the federal marshal down on our heads," Brule said. "We do this smart."

"Any lawman shows up, he'll wish he hadn't," Ritlin said.

"Let's not get ahead of ourselves."

"Easy for you to say. You like doves."

"Damn it, Ritlin," Brule said. "You do any of that, you take them off where no one will find their bodies. You hear me?"

"I'm not stupid," Ritlin said.

One Eye sat up straighter and bobbed his chin toward the entrance and said, "Lookee here."

A man had come hurrying in. He wore a cap and high boots that marked him as a timberman. He crossed to the bar and said something to the men who were drinking that caused them to gather around.

"What's this?" Axel said. "He must have news of some kind."

"Maybe about the hogs," One Eye said.

"Let's have a listen," Brule said, and rising, he led them over. Some of the cardplayers had also stood and were converging.

". . . God is my witness," the newcomer was saying. "I was delivering a load of wood. That's how I know."

"And you saw it?" a townsman asked.

"You saw *him*?" said someone else.

"Well, no," the timberman said. "But I saw the bodies. He shot each and every one in the face."

Brule shouldered in among them. "Hold on. What's this about? Who shot who?"

"You won't believe it," the timberman declared. He was enjoying the attention.

"Try me," Brule said.

The timberman took his time. He helped himself to a swallow of liquor from a glass the bartender had given him, and wiped his mouth with his sleeve. "It's like this," he said. "There's a settlement north of here a ways, called Savage."

"I've been there," One Eye said.

"Is there anywhere you haven't been?" Axel asked.

The timberman appeared annoyed by the interruption. "Some cowhands from the Bar H got into a scrape with a leather-slapper, and you won't believe who. I didn't hardly believe it myself but I talked to the barkeep, Dorsey, and he swore by his mother's grave that it was him."

"Him who, damn it?" Brule said.

"Rondo James."

"The hell you say."

Ritlin galvanized into motion, his dead eyes glimmering with sudden interest. Shoving surprised patrons out of his way, he strode up to the timberman. "You'd better not be lying, mister."

"I'm telling you," the timberman said. "Folks saw him as clear as day. White hair. Pearl-handled Navies. Dressed all in gray."

"That sure sounds like Rondo James," someone said.

"I'll be damned," Ritlin said.

"How many was it he killed?" the bartender asked.

The timberman ticked them off on his fingers and announced, "I saw seven bodies."

"By God, that's some shootin'."

"Seven at one time? I ain't ever heard the like."

"When it comes to man-killin', there's no one like Rondo James."

Ritlin turned to the last man and his hard face became harder. "How would you like to see seven men shot right here?"

"Don't," Brule said.

The man who had admired the total went pale under Ritlin's glare. "What's got you so mad?"

"Rondo James is Southern trash. The same as Jesse and Frank James and that Wales."

"Hold on," said a townsman in a suit. "I'm from the South."

"I wore blue in the war, mister," Ritlin said, "and I'm sick of hearing about all the boys in gray who get wrote up and fawned over like they were special."

"Not that again," Brule said, and put his hand on Ritlin's arm. "Let it drop. We have work to do, remember?"

"Damned, stinking Rebs," Ritlin said, and moved toward the batwings. Those in his path were quick not to be.

"Talk to him," Axel said to Brule. "We can't have him doin' this."

Brule nodded and went out. A wagon was going by, raising dust. "You've got to control that temper."

Ritlin was leaning against a post, his thumbs hooked in his gun belt. "He's ahead of me now."

"Who is?"

"Who were we just talking about? Rondo James. From what I hear, the tally was about even. Now he's ahead."

"Who cares how many he's killed?"

Ritlin's eyes blazed. "*I* care. I'm as good a man-killer as he is, but he's famous and hardly anyone has ever heard of me."

"That happens."

"It's because he's from the South. All those Southern boys get admired and talked about."

"Hell in a basket," Brule said. "It's been, what, more than twenty years since the war ended? How can you still hold a grudge?"

"I lost both my brothers to Rebs," Ritlin said. "Grudge doesn't hardly cover it."

Brule went to the post and leaned on the other side. "Listen to me. I'm one of the few friends you have, so don't hold what I'm about to say against me."

Ritlin grunted.

"Sure, you've done more than your share of killin'. But it's the kind that can get you hung or thrown behind bars. So naturally folks don't know about it."

Ritlin didn't say anything.

"Damn it, Win. Why you are always goin' on about bein' famous, I will never know. The work you do, that's the last thing you want."

"It's not fair," Ritlin said.

"Will you listen to yourself? You're a hired assassin, for God's sake."

"Hickok was famous. Longley was famous. Ben Thompson and King Fisher. Everyone talked about them."

Brule muttered something, then said, "Hickok was shot in the back of the head. Longley got himself hung. Thompson and Fisher were blasted to pieces. Is that what you want to happen to you?"

"Be serious," Ritlin said.

"I am, damn it. What did their fame get them? An early grave. And if word got out about all the killin' you've done, that's what you'd get, too."

Two women walked past. Brule smiled at them and touched his hat brim. Ritlin ignored them.

"I don't hear you agreein'," Brule said.

"I'd like to be remembered."

"Do you think anyone will remember Hickok fifty years from now? Hell, hardly anyone remembers Longley and he's been dead less than ten."

"Since I was a boy I've wanted to make a name for myself."

"Then you picked a piss-poor line of work. You should have gone into politics. Or be on the stage."

Ritlin looked at him. "I'm no talker. And it'll be a cold day in hell before I'll prance around in tights." He paused. "What I am is a killer. And I like it. Killing suits me to my marrow."

"I will admit," Brule said, "that I've never met anyone who likes it as much as you do."

"It's the one thing I'm good at," Ritlin said. "And it eats at me that no one will ever know."

"You are damned peculiar."

"It's human nature."

"Not mine," Brule said. "The both of us are better off in the shadows. Be thankful you're not famous or you wouldn't be able to do the killin' you love so much."

"I suppose."

"Cheer up, damn you." Brule grinned and clapped the man in black on the shoulder. "Tell you what. When you're ready to give up bein' an assassin, there's a quick and easy way to be as famous as anyone."

"I'm all ears."

"It's simple. You find someone who already is, and you blow out their wick where everyone can see." Brule laughed and turned and went into the saloon.

Ritlin stared after him. "Well, now," he said. "As brainstorms go, that's not half-bad."

6

Martha Sether came out of her house wearing her work gloves and carrying a small basket that contained her hand hoe, trowel, fork and weeder. She went down the steps and turned toward the flower garden.

Behind her, Sally said, "Who's that, Ma?"

Martha was startled to see a man and a horse not ten steps away. The man was dressed all in gray, with a long coat buttoned in the middle. He was holding the reins to a Palomino. "My word," she blurted.

The man took off his hat and held it at his chest and gave a slight bow. "My apologies, ma'am, if I've given you a fright," he said courteously. "I didn't mean to."

Martha saw that his hair was white but he wasn't all that old. "That's quite all right. We didn't hear you ride up."

"I didn't ride, ma'am," the man said. "I walked." He turned and gently touched the Palomino's right foreleg. "General Lee, here, has come up lame."

"Oh, my. I hope it's not serious." Martha liked the man's Southern accent.

"I'm worried it might be an infection, ma'am. I'd like to take off the shoe and have a look. Maybe give him some oats and let him rest." The man motioned at the barn. "I'd be willin' to pay."

Martha also liked how polite he was. "I'm willing but it's not entirely up to me. My husband will want his say."

"I understand, ma'am. Is he inside?"

"No, he's out at what we call the second field. Follow that track, there, past the row of trees."

"I will, ma'am, and I thank you most kindly." The man placed his hat back on. "Is it all right if I leave General Lee here?"

"It certainly is."

The man let the reins dangle and started off.

Martha didn't know what made her say, "Hold on. I'll go with you." She set down her basket and removed her gloves and placed them on top of the tools. A tug at the back of her dress reminded her she wasn't alone.

"What about me, Ma?" Sally asked. "Do I go with you?"

The man smiled at her and doffed his hat again. "I'd be delighted to have your company, as well, young miss."

"Oh," Sally said, looking flustered.

Martha took her daughter's hand. "We don't get many visitors."

"I'd imagine not, ma'am."

Martha wanted to keep him talking so she said, "That's a fine animal you have."

"General Lee is more than an animal, ma'am. You might say he's my friend."

"Named after General Robert E. Lee, I presume?"

"You presume correctly, ma'am."

Martha noticed that the man was matching his pace to theirs, something she wished Roy would do more of. It was a trial keeping up with his long strides. "And may I also presume from your hat and your coat that you served in the Confederate army?"

"Proudly, ma'am."

"We don't see many in a Confederate uniform anymore," Martha commented. "Used to be we did, the first few years after the war."

"Might I ask your name, ma'am?"

"Forgive my manners," Martha said, and introduced herself and Sally. "Might I ask yours?"

The man seemed to hesitate. "It's Mosby, ma'am. Nathan Mosby."

"Wasn't there a Confederate general by the name of Mosby?"

"What a remarkable memory you have, ma'am. If it's the gentleman you're thinkin' of, he was a colonel."

"Any relation?"

"No, ma'am. We're not kin."

"Your accent," Martha said. "Are you by any chance from Tennessee or one of the Carolinas?"

"I hail from Old Dominion, herself. The grand and sovereign State of Virginia. Some would call her the backbone of the South."

"Do you ever miss home?"

"I would if it was still there. Yankees caused it to burn to the ground during the war."

"I'm sorry," Martha said. "Was it that General Sherman I recall reading about?"

"No, ma'am. Sherman marched through Georgia."

"Do you still have family back there?" Martha was intensely curious to learn all she could. She so seldom got to talk to anyone from the South.

"My mother died in the Union shelling. As near as I could find out afterward, they mistook our house for a supply depot that was down the road a ways."

"How dreadful. And your father?"

"He died at Gettysburg." The man in gray didn't expand on how.

They were nearing the trees. Martha would have liked to carry on their conversation but she saw her husband and the boys off in the field and waved to him.

Roy was going down the recently plowed furrows looking for large rocks and clumps that would interfere with the planting. "What have we here," he said, and immediately made for his wife and the stranger.

"Is he in the army, Pa?" Matt asked. "That's a uniform of some kind, ain't it?"

"Isn't it," Roy corrected him. "And, yes, it is. A Confederate uniform. Haven't seen one in years."

"Look at how white his hair is," Andy remarked. "It's as white as snow."

A memory tugged at Roy's mind but slipped away before he could grab hold of it. "Hush about his uniform and his hair. It's not polite to talk about how people look."

"How come?" Matt said.

"Good manners, your mother would call it."

"And we know how she is about manners," Andy said.

"That'll be enough out of you," Roy said. His oldest had taken to being much too critical of late, of just about everything. Roy smiled and held out his hand and said, "How do you do. I'm Roy Sether."

"This is Mr. Mosby," Martha said as they shook. "He has a problem with his horse."

"Oh?" Roy was impressed by the other's firm handshake. He'd always believed that you could tell a lot about a man by how he shook hands.

"I'd like to have a few words about it in private, if I may."

Roy was puzzled by his wife's evident surprise. "Honey, if you'll take the kids on back," he said, and was even more puzzled at how hurt she looked.

"As you wish," Martha replied. To the man in gray, she said, "I trust it wasn't anything I said?"

"Not at all, ma'am," the Southerner said, and bestowed a kindly smile. "It's man talk, you might say."

"Lordy," Martha said. "You men and your secrets." She draped an arm over Sally's shoulders. "Come along, boys."

"But we're men," Matt said.

"Go with your mother," Roy directed. He wondered what the man could possibly want to say. It occurred to him that he was unarmed and there were suspicious bulges under the Rebel's coat.

He balled his fists, ready to defend himself if need be.

"I reckon they're out of earshot," the man in gray said. He looked Roy in the eyes. "I deceived your missus because I thought it best but I won't lie to you."

"Deceived?" Roy repeated.

"My handle isn't Mosby. I told your wife that so as not to scare her. My real name is Rondo James. Could be you've heard of me."

The memory that had tugged at Roy acquired form. Hiding his astonishment, he said, "I believe I have. You, sir, have a reputation as a gunny."

"I'm not much fond of brands," Rondo James said. "But if I have to be branded I prefer pistoleer."

"What's this about your horse?"

Rondo studied Roy. "I take it you haven't heard, then? I was in a shootin' affray up to Savage. Some cowpokes tried to throw down on me and I had to kill some."

Roy had talked to men who had been to Savage but he had never been there. "Why are you telling me this?"

"Because I need you to trust me and you won't if I lie or hold somethin' back." Rondo James unbuttoned his slicker and swept it back.

Roy had seen a lot of revolvers in his time but few with pearl handles and fewer with nickel plating. He whistled in appreciation.

"They are pretty, aren't they?" Rondo placed his hands on the pearl handles. "They've saved my hide more times than I care to count. Saved me in Savage, too. But I had to light a shuck. Shoot one cowboy and you have a whole passel after you."

Roy gazed off across Thunder Valley. "Are they after you now?"

"No," Rondo said. "I reckon I gave them the slip. General Lee can outrun most anything on four legs. I aimed to push on clear to Denver but late yesterday General Lee commenced to limp and it's gotten worse since." He fished in his pocket and produced a double eagle. "For boardin' the General in your barn for the night."

"That's too much," Roy said. It was twenty dollars. In Teton a man could put up his animal for a dollar.

"Those cowpokes had friends who might be after me," Rondo said. "They catch up, they're liable to shoot up your barn to flush me out and you'll regret I didn't give you more."

Roy was struck by the Southerner's thoughtfulness. "You're thinking of me when it's your life at stake?"

"I'm used to it." Rondo James held out the double eagle. "It'd sit easier on my conscience if you take it. That is, if you're agreeable to my proposition."

"You're the first quick-draw artist I've met."

"We're not a common breed," Rondo acknowledged. "But what's your point?"

Roy was frank with him. "The newspapers and the penny dreadfuls have it that your kind are heartless killers. I'd half expect you to go around forcing people to do your will at gunpoint."

"There are those as would, I reckon."

"I have no objection to you using my barn," Roy said. "But there's one thing you should know."

Rondo James looked at him.

"I don't lie to my wife. Never have, never will. As soon as we get back I'll tell Martha who you are and what you've done, and it might be that she won't like the idea."

"Your wife and kids." Rondo lowered his arm. "I didn't think of them."

"I'm not saying she will."

"It's not that." The Southerner scowled. "All I was thinkin' of was your barn when I should be worried for your family. I stick around, it could put them in danger."

"No man in his right mind would shoot a woman or children," Roy said. "They'd be strung up so fast, their head would swim." He smiled and made bold to give the man in gray a light clap on the arm. "Let's go tell her the truth and see what she says."

"I'm obliged. I truly am."

"I'd do the same for any man in need."

"I'm not just any man," Rondo James said.

7

Charlton Rank never went anywhere without his six "enforcers," as he called them. He also never went anywhere without Bisby, his male secretary, and Floyd, his manservant. So when he swept into Teton with his entourage, he attracted attention.

Rank didn't care. He was used to it. Lesser men were always fascinated by their betters. He drew rein at the Timberland. As a hotel it wasn't much, but it was all the town offered. When the manager found out who he was, the man fawned over him, eager to meet his every whim. Rank was used to that, too.

Installed in the most expensive suite, Rank sat in a plush chair and sipped a sherry cobbler — he brought his own oranges — that Floyd had prepared. Rank was fond of them. Some might say it was a weakness, but Rank didn't allow himself weaknesses.

Bisby was perched on the edge of another chair, awaiting orders.

"I want you to go to the Grand Lady saloon. There will be four men seated at a table. One will look like a bear, another will have an eye patch, and the third, from what I hear, likes to dress all in black."

"And the fourth?" Bisby asked.

"He's smarter. He blends in."

"Sir?"

"Don't annoy me with trivialities," Rank said brusquely. "You will go up to the bear and ask if his name is Brule, and if he confirms that he is, you will inform him that he and his cohorts are to come to the rear of this hotel half an hour after the sun goes down. You will be waiting for them and escort them up the back stairs. Am I understood?"

"You wish that they not be noticed."

"I wish it very much."

Bisby stood. "On my way."

Rank sipped, and as his secretary was reaching for the door he said, "And Bisby."

"Sir?"

"Be very careful. The bear and the one who blends in are rational enough but the other two are rabid. They bite without provocation."

"Sir?"

"They are murderous sons of bitches, Bisby. Try not to be murdered if you can help it." Rank grinned at his own wit as his secretary bustled out. No sooner did the door close than he snapped his fingers and the chief of his Enforcers stepped forward.

"Sir?"

"Follow him, Bannister. Take Tate. Be inconspicuous and stay in the background but if they try to harm him, kill the bastards."

"Inconspicuous in these?" Bannister said, and touched

the suit with a matching bowler that Rank required all of his Enforcers to wear.

"I take your point. Tailor-made apparel is rare in these parts," Rank said. He flicked a finger. "Off you go now." He watched the pair leave, and settled back. He had every confidence in his Enforcers. Three were ex-Pinkertons, one an ex-marshal, another an ex–army captain, and the last, Tate, had once been a Texas Ranger. Rank had lured them all from their former vocations by offering the one thing he had more of than most anyone: money.

"Anything else I can get you, Mr. Rank?" Floyd inquired from over at the bar.

"Not at the moment." Rank realized he had nothing to do for the next couple of hours. It was so rare for him to have time to himself that he didn't quite know how to spend it. He wasn't good at relaxing. He liked to be busy, to be on the go, to be doing this or that or the other. It was what made him successful. It was what had made him rich, and would make him richer. Because as Rank had learned long ago, he wasn't the sort to be content with his laurels. He always had to have more, more, more.

Rank gazed out the window at the pitiful excuse for a town and imagined how much bigger and grander Teton would be once his plan came to fruition. He would bring genuine civilization to this backwater bit of nothing and line his pockets and those of the board in the process.

Rank drank and dreamed and when Bisby returned to inform him all was set, he smiled and set the empty glass aside and to his mild surprise, dozed off. He rarely slept during the day. He was too much a fountain of energy to sit still long enough.

A tap on his shoulder awakened him. The window was dark and the lamps had been lit.

"They should be here in the next fifteen minutes or so," Bisby informed him.

Rank coughed and rose and went to the mirror to adjust his clothes and brush his hair. He had Bannister and Tate and another Enforcer stand against one wall and the other three against the wall opposite so that their guests would be in a cross fire should the unexpected occur. Then he went and sat imperiously in his chair by the window.

At the appointed time, Bisby hurried out. He wasn't gone five minutes when he rapped lightly on the door and opened it and stood aside for their visitors.

"Mr. Brule," Rank greeted him without rising from his chair. "It's good to see you again."

Brule nodded and indicated the others. "These here are the hombres I told you about. This tall one in black is—"

"I know who each of you are," Rank cut him off. "Did you think I would hire you and not have you investigated?" He pointed at the drab one. "Mr. Axel. He used to work as a cowhand until he became involved in the Hoodoo range war. He killed a man and was paid to kill a few more and ever since has hired his gun out."

"Those are the rumors," Axel said.

Rank pointed at the one with the eye patch. "Mr. Smith. If filth was gold you would be wealthier than me."

"Here, now," One Eye said.

"You killed your first man when you were sixteen and have been killing ever since. You lost that eye in a knife fight and were cut on the cheek, besides. You're vermin, through and through, but you always get the jobs that you are hired to do done, and you are discreet."

"That's better," One Eye said. "But what does discreet mean?"

Rank pointed at Brule. "You, sir, are the brains of this group. At least in so far as you have kept them from the gallows. Your given name is Ira Norman Brule. You've always been a brawler. It got you into trouble when you were younger and you drifted to the shadier side of the law. You enjoy beating on people with your fists, which is why you're ideal for this particular work."

Brule smiled.

"That leaves you," Rank said, and pointed at the man in black. "Winifred Ritlin. You have a cruel streak that far surpasses Mr. Brule's. The report I was given mentions acts I can only describe as despicable. There will be none of that here, do you understand? You are to leave the women and the children alone."

"I do as I please," Ritlin said.

Rank bent forward in his chair. "I'm paying you. You will restrain your baser impulses while in my employ. If you don't like it, you can leave right this second."

Ritlin stiffened and went to respond but Brule gripped his arm and shook his head.

"Ritlin will behave, Mr. Rank. You can count on it."

"He'd better," Rank said. "There's too much at stake." He sat back and folded his hands in his lap. "I must impress on you the importance of this undertaking. I represent the Wyoming Overland Railroad. The W.O.R. intends to run a spur line to Teton. As your own eyes will attest, there's timber in these mountains. Prime trees, awaiting the ax. Plus, we've found evidence of coal deposits. In short, gentlemen, this spur is worth millions of dollars to the W.O.R."

"Maybe we should ask for more," One Eye said, and snickered.

"Mr. Brule and I have already agreed on a price for your services," Rank said. "And I expect you to abide by the terms."He paused. "But to get back to the W.O.R. The most economical route for us to lay tracks is through Thunder Valley. A representative of ours approached the farmers and ranchers there about a year ago and offered to buy them out but they refused."

"How much did you offer?" Ritlin asked.

"That's none of your concern."

"Humor me, Mr. High-and-Mighty," Ritlin said.

Rank didn't like his tone or his attitude but he said, "We offered them a fair settlement."

"How much?"

"I fail to see why you want to know."

"I'll bet you offered them less than they paid," Ritlin said, "and made out like you were doin' them a favor."

"That's standard business practice."

"I thought so."

Rank looked at Brule. "What's the matter with your friend? Is he deliberately trying to provoke me? Because if he is, those six gentlemen along the walls can demonstrate how displeased I am."

"Six isn't enough," Ritlin said.

"I beg your pardon?"

"I'll get five of them myself and my pards here will do the last."

Rank snorted. "Oh, please. No one is that fast."

"I'm not fast," Ritlin said. "I'm quick." He faced the three Enforcers along the left wall. "Have them draw on me."

"You're behaving childishly," Rank said. He appealed to Brule. "Talk to your friend. The last thing I want in here is gunplay. It will attract too much attention."

"You should have them draw," Brule said. "Win won't shoot. He won't need to."

Rank resented being told what to do. He decided to

put the bastards in their place, and nodded at the three Enforcers. "If you please, Mr. Bannister. Would you and Mr. Tate and Mr. Hanks indulge them?"

"Whenever they want," Bannister said.

"Now," Ritlin said.

Bannister and Tate and Hanks were fast. They swept their hands under their jackets but before they could sweep them out, Ritlin's Colt was pointed at them and they heard the click of the hammer. All three froze.

"Hellfire," Tate said.

Ritlin let down the hammer and twirled the Colt into his concho-studded holster with a flourish and a smirk. Then he turned to Rank. "You shouldn't ought to have called me despicable."

Rank was taken aback. Bannister and Tate—especially Tate—were supposed to be supremely fast shooters. It was part of why he hired them. "We're getting off on the wrong foot here."

Brule frowned at Ritlin and turned and smiled at Rank. "He doesn't cotton to insults, is all. But you can depend on us. Honest."

"You can control your friend?"

Brule nodded. "Me and Ritlin have been pards a good long while. He'll do as I say. Won't you, Win?"

Ritlin grunted.

"Why don't you just take the land?" Brule asked. "Doesn't the railroad have, what do they call it? Em-something or other?"

Rank nodded. "The right of eminent domain, yes. But the farmers can fight it. They can take us to court. We nearly always win but courts take time and we don't have a lot of time to spare. We want the new line laid as soon as we can."

"You want all that timber money," One Eye said, and laughed.

"I can't stress enough that this must be done quietly," Rank said. "No one must link your deeds to the W.O.R. If they do, there will be hell to pay."

"For us or for the railroad?" Brule asked.

"For everyone," Rank said.

8

Moses Beard loved his life.

His farm was at the west end of Thunder Valley. Not three hours' ride from Teton, it afforded him a magnificent view of the towering mountains. He loved to look at them. There had been nothing like them in his native Rhode Island. It was ironic that he'd moved from the smallest state in the Union to the wide-open spaces.

Moses loved working with the soil. He'd had a small farm in Rhode Island and always dreamed of owning one a lot bigger.

All the talk he'd heard about "Go west, young man" had fired his imagination. Not that he was young; he would turn thirty-five this year. But the idea of one hundred and sixty acres, or more, was heady to contemplate.

Moses had the usual worries. Indians were at the top. He was deathly afraid of them. Back east, hardly a week went by that the newspapers didn't print a story about whites being massacred or scalped. They did it so often that Moses suspected they liked to print them. Journalists, he decided, were ghouls who feasted on the misery of others.

Ironically, it was his wife who put his fear to rest. Tilda reminded him that most of the tribes were tame. Many had been forced onto reservations. The few tribes still hostile were being harried by the army and it was only a matter of time before they were on reservations, too.

Moses's other worry was the weather. Winters in the Rockies were supposed to be ferocious, far worse than those in little Rhode Island.

Once again Tilda calmed him by saying that snow was only snow and cold could be endured and that the mountains were rich in trees and thus rich in firewood.

After a couple of years of seesawing back and forth, Moses asked Tilda what she wanted to do. She surprised him by saying they should head west.

So off they went, seeking a spot to settle. In Denver they talked to a man who had been to Teton and who mentioned a fertile valley ripe for the plow.

Now, standing on his porch and admiring what he liked to think of as his domain, Moses smiled and was greatly thankful to the good Lord for how well things had worked out.

The screen door squeaked and Tilda came out carrying a tray with cups and a teapot and a sugar bowl. "They're both asleep," she announced, moving to the two rocking chairs.

Moses claimed his. The tea was a nightly ritual, a way to relax after the hard work of each day. He sat and waited while she poured and spooned the sugar and stirred. "God, I love it here."

"Don't use the Lord's name in vain," Tilda said.

Moses didn't think he had but he wisely kept quiet. His wife was a stickler for the Lord. He accepted his cup and sipped and savored the taste and the warmth that spread through his body. "You make the best tea ever."

"It's passable," Tilda said. She sat and sipped and slowly rocked.

"Tell me true," Moses said. "Are you glad we came?"

"We've been here two years," Tilda said. "Have you ever once heard me complain?"

"Complaining's not in your nature," Moses complimented her. Disagreeing, on the other hand, was.

"Yes, Moses, I like it here a lot."

"More than Rhode Island?"

Tilda gave Moses what he thought of as her "putting up with him" look. "Get over your guilt, Moses. It's over and done with. Look ahead, not back."

"Yes, dear." Moses was always nettled when she took that tone. Which she did a lot.

"You shouldn't be fretting about something we did two years ago," Tilda said. "If you must fret, fret for our cows and our horses and pigs."

"Why should I fret for them?" Moses wondered. Their livestock was healthy as could be.

"Because whoever slaughtered the Klines' hogs might well decide to slaughter more."

"What's this about Tom's hogs?" Moses remembered that he had seen Irene Kline ride up while he was out in the fields. The wives were always visiting one another.

"Oh? Didn't I tell you?" Tilda took another sip of tea. "Someone killed all of them."

"What?"

"Slit the throat from ear to ear of every last hog the Klines owned."

"What?"

"There was blood everywhere, Irene told me. Their barn stank of it." Tilda indulged in another sip. "Five nights ago, it was."

Moses was dumbfounded. The Klines had their hogs killed and no one thought to tell him? What kind of neighbors were they?

His old fear returned, and he found his voice and said, "Indians, I bet."

"You'd lose," Tilda said. "Her husband and Roy Sether found tracks. It was white men."

"The hell you say."

"Don't swear, Moses. You know I can't abide swearing. It upsets me that you constantly forget."

Moses didn't see how she could be more bothered by his cussing than by the slaughtered hogs. "Whoever paid the Klines a visit might pay us one."

"Didn't I say that a minute ago?" Tilda said. "There's not much we can do about the cows. We have over twenty and you can't fit all of them in the barn. But you should take the horses out of the corral and put them in the barn and be sure you bar the door to the pigpen."

"I will," Moses said. Although a barred barn door and a barred pigpen door wouldn't stop anyone from getting in.

"Maybe now you'll agree we should have a dog," Tilda said.

Moses knew that was coming. She'd been pestering him about a dog for six months now. He never much cared for them. Dogs were noisy and smelly and forever licking your face, and who knew where their tongues had been. Cats, now, he liked. Cats were quiet and were always cleaning themselves and it was cute when they purred.

"Moses, are you listening to me?"

Moses realized he had missed something she said. "I was thinking about the cows," he fibbed.

"Think about your shotgun," Tilda said. "You never keep it loaded, and I keep telling you that you should."

"I'll load it first thing when we go in."

"That's a start. You should also keep a lantern handy in case you have to run out in the middle of the night. And it's warm enough at night that we can keep the window open and hear if there's a ruckus."

"Yes, dear." Moses hated to sleep with the window open. He could never shake the feeling that something might sneak in. "I should go talk to Roy tomorrow."

"Oh?"

"I'd like to hear what he has to say." Moses regarded Roy as the valley's unofficial leader. Olander, the rancher, acted as if he was, but Roy had the most experience working the land, and was generous with advice.

"I don't see what he can say that I haven't but if you must, you must."

"Honestly, Tilda," Moses said.

"I'm only saying."

Moses almost sighed but caught himself. She always gave him one of those looks when he sighed, as if his sighs were a great annoyance. He sipped and did more pondering. "It's too bad the county sheriff is so far away."

"There you go again," Tilda said. "He is and that's that. Deal with it."

Moses felt anger stir. "I won't be talked to like that. You hear me, woman?"

"I am your wife, Moses Beard. Use my name. Don't address me as if you've just met me on the street."

Moses backed down. When she used that tone, he was on the brink of a tongue-lashing. And if there was anything he hated more than the marks of her tongue on his back, he had yet to come across it. "I'm flustered by the hogs," he sought to justify his lapse.

"Perfectly understandable," Tilda said. "I'm concerned, too. Although if I'm right, we don't have a whole lot to worry about."

"We don't?"

"Think, Moses. We know they were white men. Who in their right mind would do such a thing? The answer is no one. Then why did they do it? The answer is obvious." Tilda paused. "They were under the influence."

"Could well be," Moses said.

"No could about it," Tilda said. "Men and their liquor. They were drunk. No sober man takes a knife to an animal's throat."

"A mean man would."

"A mean man would pick on other men," Tilda said. "Not on innocent hogs."

Moses wasn't sure he agreed, but then, this was his first hog slaughter. "There's some men who will kill anything."

"They are few and far between and we don't have any in this part of the country," Tilda declared. "No, the devil's poison was in their veins and it clouded their judgment."

Moses dropped the subject. Her dislike for liquor was so strong, she refused to let him have a drop of it anywhere in the house. Once, shortly after they were married, he'd snuck a bottle home and hid it in the pantry.

She'd found it and called him outside and made him watch while she upended it and wasted all that wonderful whiskey on the grass. "Yes, if it was white men, that makes sense."

"They wore boots, Moses."

Moses had a startling thought. "Indians wear boots sometimes."

"Not many," Tilda said. "They prefer moccasins."

"Still," Moses said.

"White or red, the important thing is we protect our own. We'll sleep with the window open for the next week or two, to be safe."

The sun was setting and bright hues of red, orange and yellow painted the sky above the Tetons. Normally the sight stirred Moses to his soul but not this evening. "I might go into town tomorrow and see if anyone has any pups they're giving away."

"Could be you could go in with Tom Kline," Tilda said. "Irene told me he's anxious to buy new hogs."

"I'll ride over to their place as soon as I'm done milking the cows."

Tilda nodded.

"Want me to ask Irene if she'll come and stay with you?"

"What for? I'm a grown woman. I don't need a nursemaid, thank you very much."

"Just thought you might like her company," Moses said.

"No. I have too much work to do around the house. Tomorrow is laundry day, remember?"

Moses did indeed. On Mondays she cleaned the house from top to bottom. On Tuesdays she sewed and worked on her quilts. Wednesday was laundry day. Thursday she worked in the vegetable garden and on Fridays it was general chores. She was much more organized than he was, he had to give her that. He looked at the comma of hair that fell over her forehead and at her lips as she sipped, and he cleared his throat. "You sure look pretty this evening."

Tilda sipped and cradled the cup in her lap. "You know better, dear. It's not Saturday, is it?"

Moses almost sighed.

9

---·---

Rondo James woke up and was instantly alert. He nearly always did that. He'd trained himself to years ago, during the war. Groggy on a battlefield could get a man killed, and Rondo was fond of breathing. He'd proven how fond by not only surviving the bloodiest conflict on U.S. soil but the fourteen shooting affrays he'd been in since.

Fifteen, Rondo realized, counting the affair at Savage.

He hadn't wanted to kill those cowhands but that was the way it always was. He'd be minding his own business and someone would try to blow out his wick. Or stab him in the back, like that time in Newton.

Rondo sat up. The first thing he did was place his hands on his Colt Navies. It was the first thing he always did, to reassure himself they were there. He always slept wearing them.

When on the trail, he propped his back on his saddle. When in a bed, he propped pillows behind him and sat with his back to the headboard or the wall. He hadn't slept on his side since the war. It was another thing he had trained himself to do.

Rondo cast off his blanket and stood. The barn was quiet and dark. He went to the double doors and opened one wide enough for him to step out.

Thunder Valley lay peaceful under a vault of stars that would soon fade. To the east a golden glow heralded the impending dawn.

Over in the chicken coop the rooster gave voice to his first crow of the morning.

The air was cool, and Rondo felt his skin break out in goose bumps.

A light was on in the Sether farmhouse, toward the back, where the kitchen would be. The mother, Rondo figured, preparing breakfast.

Rondo went to the pump. He cranked the handle and when water spouted, he cupped his hands and splashed some on his face and drank a handful. He was turning when he sensed a presence to his left and he whirled, his hands on the Navies and the Navies starting to rise when he saw who it was. "What are you doin' out here, boy?"

Matthew Sether timidly approached and gazed up at him. "I wanted a look-see."

"At me?" Rondo said.

The boy nodded.

"Do your folks know you're out here?"

"Ma is cooking and I heard Pa up and about in their room," Matt said.

"So the answer is no, they don't know," Rondo said. He'd noticed the boy staring at him a lot. "Why are you so interested in me?" As if he couldn't guess.

"Andy says you're a shooter."

"Don't you mean shootist?" Rondo knew the term was used a lot in the newspapers.

"No, Andy said shooter," Matt said. He stared at the pearl handles at Rondo's waist. "He says you shoot people."

"I've shot a few."

"My pa hasn't ever shot anybody."

"Good for him." Rondo turned and hadn't taken two steps when the boy was at his side.

"Why is that good?"

"A shooter is another name for a killer and in this day and age killers aren't popular."

"This day and age? Does that mean now?"

"It does," Rondo said. "There have been other days, other ages. Ever hear of the Greeks?"

"No, sir."

"They lived a long time ago. They didn't have guns so they fought with swords and such. Some were good at it and they killed a lot of other men and folks looked up to them and called them heroes."

"How do you know all that?"

"My grandpa used to read to me when I was your age. From a book that tells all about it. Can you read, boy?"

Matt nodded. "I'm fair at it. My ma taught me. Pa helped some but it's mostly Ma who does our schooling."

"Good for her," Rondo said. "Learn all you can and you'll be better off for it." He stopped at the door and pulled it wider.

"How's your horse?" Matt asked.

"General Lee has an abscess in his hoof. Do you know what that is?"

"I heard Ma and Pa talking about it."

"I have to treat it before I can ride him again," Rondo

said. "Could take a few days." Or more, he reflected, and frowned.

"Ma and Pa say you're welcome to stay as long as you like."

"I know," Rondo said. "And I'm grateful." He was also worried but he kept that to himself. "Shouldn't you be goin' in now? Your ma will have breakfast ready."

"She'll clang the bell when it's time."

"Bell?" Rondo said.

"A cowbell. She keeps it on a shelf in the kitchen. When she wants Andy and Sally and me to come, she clangs it."

"Most folks call that ringin' a bell."

"Sounds like a clang to me," Matt said.

Rondo smiled. He went to the stall General Lee was in and patted the Palomino's neck. "Mornin', big fella. I hope you're feelin' better today."

"That's a fine horse, mister."

"He's more than that. He's the only friend I have in this world."

"How come? Pa makes friends all the time. He says it's good to have them."

"You listen to your pa, boy." Rondo wanted to examine the afflicted hoof but it wasn't light enough in the barn yet. "He's a good man."

"He said the same about you."

Rondo glanced down sharply. "No one has called me good in so long, I can't remember when. You sure that's what your pa said?"

"I heard him and Ma talking," Matt replied. "They were talking about the men you've shot. Pa said he didn't care what people say about you, he can tell how a man is, and he thinks you're a good man."

"Well, now," Rondo James said.

"Well what?"

"Nothin'." Rondo entered the stall and hunkered and lifted the right foreleg to look at the hoof. He had been soaking it in warm water with Epsom salts, courtesy of Mrs. Sether, and then thoroughly drying it and applying a poultice. He always kept black ointment in his saddle-bags, just in case.

"Can I ask you a question?" Matt said.

"Isn't that what you have been doin'?"

"How else do you find things out if you don't ask?" the boy returned.

Rondo grinned. "You've got me there. What's your question?"

"Can I see you shoot sometime?"

"No." Lightly probing with his fingertips, Rondo gauged that it would be a day or two yet before the abscess blew out.

"Why not? I asked nice."

"I'm not a monkey on a rope," Rondo said. He chuckled at the boy's confused expression. "I saw one once, down to New Orleans. An old man had a small monkey on a rope. The monkey did tricks, and people would drop coins in a cup."

"If I give you a penny will you shoot?"

"That's not the point," Rondo said. "Other folks might think of me as a spectacle but I'm not."

"I wouldn't know about that," Matt said. "But Andy told me you can probably shoot the wings off a fly. I just wanted to see you do it."

"That would be some shootin'." Rondo sighed. "Next thing you know, they'll have me shootin' the fleas off a dog."

"I'd like to see that too, only we don't have a dog. Ours died a while back from old age."

"I have my druthers," Rondo said, "I'd like to die from the same affliction."

"So you really won't shoot for me?"

"I won't shoot for anyone."

The boy might have pestered Rondo more but his sister came down the aisle.

"Here you are," Sally said. "Ma sent me to look for you. Why aren't you washing up for breakfast like you're supposed to be doing?"

"I wanted to talk to Mr. James," Matt said sulkily.

"Get yourself inside. I, for one, am hungry, and we can't eat until we're all at the table to say grace." Sally motioned, and Matt reluctantly moved past her.

"I'm obliged, princess," Rondo said.

Sally blushed. "No one has ever called me that before." She took a step. "Aren't you coming?"

"I don't want to impose."

"Ma said I was to bring you. She said she's asked you to join us for each meal but you always refuse and I'm not to take no for an answer."

"Your ma is a gracious lady."

Sally nodded. "Pa feels the same. He said it's not right, you eating jerky out here in the barn while the rest of us have home cooking." She held out her hand.

Unfurling, Rondo let her lead him out and across the yard and around to the rear.

"After you."

"That's not how it works." Rondo held the door for her.

Sally dipped in a curtsy. "Thank you, kind sir."

The moment he stepped inside, Rondo was assaulted

with memories. Their kitchen was smaller and the walls were yellow and not white but the smells were the same and the warm comfortable feeling was the same and the family at the table might just as well have been the James family before all they had went up in the smoke of war.

"Don't be shy, Mr. James," Martha said. "We have plenty to share."

"It's not that, ma'am." Rondo removed his hat. A chair on the other side had been left empty and he pulled it out and sat. "This is awful kind of you."

"We'll talk more after grace," Martha said. "Roy, would you do the honors?"

Rondo bowed his head and clasped his hands. He remembered the plantation, the magnolias, the mint juleps his mother liked, the cigars his father smoked. He remembered it all, and he hurt so much inside, it was all he could do not to get up and leave.

"And we thank you, Lord, for our bounty," Roy concluded. "Amen."

All of them said the same, and Martha smiled. "Dig in, everyone."

Rondo looked at her and saw instead his mother with her golden curls and gay dresses, always smiling and laughing and happy until that terrible day.

"Is something the matter?"

"No, ma'am," Rondo said. To cover his embarrassment he ladled eggs onto his plate.

"Before I forget," Roy said as he buttered a slice of toast, "I'm going into town this morning with a couple of neighbors. You're welcome to come along."

"I shouldn't," Rondo told him.

"If someone was after you they'd have shown up by now." Roy took a bite of toast. "No one in Teton knows you, so you should be perfectly safe."

"I don't know."

Martha was selecting a strip of bacon. "You really should get away for a little. You've been cooped up in that barn for too long."

Rondo heard himself say, "There are a few things I need to buy." Ammunition was one.

"Good," Roy said. "We'll have a good time. And don't you worry. Everything will be fine."

"I hope so," Rondo James said.

10

Axel owned the spyglass. He was the cautious one, the one who thought things out, the one whose judgment the others relied on although Brule acted like their leader most of the time.

From a rise on the south side of Thunder Valley, Axel fixed his spyglass on a buckboard. "Four men. Two in the seat, two in the bed. The two in the seat are farmers. Can't tell much about the two in the bed. One has his head down on his chest and his hat pulled low but he's wearin' a slicker and farmers don't usually wear slickers."

"Headin' for Teton, by God," One Eye said, and cackled. "How nice of 'em."

"It would help to know which farms they're from," Brule said. "We'll have to spy on all of them and keep track of who's who."

"Spy hell," Ritlin said. "We pick one and ride up to it." He indicated a farmhouse and barn half a mile away. "That one will do."

"In broad daylight?" Brule said.

"Why not?"

"You know damn well why. You heard Charlton Rank. We're to do this quiet."

"They'll see us in broad daylight," Axel said, folding his spyglass.

"I don't give a damn," Ritlin said.

"Me either," One Eye echoed.

"I don't know what has gotten into you lately," Brule said to Ritlin. "The work we do, we can't afford mistakes."

"When do I make any?" Ritlin said, and with that, he tapped his spurs to his sorrel and made for the farm.

One Eye chuckled and followed.

Axel looked at Brule. "This isn't good."

"He's got a burr in his backside," Brule said. "Been that way since we heard about Rondo James."

"That's childish," Axel said.

"I agree. But he's my pard. What else can I do?" And Brule gigged his mount.

Axel frowned, and clucked to his. He shifted to stare after the receding buckboard and didn't stop watching until it was out of sight.

A farmer was chopping wood. Although it was spring, families needed wood for cooking and the occasional chill mornings. He paused to mop sweat from his brow with his sleeve, and when his plow horse in the corral whinnied, he looked up and saw them.

The farmer wasn't alarmed. He was used to people passing by now and then. He smiled and waited with the ax handle across his shoulder as they came around the corral and drew rein. "Morning, gents."

"Mister," Brule said.

"Nice day if'n it don't rain," One Eye said, and tittered.

"I hope it doesn't," the farmer said. "It's planting time and the seeds get washed away if it rains too hard." He placed the ax head on the ground and leaned on the handle. "I'm Frank Jackson, by the way."

Ritlin stared at the farmer until Jackson nervously shifted. From inside came the sound of a woman, humming. "That your missus?"

"Sure is," Jackson said, and boasted, "The sweetest gal around."

"Any sprouts?" Ritlin asked.

"Unfortunately, no," Jackson said. "We've wanted some but it hasn't worked out."

"Try a lot, do you?" One Eye asked.

"That's none of your business," Jackson said, coloring.

Brule turned to Ritlin. "If we're goin' to do it, you'd better get to it. We shouldn't sit around in the open like this."

"Do what?" Jackson asked. He was growing uneasy. He didn't like how the tall one in black stared at him nor how the runt with one eye kept grinning and chortling.

Ritlin swung down. "We'd be obliged for a drink of water."

"The pump is yonder," Jackson said, nodding. "Help yourselves."

His spurs jingling, Ritlin walked over. He took off his black bandanna, worked the lever, and got the bandanna soaking wet. Then he wrung it out, wiped his face and his neck, and retied it. The whole time, he stared at the house. When he was done he returned to his horse.

"You said you wanted a drink," Jackson mentioned. It struck him as peculiar that the man hadn't.

"Have any cows for sale?" Brule asked.

Jackson had his attention on the man in black. "What?

Oh, no. I don't ever sell one unless it won't give milk and all my cows are giving milk just fine."

"Ain't you lucky?" One Eye said, and laughed.

"I don't know what luck has to do with it," Jackson said. "Cows are cows."

"Are all your critters off in the pasture?" Brule asked.

"No," Jackson answered. He was stumped by this sudden interest in his cows. "I keep my best milkers in the barn."

Brule dismounted, his saddle creaking. "Show me."

"You want to see my cows? I just told you I don't have any for sale."

"If you'd be so kind," Brule said with a friendly smile.

Jackson would rather not but he figured he'd be shed of these men sooner if he humored them. He held on to his ax. It lent him a sense that they wouldn't try anything, even though an ax against pistols was little use. When he reached the barn he saw that it wasn't just the wide one who had tagged along. The man in black and the runt with the patch had trailed after him. The one who dressed like a cowboy was still on his horse. "Here they are."

Brule regarded the stalls and the cows. "Holsteins, aren't they?"

"You know your cows," Jackson said. "They give more milk than any other breed."

"Do they give more blood?"

"How's that again?" Frank Jackson wasn't sure he'd heard right.

"Do cows bleed out as fast as hogs?"

Jackson had heard about poor Tom Kline. A chill washed through him as he realized these might be the men responsible. He took a step back, or tried to, and was gouged in the spine by something hard. He glanced over his shoulder. The runt had a six-shooter pressed against him. "What's the meaning of this?"

One Eye grinned at Brule. "Not too smart, is he?"

"Can't blame him," Brule said. "It's not every day he has visitors like us." Drawing his large knife, he moved to the first stall.

"What in God's name are you doing?" Jackson said.

"What do you think?" Brule patted the cow on the head and rubbed its neck. The cow went on chewing its cud. "Dumb brutes," he said.

"Quit waving that knife around," Jackson said. "You might hurt her."

"That's the whole idea," Brule said, and with a quick motion, he slashed the cow's throat. Blood spurted, and the Holstein gave a start.

"My God!" Jackson exclaimed, aghast. Forgetting himself, he started toward the stall. Suddenly his head seemed to explode, and the next thing he knew, he was on his knees and overcome with pain and nausea.

"Behave yourself, cow-lover," One Eye warned, "or I'll cave in your skull."

"My cow!" Jackson lurched to his feet.

The whole front of the Holstein was scarlet and blood was continuing to flow. She swayed and raised her head and mooed, which caused more blood to gush.

"God, no." Jackson took another step and a foot hooked him from behind and he was shoved to his hands and knees.

"Stay down," One Eye growled.

Brule stepped to the next stall. His knife dripping red drops, he held it close to the next cow's neck and grinned at Jackson. "Ask me real nice and maybe I'll spare her."

"Don't," Jackson pleaded. "Please don't."

"That wasn't nice enough." With a savage swipe and a

twist, Brule cut the cow wide. He quickly stepped back as blood sprayed like rain.

"Oh Lord." Jackson pushed up but a blow to the side of his head felled him again.

"You don't listen worth spit," One Eye said.

"My cows," Jackson wailed. "Not my cows."

"Be thankful it ain't you."

Jackson saw the wide one move to the next stall, and the next. In shock and horror he heard the sickening *thuck* of the blade and saw the showerlike spray of death. "Please," he said, near tears. "Please don't."

Brule strolled back up the aisle and squatted. He grinned and wiped his knife clean on Jackson's shirt and slid it into its sheath. "Are you payin' attention?"

"Yes. Please, mister, don't kill any more of my cows. I'll do anything you want. Give you whatever you want. I'm not rich but I've got a few hundred dollars."

"You'll need it wherever you end up," Brule said.

"What?"

Brule swiveled on his boot heels and indicated the red pools spreading from the stalls. "You don't want to live here after today."

"What?" Jackson said again.

"I thought you were payin' attention?" Brule reached out and cupped the farmer's chin. "Look at me."

"I am."

"You have one week to pack up all your things and go, and never, ever come back."

"You want us to leave?"

"You're slow but you're gettin' there."

"You want us to give up our farm? Our home? All that we've worked so hard for?"

"It's either that," Brule said, "or lose every damn cow you own."

"And your own hides, besides," One Eye said.

"But . . . but . . . but . . . ." Jackson sputtered.

Brule drew his Smith & Wesson and held it so the muzzle practically touched Jackson's right eye. "Are you sure you're payin' attention?"

"Yes, God, yes."

"There's no buts. Either you do what the hell we tell you, or we come back. And the next time we won't be as nice as we're bein' now."

"You just killed my best milkers!" Jackson shrieked.

Brule cocked his revolver. "I'd calm down, were I you. Splatterin' your brains would mean no more to me than slittin' cow throats."

"You don't know what you're asking. You want us to give up *everything*. How will I explain it to my wife? She'd never agree. She loves it here."

"You still don't savvy," Brule said. "If you're still here a week from now, you'll be here permanent. Only it will be six feet under."

"I can't believe this is happening," Jackson said. "I just can't."

"You'd better. And you'd better believe a few other things. Go to the law and you're a dead man. Tell your friends and you're a dead man. Do anything but what we tell you and you're a dead man." Brule stood and let down the hammer and shoved the Smith & Wesson into his holster. He looked at One Eye and then past him. "Where did Ritlin get to?"

"Where do you think?"

From inside the farmhouse came a muffled scream.

Frank Jackson started to stand but Brule slammed him down and put a boot on his back. "Stay put, mister. You go runnin' in there, you're as good as dead."

"Beth!" Jackson cried.

"I wouldn't worry about explainin' things to her." Brule grinned and winked. "When my pard gets done with your missus, she'll want to leave Thunder Valley more than she's ever wanted anything."

"Dear God in heaven," Frank Jackson said.

11

—————— ·•·———

Roy Sether almost laughed when he noticed that Tom Kline was doing the same thing he was. They were on the buckboard seat with Tom holding the reins. In the bed behind them sat Moses Beard and Rondo James.

Every so often, Roy would turn his head just enough to glance at the notorious man-killer out of the corner of his eye. He saw Tom doing it, too. And once, when he looked over his shoulder, Moses was flat-out staring at the man.

Rondo James had his head bowed and his hat brim low over his face and apparently wasn't aware they were fascinated by him.

Or was he? Roy wondered. He couldn't imagine what it was like to have shot so many men. Or to be so famous. He remembered first hearing about Rondo shortly after the Civil War, in what was called the Gallatin Bloodbath. The newspapers made it a point to mention how Rondo shot each of them in the face. That became Rondo's trademark, you might say—he always shot men in the face.

That was more than two decades ago, Roy reflected. Back then, shooting affrays were widely written about in the newspapers. The exploits of the likes of Wild Bill Hickok and Jesse James were on everyone's tongue. That reminded him. He cleared his throat and said, "Mr. James, do you mind if I ask you a question?"

From under the hat came the low reply, "I've asked you to call me Rondo, Roy. I'd be grateful if you did."

"Sorry," Roy said. He had to admit he was more than a little awed by the pistoleer's celebrity. "But I've been meaning to ask. Are you any relation to Jesse and Frank James, you having the last name?"

"So far as I know," Rondo James said, "our blood never mixed. They're not kin of mine."

"That's too bad," Moses said.

Rondo raised his head, his eyebrows pinched over his nose. "Why bad, Mr. Beard?"

Roy didn't know what to make of the fact that while Rondo James called him by his first name, he always referred to Tom and Moses as Mr. Kline and Mr. Beard.

Moses uttered a nervous laugh. "Well, you know. Him being so famous and all. If you were related, that would make you doubly famous, wouldn't it?"

"You are a wonderment," Rondo James said, and bowed his head again.

Moses smiled at Roy and Tom as if he had just been given the greatest compliment in the world.

Tom looked at Roy and rolled his eyes.

Now that the silence had been broken, Moses said, "I sure hope I can find some pups for sale. Or better yet, free."

"Didn't think you were all that fond of dogs," Roy recalled.

"I'm not," Moses confirmed. "Tilda wants one and what Tilda wants, Tilda gets."

"Better watch out," Tom teased. "She'll be cuddling it instead of you."

"Don't ever tell her I told you this," Moses said, "but when it comes to cuddling, there are days I suspect she'd rather cuddle a tumbleweed than cuddle me."

"Women," Tom said.

"She wants it for a guard dog, mainly," Moses said. "So what happened to your hogs won't happen to our animals."

"A puppy isn't much of a guard dog," Roy said.

"I still can't get over someone doing that," Tom said bitterly. "Slitting the throats of all my hogs. What sort of man does such a thing?"

"There are all sorts in this world," Moses said.

"Nothing else has happened so maybe my wife is right and it was a bunch of drunks."

"It sure is strange they picked your hogs," Moses remarked.

Roy saw that Tom was becoming upset. "Enough about the hogs. It's been weeks since I've been into Teton. I'm looking forward to it."

"Did you hear about the high muck-a-muck who stopped for a night at the Timberland?" Moses asked. "Eb Harper was in town and saw them with his own eyes. He stopped and told me about it on his way to his farm."

"Didn't hear," Roy said.

Moses nodded. "Some fancy pants in a suit and a derby. He had six men with him, all dressed as fancy."

"He have a name?"

"He signed the register at the hotel as John Smith. But McCarthy over to the general store told Eb he thought he'd seen the gent before." Moses paused. "Thought he was a railroad man."

"Not them again," Tom said. "We already told them we're not interested in selling our land."

Roy was vaguely troubled by the news. The railroad representatives had been persistent in trying to persuade them to sell. Which was an understatement. They'd practically demanded it. He'd finally had to tell them to get off his land and stay off.

"No railroad is getting my farm," Moses said. "Tilda loves it here and she means to stay."

Roy gazed to the west. He never tired of admiring the Tetons. They were magnificent. They rose so high and so sheer, it was as if they thrust up out of the earth ready-formed. He especially liked how they seemed to change colors. At sunrise they were splashed with rosy hues. Midday, they were mostly brown with white patches. In the evenings they were sometimes bluish and sometimes purple, depending on the sky.

"You know," Tom said. "I have an idea. We should ask around at the saloons when we get there, find out if anyone has been bragging about killing my hogs."

"Who would brag about that?" Moses asked.

"You never know," Tom responded. "Drunks tend to run off at the mouth."

"Tilda doesn't like me to go in saloons."

"Are you a man or a mouse?" Tom said.

"Need you ask?"

Roy laughed. Come to think of it, he liked the idea of visiting a saloon. He hadn't been inside of one in months.

12

The road wound around a small lake with stands of cottonwoods along the shore. Out on the water, ducks and geese swam. A large fish jumped with a loud splash.

"Look there," Tom said, and pointed.

A cow elk was slaking her thirst. She'd waded a few yards out and her muzzle was in the water.

"Lordy, I love it here," Moses said. "Except for the snow and cold in the winters, it's the Garden of Eden."

"I wouldn't go that far," Tom said.

Roy spotted a bald eagle high on a spruce. The eagle was scouring the lake for prey. Even as he watched, it took wing and swiftly rose. It circled and suddenly dived, its talons extended. There was a flurry of spray and a flash of silver, and the eagle rose again, a fish clutched tight.

"How about you, Roy?" Moses asked. "Do you love it here as much as I do?"

"I surely do," Roy admitted.

They entered forest and lost sight of the lake. Roy smelled the aromatic scent of the pines, and breathed deep.

A yellow finch and its mate flitted from tree to tree, and somewhere a jay screeched.

"Either of you heard if hostiles have been seen around here lately?" Moses nervously brought up.

"I haven't heard of any," Tom answered.

Roy shook his head.

"I know the army says it has them under control," Moses said, "but that's not true and everybody knows it."

"Are you saying our government lies?" Tom said, and acted shocked.

"It would to lure in settlers," Moses said.

Roy had heard the same rumor. Namely, that the bigwigs in Washington wanted more people from east of the Mississippi River to move west of it. A lot of folks were understandably reluctant after hearing about all the massacres and scalpings. To counter that, the politicians kept crowing about how safe the frontier had become. But then, politicians and lies went hand in hand.

The road climbed slightly. Presently, in the distance, squares and rectangles were silhouetted against the backdrop of a towering mountain.

"Teton," Tom said.

"We've got eyes," Moses said.

Roy had been so engrossed in the scenery and their talk that he'd nearly forgotten about the man in gray. He was reminded when Rondo James sat up and shifted so his back was to the side of the buckboard.

"We have to talk, Roy."

"What about?"

"I don't want any harm to come to you on my account," Rondo James said.

"Why would it?"

"Because I am who I am," Rondo said in that slow drawl of his. "If word gets around I'm in town, there's no tellin' what might happen."

"I'm sure I speak for my friends when I say we won't tell anyone."

"You wouldn't have to. Thanks to the damn newspapers and those silly stories that've been written about me, I get recognized." Rondo stressed with a scowl, "I get recognized a lot."

Roy shrugged. "If it happens, it happens. We'll cross that bridge when we come to it."

"No," Rondo said. "We'll cross it now. I aim to wander around by my lonesome and meet you at the buckboard when you say to."

"We'll wander together," Roy said. He had no specific purpose in going to town other than to be with his friends. "Don't worry about me. I'll be fine."

"That's just it," Rondo said. "I like your missus and I wouldn't want her to become a widow and have it be my doin'."

"You can't blame yourself if others are looking for trouble."

"I'm the piece of meat and they're the flies."

"What a curious way to describe yourself," Moses said.

Rondo didn't seem to hear him. "Usually I try to slip into towns quiet-like and slip out again without anyone guessin' who I am but it doesn't always work out."

"Pull your hat low and button your slicker," Roy suggested.

"It's not always enough."

Roy put it from his mind. As Martha was fond of saying, what would be, would be.

The road curved through another patch of woodland and when the buckboard rattled into the sunlight, there Teton was. Main Street spread before them, bustling with people on foot and on horseback. They passed the livery and the church with its white steeple and the Timberland.

"The hogs and a pup can wait," Tom announced. "First thing we do is wet our throats."

"I'm for that," Moses agreed.

Roy licked his lips at the prospect. He was about to comment that he was for it too when he spied several men in blue uniforms lounging in front of the general store. "Why, there are soldiers in town."

"They must be on patrol and stopped to rest," Tom speculated.

"Or they're after redskins," Moses said.

"Or it could be," Rondo James said, "they're after me."

13

The surrender at Appomattox not only brought about the end of the war, it almost brought about the end of the South. The North wasn't content with its military victory. The end of the conflict was the start of a new campaign to reduce the South to a helpless ruin.

The North unleashed their dogs of avarice under the guise of rebuilding. The politicians were behind it. Using new laws they passed, they created an opportunity to plunder and pillage to their greedy hearts' content.

Like ravaging locusts, a horde of carpetbaggers descended on the Southern populace. The Northerners bought up all the land they could get their hands on, for cheap, then hired the recently freed blacks to work their farms and plantations, for cheap. They reaped profits hand over fist.

The carpetbaggers took over industry after industry, from railroads to cotton production. All under the banner of reconstruction. Southerners were reduced to slaves of a new kind; they were in economic servitude to their Northern masters.

The South wasn't just defeated. It was pummeled with the sledgehammer of righteous reform and then its bleeding carcass despoiled of its lifeblood.

For the men who served in the Confederate army, life was especially harsh. They were reviled by the new elite. They were despised for their service. They were looked down on and literally spat on and there was nothing they could do but grit their teeth and bear it or they would be thrown behind bars.

The few who refused to bear it became folk heroes. The James brothers and their ilk, sons of the South who resisted the Northern tyranny by doing plundering of their own.

And then there were men like Rondo James.

Rondo was in Dodge City when he started on the road to unwanted fame. He was in a saloon, minding his own business, playing cards. As always, he was wearing his Confederate gray.

Four Yankee soldiers were drinking at the bar. Rondo saw them glance his way a few times but he didn't think much of it until they swaggered over to the table. The other players promptly got out of there.

A big bulk of a sergeant sucked down some bug juice, wiped his mouth with his sleeve, and sneered, "What do we have here?"

"You don't want to do this," Rondo told him without looking up.

"Listen to the Johnny Reb," the sergeant growled.

"Who does he think he is?" another trooper demanded. "Telling us what we can do?"

"Why are you wearing that uniform, Reb?" said the big bulk. "Didn't you hear the war is long over?"

Rondo had set down his cards and placed his hands flat on the table. "This will end badly," he'd warned them.

"Take it off," the sergeant said.

Rondo had looked at him.

"You heard me. Take off that Reb uniform. Right here and now."

Rondo hadn't moved.

"We mean it, Reb," the sergeant had said. "I lost a brother to you stinking Confederates. Get shed of it, or else."

"No."

The trooper across the table had laughed. "He thinks he has a choice."

"Dumb as stumps, these Rebs," said the fourth trooper.

All of them put their hands on the flaps to their holsters and the sergeant placed his other hand on Rondo's shoulder.

"You have one minute to start peeling those buttons."

Nearby tables had been vacated. Patrons were moving as far back as they could. The bartender yelled that he didn't want trouble in his place but the soldiers ignored him.

"Didn't you hear me, Reb?"

"Don't hold your breath," Rondo had replied.

"Enough of him," said the trooper across the table, and he jerked at his revolver.

So did the others.

They all nearly had their hardware out when Rondo moved. He drew as he rose, flicking his pearl-handled Colt Navies up and out, and he shot the sergeant in the face with his left Colt even as he shot the trooper across the table in the face with his right Colt. The soldier on his left was raising his weapon and Rondo shot him in the face and shifted, and then he shot the last trooper in the face just as the man squeezed the trigger. The slug plowed into the table and the trooper crashed on top of it, and the table and the four soldiers crashed to the floor and were still.

Rondo had backed out of the saloon with a smoking Colt in each hand. No one tried to stop him. He left Dodge on the fly. He was surprised that no one came after him. He was even more surprised that the army didn't hunt him down. Later he learned that since the four soldiers were off duty and drunk and witnesses told the marshal that the soldiers started it, no charges were brought against him.

Still, from then on, Rondo made it a point to stay shy of troopers. "It could be these here have heard about Savage," he concluded his account after Roy Sether had Tom Kline wheel the buckboard into a side street and park.

"They're not the law," Moses Beard said. "They don't go around arresting people."

"I doubt you have anything to worry about," Roy agreed.

Rondo thought it safer that he stay in the buckboard, and said so.

"And not have a drink with us?" Roy hopped down. "Come on. I have an idea."

Rondo indulged him. With Roy in front and Tom and Moses to either side, they headed down Main Street. He pulled his hat low and shoved his hands in his pockets and pulled his slicker close around him so no one could see his Navies. He tensed when a pair of bluecoats came ambling the other way, but neither so much as glanced at him.

"See?" Roy said, and grinned.

They entered the first saloon they came to. It was called The Ax and Stump. A dozen or so timbermen and others were getting an early start on their drinking.

Roy offered to buy the first round. They carried their glasses to a corner table and Moses was about to sit in the chair against the wall when Rondo James said, "That one's mine."

"A chair is a chair, isn't it?" Tom said.

"Not for me." Rondo walked around and Moses moved and the Southerner sank down. "I never sit with my back to a room." He leaned back. "Any room."

"It must be rough being you," Roy said.

Rondo grunted.

The three farmers drank and talked about their families and the crops they hoped to harvest and joked and laughed and had a good time.

Rondo mostly listened. He had forgotten what it was like to be ordinary. He had forgotten how it felt to spend a carefree hour with friends. Hell, he told himself, he hadn't had a friend in so long, he'd forgotten what that was like, too. He marveled that these three treated him no differently than they treated one another. He was used to being feared and shunned and despised. Suddenly he realized Tom Kline was talking to him.

". . . a last round on me? What do you say?"

"I'm obliged," Rondo said.

Tom got up and went to the bar.

"Remember," Moses said to Roy. "No mention of this to Tilda or she'll make me wish I was never born."

"She's not that bad," Roy said.

"Do you live with her? Or do I?" Moses actually shuddered. "She's fearsome when her dander is up."

"Martha thinks highly of her," Roy said. "When we have you over, Tilda is always nice."

"With others she doesn't show her fangs," Moses said.

Roy chuckled and turned to Rondo. "How about you? Have you ever been married?"

Just when Rondo was starting to relax and enjoy himself, a cloud settled over him. "No," he said simply.

"Never found a gal you could love?" Moses asked.

"I don't like people pryin' into my personal life," Rondo said gruffly, and regretted it when Moses Beard recoiled as if he'd been struck. To ease the sting he said quietly, "I don't have the right to inflict myself on a woman."

Tom came back carrying a tray with their beers. He set a brimming glass in front of each of them and settled into his chair. "What did I miss?"

"Rondo was just saying he can't inflict himself on a female," Moses said.

Tom smiled at Rondo. "Inflict yourself how?"

"Marry," Rondo said.

"It can be an affliction when the wife is in a mood," Tom said, and laughed, "but how can it be an infliction?"

"Listen to you, big words," Moses said.

All three looked at Rondo. He raised his glass to his lips and swallowed and smothered a frown. They were only being friendly, he reminded himself. "How could I marry a gal, never knowin' when someone might show up on our doorstep wantin' to buck me out in gore?"

"There are men who have done that?" Tom said. "They come hunting you, I mean?"

Rondo told them about Warm Springs, Texas.

It was three years after Dodge City. He'd been wandering

where whim took him, winning enough at cards to keep food in his belly and to take rooms in seedy hotels. That night he'd won a sizeable pot and returned to the Lone Star to get some sleep before he headed out in the morning.

Rondo had taken off his boots and spurs and set his hat on the table. He'd unbuckled his gun belt and hung it over the back of a chair. Sliding the Navies from their holsters, he lay on his back, propped by his pillows. As he always did, he placed a pearl-handled Colt on either side of him, within easy reach, and let himself drift off.

Well past midnight, Rondo was awakened by a noise. It took him a few seconds to realize it was the scrape of his window being slowly raised. His room was on the second floor at the front, above the porch overhang. Someone had climbed up and was trying to slip in undetected.

Rondo had reached for his pistols. He heard whispers and realized there was more than one. Sliding off the bed, he'd crouched beside the table.

The room was dark but the moonlight spilling in revealed the two figures who slipped over the sill and straightened. They turned toward the bed and gun hammers clicked.

Rondo shot them. He couldn't see their faces but their heads were good targets and he triggered shots at each black circle. When he lit the lamp, he found them slumped in a pile, their brains splattered over the wall and window.

The marshal was summoned by the hotel owner. It was a clear case of self-defense so the lawman didn't try to take him in.

The next morning, as Rondo was about to ride out, the marshal showed up. Apparently he had asked around and learned that one of the two men was the brother of one of the soldiers Rondo had killed in Dodge.

"Now you know why I've never had a wife," Rondo finished. "Or any friends, for that matter."

"Well, you have some now," Roy said, and Tom and Moses nodded.

"I'll be damned," Rondo said.

14

The McWhirtle farm was next to the Jackson farm. Aaron McWhirtle was fifty-seven and from Illinois. He'd come west later in life than most. His family said he was crazy to start over at his age. But not Maude. She'd hankered after a new life and new challenges as much as he did. That was why they'd been married for thirty-one years. They always thought alike.

Now, busily stringing a fence at the rear of the chicken coop, Aaron thought about how much he loved that woman, and how blessed he was that she chose him for her husband. He whistled as he worked. He was content and at peace with the world.

When Aaron heard the thud of hooves and saw four riders cutting across his recently planted field, he lost some of that sense of peace. Strangers should know better, he told himself.

The hammer in his hand, he moved to meet them. Although he was angry he did the neighborly thing and smiled. "Hello, gents," he greeted them when they drew rein. "To what do I owe this visit?"

"Two in one day," said a short man with an eye patch.

"Two what?"

"Lunkeads," a rider as wide as a buckboard answered. "You live so close to Frank Jackson that we figured we might as well."

"I'm afraid I don't understand."

"That's because you're a miserable dirt farmer," declared a tall rider in black. "And your kind are as dumb as stumps."

"Have a care," Aaron bristled. "You have no cause to insult me."

"Sure we do," said the man in black, and with a jab of his spurs he caused his horse to bound forward.

Aaron was caught unprepared. The animal slammed into his chest and knocked him down. He braced for the stomp of heavy hooves but the man in black had drawn rein. His chest a welter of pain, Aaron gaped in disbelief and blurted, "What in hell did you do that for?"

"They're always slow as molasses, these sodbusters," said the man with the eye patch.

"I reckon we'd better explain it to him," said the last of the riders, whose cowboy garb lent the illusion he had drifted in off the open range.

Aaron was slow getting to his feet. It wasn't bad enough he'd been ridden into; he had a sense that he was in great danger. "There must some mistake," he said. "I don't know you gentlemen."

"No mistake at all," said the wide one. "We're givin' you twenty-four hours to clear out."

"To do what?"

"To pack your things and light a shuck," said the man

with the patch. "We don't care where you go just as long as you are gone."

"That's insane," Aaron declared.

The tall man in black swung down. "Is your wife as old as you are?"

"Maude?" Aaron said. "We're the same age. Why?"

"Too bad," the man in black said. "I don't like them old. So you will have to do."

"I'm terribly confused."

"Let me set you straight," the man in black said, and in the blink of an eye his ivory-handled Colt was in his hand and he smashed the barrel against Aaron's temple.

Aaron had no time to duck or yell in protest. His head exploded in agony and he was felled where he stood. Dimly, he was aware of being on his hands and knees and the world churning like butter in a churn.

"Twenty-four hours," the man in black said, "or we'll come back."

"And the next time we won't be as nice," the man with the patch said.

"You call this nice?" Aaron fumed. He was afraid but he was mad and his fury trumped his common sense. "I'll have you arrested for this."

"You reckon?" said the man in black, and his leg swept up and in.

To Aaron it felt as if the man's boot drove his stomach into his spine. Overcome by torment, he collapsed. Bile gouted from his mouth and he thought he might vomit. All his strength left him. "No," he said. "Don't."

"We can't hear you," said the man with the patch.

"Please," Aaron begged.

The man with the patch cackled. "I love it when they grovel."

The man in black hiked his boot over Aaron's head. "I should stomp your brains out."

"No," said the wide one. "We're not to kill yet."

Aaron was relieved beyond measure when the man in black lowered his leg. Inadvertently, he swallowed his own bile, and grimaced.

"I hate havin' a leash on me," the man in black said. Bending, he seized Aaron by the shirt and hauled him to his feet. "Twenty-four hours, mister. If you're still here, my pard won't stop me from puttin' you under."

"What is this about?" Aaron said. "What did I do that you're treating me like this?"

"Jackass," the man in black said, and punched him in the gut.

Aaron would have fallen if the man wasn't holding him. As it was, he sagged and nearly passed out. The man shook him, hard, until it felt as if his bones were about to burst from his skin. The shaking stopped and he thought his ordeal was over. Then a knee caught him in the groin.

A veil descended. The next Aaron knew, he was lying facedown and tasted dirt and blood in his mouth. He groaned and struggled to roll over.

Iron fingers clamped on to his shoulders and he was slammed onto his back. "Have a good nap?" the man in black said.

"No more," Aaron said. "I'll do whatever you want."

"You might be fakin'," the man said, and kicked him in the side.

Aaron couldn't stop himself—he cried out from the pain, and clutched his side.

"Careful," the wide man said to the man in black.

"Quit naggin'," the man in black said. Reaching down, he gripped Aaron's chin. "How many teeth you got?"

"What?" Aaron was so awash in agony he couldn't concentrate.

The man in black punched him in the mouth.

Aaron's head rocked to the blow. More pain flooded through him. Blood filled his mouth and bits of teeth fell on his tongue.

"How many now? Twenty-four hours," the man in black said yet again, and straightened. "I reckon that's enough." He turned toward his horse.

From near the rear of the chicken coop came a voice tinged with fury and choked with emotion. "Hold it right there, you scalawags."

Aaron was spiked by terror. He raised his head and had to squint to see Maude, holding the shotgun. "No!" he gurgled through the blood.

The man in black and the three on their mounts had frozen.

"What have you done to my husband?" Maude demanded, coming around the partially completed fence. She glanced at Aaron and stifled an outcry. "You animals. You awful animals."

The wide man looked amused. The man with the eye patch was grinning. The cowboy showed no emotion.

As tense as taut wire, the man in black said, "Look what we have here."

"Why did you do this?" Maude shrilled, gesturing with her elbow at Aaron. "Explain yourselves."

"Lady," the wide man said, "if you know what's good for you, you'll put that howitzer down."

"I hope she doesn't," the man in black said.

"Darned right I won't," Maude said savagely. Tears were in her eyes. "I should shoot you where you are. I've got buckshot in these barrels, and it will blow you to pieces."

"Killed a lot of men, have you?" taunted the man with the eye patch.

"No," Maude said, then said fiercely, "but don't think I can't to protect the man I love."

"Ahhhh, how sweet," said the man with the patch.

Aaron was collecting his wits. He spat out blood and pushed to his knees. "Maude, you have to get out of here. Give me that shotgun and go."

"No," Maude said, not taking her eyes off the four men. "I'm not leaving you, Aaron."

"They'll hurt you, or worse."

"Like the dickens they will." Maude put her cheek to the shotgun. "Take off your gun belts and drop them."

"Like hell, lady," said the man with the patch.

"I mean it." Maude pointed the shotgun right at him. "I will by God blow you in half."

"We've got us a regular she-cat," the wide one said, and laughed.

"This isn't funny," Maude said. "Not even a little bit." Her face was steel and resolve. "Now do as I say or I squeeze these triggers."

"Maude, no," Aaron said. Fighting the torture, he made it to his feet, and swayed. He hurt all over, his head most of all, and blood seeped over his lower lip. He spat again and said, "Give me that shotgun."

"No," Maude said.

Aaron wished she would listen. This wasn't like her. They hardly ever argued or had a cross word for one another. She was mad, he realized. More mad than he'd ever seen her. Watching the four hard cases, he went to her, careful not to step in front of those twin barrels. "Maude, I don't want you hurt. Give me the shotgun, please."

"No."

The man in black did a strange thing. He smiled. "Must be my lucky day."

"Don't," said the wide one.

"You see her, Brule."

"Damn it, Ritlin. We have been told not to until it's necessary."

"It's necessary now," Ritlin said.

"I'm with you," said the man with the eye patch.

The one who looked like a cowboy and who hardly ever spoke said, "One Eye and Ritlin are right. We can't let her run us off."

"Damn it to hell," Brule said.

Maude raised her head. "How can you talk like that with me pointing this at you? Take off your guns, I say. And do it before I lose my patience."

"You've lost more than that," Ritlin said. His hand was a blur and his ivory-handled Colt filled it and there was the boom of the shot.

Aaron saw a hole blossom in the middle of Maude's forehead, saw her head snap and the back of her skull burst with hair and bone and gore. He saw the life fade from her eyes and he screamed at his loss and grabbed for her to catch her before she fell. He was thinking only of her. Too late, he glanced at the four monsters who had invaded his life. All four held revolvers. He opened his mouth to curse them and his world crashed with noise that nearly deafened him. Then he was on the ground with no sense of having fallen. A dark figure blotted out the sun and he heard the last words he would ever hear.

"Let's kill the chickens and cows, too."

15

Roy and his two friends and the Southerner were on their way home from Teton.

A cute puppy lay in Moses's lap. Thanks to a tip from a bartender, they'd found an old woman whose dog had a litter about a month ago, and she was giving them away.

Tom had made a deal with the owner of the general store to buy four hogs from him just as soon as they were weaned from their mother.

"Yes, sir," Tom was saying. "Irene will be tickled as can be."

"So will Tilda," Moses said, rubbing the pup.

Roy glanced at Rondo James. "We could have gotten a pup for you, too."

"First you want me hitched and now you want to saddle me with a dog?" Rondo shook his head. "Next you'll be sayin' I should have kids."

"They make a difference in a man's life," Roy said. "They bring out the best in us."

"If he has any best to bring out," Rondo said.

"All men have some good in them."

Rondo peered up from under the hat brim. "No," he said. "Some don't."

"My Martha likes to say that every barrel has its bad apples but the bad spots can be cut out and the apple made good again."

"With all respect, suh," Rondo James said, lapsing into his most pronounced drawl yet, "your missus is mixin' apples and people. Some people are as evil as can be."

"I've yet to meet one," Roy said.

"I pray to God you don't."

Roy figured that was the end of it and swiveled in his seat but he was mistaken.

"The life I've led," Rondo said, "I've spent most of it on what folks would call the wrong side of the tracks. I've seen men, I've *killed* men, who'd think no more of guttin' you than they would squishin' a fly."

"We've lived in whole different worlds, then," Roy said. He'd lived his on the right side of the tracks. His family had a lot to do with it, but then again, he didn't have it in him to kill or spend all his nights drinking and carousing.

"I reckon," Rondo said.

They were past the forest and the lake and nearing the first of the farms.

Tom sat up and said, "What's that all about?"

The farm belonged to Frank Jackson and his wife Beth. They owned a buckboard, and they were barreling down the rutted track from the farmhouse to the road as if the hounds of Hades nipped at the rear wheels.

"Look! They have a lot of their belongings in the back," Moses observed. "Where could they be going?"

Roy wondered the same thing. He didn't know the Jacksons all that well. He'd socialized with them a few times but he wasn't as close to Frank as he was to Tom and Moses.

Tom brought the buckboard to a stop.

The Jacksons barreled toward them and for a few moments it appeared that Frank Jackson might not stop and would smash into them. Then, hauling back, Jackson brought his buckboard to a stop in a swirl of dust. "Out of our way."

"Howdy, Frank," Tom said. "And how are you, Mrs. Jackson?"

The woman didn't answer. Her head was bowed and her fingers were entwined in her lap. She was wearing a bonnet and shawl; the bonnet wasn't tied and the shawl hung unevenly.

Frank motioned and said, "Didn't you hear me, Kline? Move. We need to get by."

"What's your hurry, Frank?" Moses asked. "You keep going like you are, you're apt to roll."

Frank Jackson glanced over his shoulder at his farm. "That's the least of our worries."

"Is something wrong?" Roy asked. He thought he saw tears glistening on Beth's cheeks.

"We're leaving," Frank said.

"To Teton?" Tom asked.

"For good."

Roy looked at Tom and at Moses and they all looked at the Jacksons.

"Kind of sudden, isn't it?"

"Not sudden enough," Frank Jackson said.

"When did you sell your place?" Moses asked. "I didn't know it was for sale."

"We didn't sell—" Jackson said, and stopped. "Listen, will you get out of my road? We have a lot of miles to cover before dark."

"Hold on," Roy said. This made no sense. "If something's wrong, we'd like to help. We're your neighbors."

"If you're smart you'll leave too."

"Leave Thunder Valley?" Tom laughed. "That'll be the day. Irene loves it here more than she's ever loved anything. Including me."

The humor was wasted on Frank Jackson. "By God, if you won't move, I'll go around you." He slapped the reins and bumped over the corner of a tilled field to reach the road. With another slap and a shout, the buckboard rumbled off to the east.

"What in God's name was that all about?" Tom said.

"She was crying," Roy said.

"Who?"

"Beth. Didn't you see her face?"

"We should catch up to them and make him tell us what's going on," Moses proposed.

"I can try," Tom said.

Roy clung to the seat as it bounced under him. For a while it appeared they were gaining. Then Frank Jackson looked back and said something to his wife and went faster.

Finally Tom slowed and said, "It's hopeless."

Roy let go of the seat.

After a while the next farmhouse appeared, set a quarter mile back from the road.

The McWhirtle place. Roy liked Aaron and Maude. They had kindly natures, maybe because they were older than the rest of the farmers in the valley.

In the glare of the afternoon sun Roy almost missed the black specks in the sky. Shielding his eyes, he saw the specks more clearly. After what just happened with the Jacksons, they filled him with alarm.

The specks were vultures.

"Stop the buckboard," Roy said.

Tom didn't ask why. He brought it to a halt and joked, "Is that beer catching up with you?"

Roy pointed. "What do you make of that?"

Moses leaned over the side for a better look. "Good God. Are those buzzards?"

"They are," Roy said.

"There must be seven or eight," Moses said. "Why are they circling over Frank's place?"

"Maybe a cow is down," Tom said.

"Aaron wouldn't leave it lying there," Roy said. Farm animals that died were nearly always buried as soon as possible.

"Let's have a look-see," Tom said.

"Go slow," Rondo James cautioned.

Once again Roy had almost forgotten the pistoleer was there. The Southerner was so quiet, it was easy to do. "Do you know something we don't?"

"Slow keeps a man alive longer than reckless," Rondo said.

More vultures were winging in from various points of the compass. From the size of the gathering, whatever drew them must be a virtual feast.

"Stop," Rondo James commanded when they came within hailing distance of the house. Lithely swinging up and over, he landed lightly on the balls of his boots. Sweeping his slicker aside to reveal his pearl-handled Navies, he hollered, "Hallo the house."

No one came to the front door or poked a head out a window or came from the barn.

Rondo crossed to the front porch and knocked loudly. As before, no one appeared. He came down the steps and on around the side, gesturing for them to stay where they were.

Roy lost sight of him.

"You see how he moves?" Tom said. "He reminds me of a panther on the prowl."

"It reminds me not to provoke him," Moses said.

"He wouldn't hurt us," Roy said.

"He's a killer," Moses said. "Give him an excuse and he'd shoot any of us."

Roy might have believed that, once. Now that he'd gotten to know the Southerner, he'd discovered a core of integrity that ran bone deep.

Rondo James reappeared, making for the chicken coop. Once more he was lost to sight. This time when he reappeared he moved slowly and his body was slumped as if in great sadness. He beckoned.

It wasn't until they passed the house that Roy saw dead chickens everywhere. From the manner in which their heads were bent, someone had caught chicken after chicken and wrung their necks.

"What in the world?" Moses blurted.

Over by the barn a calf was on its side in a pool of blood.

Just inside the barn lay a cow.

Tom was aghast. "It's my hogs all over again."

A new fence was being strung to keep the now-dead chickens in, and just beyond, Rondo James stood over two still forms.

Roy was off the buckboard before it stopped. He ran over and was horror-struck by the bullet holes and expressions on Aaron and Maude. They had died ugly, violent deaths. "It can't be."

"Did you know them well?" Rondo James asked.

"Well enough." Roy scanned the farm and the fields. "Who could have done this?"

"I can track them if you'd like."

"You do, and I'll go with you."

Tom and Moses would only come so close.

"Awful, just awful," the latter said.

"It's indecent, them lying there like that," Tom said. "I'll fetch a blanket to cover them with."

"How long do you figure they've been dead?" Moses said.

Rondo James squatted and put his hand on Aaron's neck and his forehead, then gripped a wrist and flexed the fingers. "About two hours, give or take."

"We can catch them if we hurry," Roy said. "Aaron has some good horses we can use." He ran to the barn, giving the dead cows a wide berth, only to be brought up short by the grisly spectacle inside.

The horses were dead in their stalls. Cows had been brought out and slaughtered. A pigpen contained only dead pigs. A rooster with a broken neck was under the ladder to the hayloft.

Roy was dumdfounded. The carnage was beyond comprehension. To murder Aaron and Maude was bad enough—but to kill cows and pigs and horses. What had they ever done to hurt anyone?

"The hombres who did this did it for the fun of it," Rondo James said behind him.

Roy hadn't realized he'd asked the question out loud. "All the horses have their throats slit. We can't go after whoever did this."

"We can if we hurry to your place," Rondo said.

"Then let's go," Roy replied. "Tom and Moses can stay and tend to the bodies."

"It's best if I go alone," Rondo said. "There might be gunplay."

"I hope there is," Roy said.

16

It surprised Roy, this sudden and unexpected urge to kill. He'd never had an urge to harm a human being in his life. He didn't have much of a temper and tended to take what life dished out in stride. Martha once said that it was one of the traits that attracted her to him. He wasn't like a lot of men who got angry at every little provocation.

But Roy was angry now. He was more than angry. Aaron and Maude McWhirtle had been good people. They didn't deserve to die so brutally, so coldly. To him it was inconceivable that men could be so vile.

His rage must have showed on his face when he brought the buckboard racing up to the farmhouse and sprang down and rushed onto the porch.

Martha and the children had heard him coming and hurried out to meet him, and the shock on their faces gave him pause.

Roy stopped and said simply, "Aaron and Maude have been shot dead."

"Dear Lord, no," Martha breathed, a hand to her throat.

"There's more but I don't have time," Roy said, opening the door. "We're going after the killers."

"We?" Martha said.

"Rondo and me." Roy ran down the hall to the parlor. He'd left his Winchester propped against the china cabinet. The ammunition was in a drawer in the kitchen. He took the box out and shoved it into a pocket.

His family had followed him. Fear was writ on Martha's features and anxiety on the children's.

"Why must you do this?" Martha asked in that quiet way she had when she was extremely upset.

"Someone has to."

"But why you?"

"They were our friends."

"Granted. But you're not a lawman. You've never shot anyone."

"Rondo has."

"He's a man-killer. He's used to it. You're not. Please forgive me, but you might be getting in over your head."

"We have to stand up for our own. That includes our friends. The nearest law isn't near at all. When something like this happens, we have to deal with it. No one else will."

"Then round up some of the other men to go with you."

"There's no time. It's late in the day. I take the time to go to the other farms, dark will fall, and we won't be able to head out until morning. By then the killers will be long gone."

"Killers," Martha said. "Plural. How many are we talking about?"

"Rondo says there are four."

"You're relying on him a lot."

"It's a stroke of luck he's here. He can track, he can shoot better than most anyone. You won't have to worry when I'm with him."

"In point of fact I will," Martha said. "Four against your two. What if they see you are after them and lie in ambush?"

Roy started to go.

"Didn't you hear me?"

"I can't predict what will happen," Roy said. "I'm going and that's final."

"Oh, Royden."

"Can I come, Pa?" Andy asked.

"No."

"I'm old enough. And I can shoot."

"You're to stay with your mother and keep watch." Roy stopped again. "Whoever these men are, they might have done something to the Jacksons, too. I'll explain later. But it could be they haven't left. It could be they're still in Thunder Valley. So I want you, Andy, to load your rifle and sit out on the front porch and keep watch. Stay alert. Matt, you can help by looking out the upstairs windows. Go from room to room so you can see in all directions. Sally, you stay at your mother's side."

"Is all that really necessary?" Martha asked.

"If you'd seen what I've seen," Roy said, "you would know it is."

"What if they come here, Pa?" Sally asked. "What should we do?"

"Any riders come, anyone you don't know, you bolt the doors and fire a warning shot out the window."

"I don't like you leaving us at a time like this," Martha said.

Roy didn't, either. But if he had a chance to catch the killers, he had to take it. He told himself his family would be all right. It occurred to him that Tilda Beard and Irene Kline were alone at their farms, and he thought about sending Andy to warn them. But he didn't. And felt bad for not doing so.

He hurried upstairs for his coat. He figured to be out all night. When he came back down, Sally was waiting at the bottom of the stairs.

"Ma is fixing food for you to take."

Roy went to the kitchen.

Martha was briskly going about from cupboard to cupboard.

"It won't be much but it will keep you from going hungry. Some bread and dried beef and a couple of apples."

"It's thoughtful of you."

"I'm scared, Roy," Martha said as she got twine from the pantry to wrap the bundle. "I'm terribly scared."

"You should be all right."

"Should be?"

Roy leaned the Winchester against the kitchen table and walked over. She turned and he enfolded her in his arms. He was startled to feel her tremble. "I wish there was another way."

"Why can't . . ." Martha stopped, then took a deep breath. "Why can't Rondo go by himself?"

"That wouldn't be right. They weren't his neighbors. They were ours."

"I bet he would if you asked him."

"I bet he would, too. But I can't do that, Martha. I'd never live the shame down."

"There's no shame in putting your family first."

"There's shame in being a coward. And that's what it would amount to."

Martha hugged him fiercely and astonished him by

passionately kissing him full on the mouth. She rarely did that unless it was night and they were in the bedroom with the door closed and the kids were all asleep.

"Be careful," she breathed into his ear.

"Rondo will be with me."

Martha drew back. "You think too much of that man. Will he take a bullet for you, too?"

Roy took the bundle and got his rifle. He could feel her eyes bore into his back.

The kids were on the porch. Andy had his rifle. Sally looked ready to cry. Matt was grinning excitedly.

"Listen to your mother," Roy instructed them.

Andy and Sally nodded and Matt said, "We'll do everything she says to, Pa."

"I don't expect to be gone more than a day or two," Roy said.

"That long?" Martha said.

Just then Rondo James came around the house leading two of Roy's horses. Roy's saddle was on one and Rondo's on the other.

"I wish General Lee was fit to ride."

"These are good animals," Roy said. "They have a lot of stamina."

"They'll need it." Rondo swung up. "We'd better light a shuck. We're losin' daylight."

Roy turned and touched Martha's cheek and got out of there while he still could. Guilt burned his gut like red-hot coals. Since he didn't have a scabbard for his rifle, he had to hold on to it as he climbed on and raised the reins. "I'll be back," he promised.

"You'd better be," Martha said.

Roy nodded at Rondo and jabbed his heels. It wasn't until they were on the road, heading west, that either of them spoke.

"You don't have to do this," Rondo James said.

"You sound like my wife. But I do. This is our home. It was our neighbors who were shot. If I don't have to do this, who does?"

Rondo made no reply.

Roy wondered, though, if that was his real reason. He had to admit, it was exciting riding with one of the most famous shootists in the West.

As if the Southerner were privy to his thoughts, Rondo said, "A man has to know when not to bite off more than he can chew."

"I'll hold up my end," Roy said, even though he wasn't exactly sure what that would entail.

Tom and Moses were digging when they got to the McWhirtle farm. One grave was done and they were working on the second. Both had stripped off their shirts and were sweating profusely.

"As soon as you're done, head for your own places," Roy advised.

Tom nodded and wiped his forehead with his forearm. "We aim to. The dead animals will have to wait until we call a meeting of every last man in the valley."

"We can't bury all of them," Moses said. "It would take a week."

"Think of the stink if we don't," Tom said.

"We'll deal with it when I get back," Roy said. "First we catch the culprits."

"We don't have time for all this gab," Rondo James said.

Roy wasn't done. "If by some chance I don't make it back, look after Martha and my family, will you?"

"You can count on it," Tom assured him.

Moses nodded.

Rondo wheeled his mount and used his spurs.

Smiling grimly at his friends, Roy rode to catch up. Now that they were starting out, the risk he was about to take hit him with the force of a blow. They could be killed. Even the great Rondo James.

"Are you all right?" the Southerner asked. "You're lookin' peaked."

"I'm fine."

"If you say so."

The tracks were plain enough that even Roy could follow them but he let the pistoleer do the honors. Whenever Rondo bent to examine the sign, Roy scanned the horizon for a glimpse of the killers.

The four had struck off due west until they were past the last of the farms and then veered to the road and taken it toward Teton.

"The nerve," Roy said. "Riding right out in the open."

"No one knows what they did," Rondo said. "We do, but we don't know what they look like."

"You're saying that if they reach Teton ahead of us, we'll never find them."

"I'm saying we should ride like hell."

They did, and since Roy wasn't the best rider in the world and had to concentrate to keep up, he didn't notice a bank of dark clouds until Rondo pointed them out.

Leagues to the west was a thunderhead; a storm front was sweeping down on Thunder Valley. In the spring storms were so common that ordinarily Roy didn't give them a second thought. "That's not good."

"It sure ain't," Rondo agreed.

As if it were an omen, thunder rumbled.

17

Axel peered through his spyglass. He lowered it and raised it to his eye again and said, "I'll be damned."

"What?" One Eye said.

They had stopped on a low grade so Brule could tighten his cinch. Brule was always doing that. He claimed he could feel when it was loose but others suspected it had more to do with the time years ago when a cinch came loose and he took a spill and broke his left arm in two places.

"Two riders are after us."

Brule looked up from his saddle. "The hell you say."

"Are you sure it's us they're chasin'?"

"They're ridin' hell-bent for leather."

One Eye swore. "I told you we shouldn't be takin' our sweet time. But would any of you listen?"

"I don't run from farmers," Ritlin said. He was leaning on his saddle horn and had that rare contented look he always had after he'd indulged in what he called his "fun."

"One of them might not be," Axel said, his eye still to the glass. "They're a long way off yet and it's hard to be sure but I think one is wearin' a slicker."

"Maybe a rancher," Brule said, "or a cowhand who works for one of the ranchers."

"We should fan the breeze," One Eye suggested.

"Like hell," Ritlin said. "We pick a spot and wait for them and shoot them to ribbons."

"Why do I have to keep remindin' you that we're not supposed to kill any of them yet?" Brule said.

"A little late for that."

"Mr. Rank isn't goin' to like it," Brule said. "He was plain as could be on how he wanted us to handle this."

Ritlin shrugged. "Rank's not here."

"How long do you reckon we have?" One Eye asked Axel.

"Half an hour, about."

Brule climbed on his mount and they rode until they came to where woodland brushed the road.

"This should do," Ritlin said. "Brule and me will take the right side, you two take the other."

Axel reined left into the trees and One Eye followed, muttering. They concealed their horses and sought cover close to the road. Finding suitable trees to crouch behind, they squatted with their rifles at hand.

One Eye did more muttering.

"What's in your craw?" Axel asked.

"I'm tired of those two lordin' it over us," One Eye said grumpily. "If one ain't givin' us orders, the other is."

"It's Brule mostly," Axel said. "And it's not as if we have to go along with what he says."

"We don't and Brule wouldn't like it one bit. He reckons as how he's the boss."

"You're makin' a mountain out of a molehill, like you always do."

"You think so? Buck them, then. I dare you to buck Brule or Ritlin and watch what happens."

"I'm not afraid of them."

"Me either," One Eye said. "Well, maybe Ritlin, a little. He's plumb loco."

"He can die the same as anyone."

"Will you listen to yourself? He's loco but he's also the quickest son of a bitch I've ever seen."

"There are quicker," Axel said, his spyglass fixed on the road.

"Not many. And that's beside the point. The point is that the two of them are too damn bossy. If you don't agree, fine. If you do, maybe we should start standin' up for ourselves more."

"I stand up for myself when I have to," Axel said.

"Hardly ever, as I recollect," One Eye said. "Come to think of it, of the three of you, I know less about you than I do Ritlin and Brule."

Axel looked at him. "How did that come up?"

"You hardly ever talk. This is the most I can remember in all the time we've ridden together."

"You can shut up now," Axel said.

One Eye's good eye narrowed and his face twisted with resentment but he didn't say anything. He leaned against the pine and looked the other way.

Across the road, Brule hollered, "Any sign of them?"

"I can see them," Axel answered, his eye to the spyglass. "They'll be in range in a couple of minutes."

"Brule will pick 'em off with his Winchester as slick as

can be," One Eye predicted. "He's the best rifle shot of any of us."

"There's one better," Axel said.

"Who?"

Axel didn't answer.

"You don't mean you, do you?" One Eye scratched his chin. "Come to think of it, I ain't ever seen you shoot a rifle. Our killin's has mostly been done with six-shooters and knives, and that time I strangled that gal with a rope."

Axel was using his spyglass again.

"Damn," One Eye said. "Now that I think about it, I ain't ever seen you draw, either."

"They're comin' fast," Axel said.

"I remember you shootin' folks but I don't remember you drawin'. How can that be?"

"You spend too much time in your head."

"What the hell kind of thing is that to say? What does it even mean?"

"You don't pay attention to what's goin' on around you," Axel said.

"Like hell I don't. I pay as much attention as you do."

"No," Axel said. "You don't."

"You know, maybe it's better when you don't gab. You say strange shit."

A calm came over the woods. The trees were still, the birds and insects quiet. It was as if the wild things were holding their collective breath. But it didn't last. There was a great sigh, as of air escaping from a bellows, and the tops of the trees swayed. Then it was the lower branches as the wind gradually increased in intensity. Overhead, the sky darkened by degrees. Black clouds scuttled in, replacing the fluffy white cumulus.

"There's a storm comin'," One Eye said.

"Didn't you see it earlier?"

"I was watchin' behind us."

"I told you," Axel said. "You don't observe much."

"Go to hell."

The wind became a shriek.

"I hate gettin' wet," One Eye said. "It's why I don't take baths."

"I hate sittin' near you," Axel said. "It's why I don't breathe deep when I do."

"Hell to you twice over," One Eye said. "I never could stand it when my ma would shove me in a washbasin and scrub me until I was raw. She did a lot of things that riled me. It's why I killed her."

A limb broke with a loud crack and tumbled from on high.

"You should have seen the look on her face," One Eye reminisced, and chuckled. "She could hardly believe it."

"They usually don't. Most folks hope to live to a ripe old age."

"Not me. I don't care when I die. Just so I don't go lyin' in bed."

"Oh?" Axel said, and set down his telescope and wedged his rifle to his shoulder.

"I don't want it to be slow," One Eye said. "I'd like so there's no pain."

"We don't always get to choose."

"I know that, damn you. I'm not stupid."

"No one thinks they are." Axel put his cheek to his Winchester. "Hush now. They're almost on us."

One Eye peered through the trees.

A pair of riders were approaching at a gallop. The wind was buffeting them so hard, they had to hold on to their hats.

One wore a slicker and it was flapping like the wings of a bird trying to take flight.

"They'll ride right into our lead," One Eye gloated.

Axel gestured sharply and then became rigid. His trigger finger curled.

One Eye sensed that he was about to fire and he tittered in anticipation.

With a nigh-deafening crash of thunder and a blazing bolt of lightning, the deluge was unleashed. The rain fell in sheets, a seemingly solid wall of wet that cascaded like a waterfall.

In a span of seconds One Eye couldn't see his own hand in front of his face. "Hell," he said, and couldn't hear his voice for the keening of the wind.

Axel was suddenly at his side. He put his mouth to One Eye's ear. "The rain ruined my shot. I'm goin' to the road. Stay with the horses."

One Eye frowned. Once again someone was telling him what to do. He was about to say he'd go to the road too when he thought he heard a shrill whinny. He swore and got up and ran to his sorrel. It was skittish about thunderstorms, and it was stamping and pulling on the reins. Grabbing the bridle, he kept it from running off.

The trees were having fits. Not far off there was the crash of one falling. Limbs snapped and crackled.

One Eye was soaked, and hated it. He held on to the sorrel and cursed thunderstorms and skittish horses and stupid dirt farmers and Brule and Ritlin and Axel.

One Eye kept expecting to hear the boom of shots. If not for the damn storm, the farmer and the cowboy would already have been blasted from their saddles.

The rain was cold, and before long One Eye was shivering. He cursed his goose bumps, and promised himself enough hot coffee to drown an ox once they made it to town. To be followed by a night of whiskey and cards. Maybe he'd treat himself to a dove, too. He wasn't like Brule, who liked pokes more than anything. Once or twice a month was enough for him. Ritlin didn't do it that much, either, and when he did—One Eye almost pitied the women. As for Axel, One Eye had to think back. Now that he did, he couldn't recollect a single instance of Axel ever payin' for it, or, for that matter, ever lyin' with a woman. That struck him as peculiar.

As quickly as it swept down on them, the storm rumbled to the east. The rain went from a downpour to a drizzle. The wind was lessening, too.

The sorrel's eyes were wide but it had stopped shaking and stomping.

One Eye let go of the bridle and ran for the road. He hurried around the last tree and almost collided with Axel, who was staring to the east, his rifle at his side.

Across the road stood Brule. He, too, was looking back the way they had come.

"What happened?" One Eye said. "Why didn't you shoot them?"

"There wasn't anyone to shoot," Axel said.

Brule crossed over, saying, "I thought for sure we had them until that damn rain commenced."

"Maybe you just didn't see 'em, the rain was so heavy," One Eye said. "They could have gone right by and you wouldn't know."

"They turned back," Axel said.

"That's my guess," Brule agreed.

"Well, hell," One Eye said. "Leave it to the Almighty to spoil our fun."

18

Roy Sether was feeling glum as he rode up to his house and dismounted. The sun had set and stars were out. His clothes were still damp from the drenching he'd taken and he couldn't wait to change into dry ones.

Andy came off the porch carrying his rifle. "Did you catch them, Pa?"

"We had to turn back because of the storm."

Rondo James didn't climb down. He gigged his mount up next to Roy's, leaned over, and snagged the reins. "I'll see to the horses. You go be with your family."

"Thanks for trying," Roy said.

"It's a shame," Rondo said, and rode off.

"Anything happen here while I was gone?" Roy asked as he tiredly trudged up the steps.

"It's been real quiet," Andy said.

Martha and Sally were in the parlor. His wife was knitting and his daughter was reading.

"You're back!" Martha said in delight. Putting down

her needles, she came to him and they embraced. "I was so afraid."

"We never got so much as a glimpse," Roy said. "When the storm struck, we realized we wouldn't overtake them this side of Teton. Rondo decided we should turn around and here I am."

"Thank God," Martha said.

"Those murderers are still out there." Roy refrained from mentioning that the next time it could be their house the killers paid a visit.

"You're not a lawman," Martha said. "You had no call to be traipsing off after those vermin."

"We've already been through that. This is our valley, our home."

"I'd like to keep it that way," Martha said.

Roy refused to have her draw him into an argument. "I need to get out of these clothes." He gave his Winchester to Andy. "Would you put this away for me?"

"Sure thing, Pa."

Roy had forgotten that Matt was to keep watch from upstairs. His youngest was in a chair near the bedroom window, asleep. Carefully picking him up, Roy carried the boy to his own bedroom and gently laid him down. Matt mumbled but didn't waken.

Donning an old shirt he took from a peg on the closet door, and a clean pair of pants, Roy went back down. The aroma of brewing coffee and food drew him to the kitchen.

Martha was at the stove, slicing a carrot into a pot. "I'm making stew," she remarked. "You need something hot in your belly."

The coffee would have sufficed but Roy sat at the table. "Where are Andy and Sally?"

"I sent her up to get ready for bed. It's late." Martha

finished with the carrot and picked up a potato. "I don't know where Andy got to."

"Tomorrow I'm sending him to the farms and the ranches," Roy said. "We'll hold a meeting here tomorrow night."

"What do you make of it all?"

Roy had been pondering that question all the way home. "The Jacksons leaving. Aaron and Maude murdered. Tom's dead hogs. Plus the other animals that were slaughtered." Roy paused. "Someone has it in for us."

Martha whittled at the potato, leaving the skin on. "By us you mean everyone in Thunder Valley?"

"Could be."

"It's only been farmers," Martha noted. "Not the ranchers, Olander or Buchanan. Maybe one of them is behind it."

"To what end?" Roy countered. "Olander thinks he's king of Thunder Valley but he's never so much as hinted he'd like to drive us out and take it over."

"We don't know much about Buchanan," Martha said.

"He keeps to himself. The few times I've seen him, he didn't strike me as the kind who would do this kind of thing."

"You never know."

No, Roy thought, the devil of it was, they didn't. "I still don't think it's them. Olander has a dozen punchers riding for his brand. Buchanan has eight or nine. No one can get anywhere near their houses without being seen."

"So you're saying whoever is behind it figured farmers are easier pickings?"

"Something like that."

"But why?"

"It could be outlaws," Roy speculated. "They are as common as fleas in some parts."

"Outlaws would steal money and other valuables. Were Aaron and Maude robbed?"

Roy was almost ashamed to admit that "I never thought to look to see if anything was taken."

"So we really don't know anything at all."

Roy felt more glum than ever.

"We should send someone for the marshal."

"I'll ask Olander and Buchanan. One or the other can send a cowhand."

"I know one thing for sure," Martha said. "You're not going off again and leaving us alone."

"I won't," Roy said.

"You promise?"

"As I live and breathe."

Rondo James stripped the horses and placed them in their stalls. He was about to climb to the hayloft and spread out his bedroll when out of the corner of his eye he glimpsed movement in the barn doorway. He flashed his right hand down and up.

"It's Andy Sether," the oldest boy said. "Sorry if I startled you."

As swiftly as he had drawn, Rondo twirled the Colt into its holster. "Don't ever sneak up on a man like me."

"You wouldn't shoot someone you know, would you?"

"Not on purpose," Rondo said. "But men like me are liable to put a slug into you before you can blink."

Andy came over. "Why do you keep saying men like you? You're not a badman. My pa said so."

"I like your pa. He doesn't go around judgin' a book by its cover, as the sayin' has it."

"You're a book?" Andy said.

"Everyone is. 'Course, you can't really tell about a person until you get to know them, but nine times out of ten, their face and the little things they do will tell you how they are."

"If you say so," Andy said uncertainly.

"Just remember what I said about sneakin' up on me and we'll get along fine." Rondo figured the boy would take the hint. He reached for the ladder.

"Do you like people much?" Andy asked.

Rondo stopped with a boot partially raised, and lowered it.

"I've never been asked that before."

"Ma says that outlaws must hate people or they wouldn't be outlaws. The same must be true for shooters."

"Don't mix apples and oranges. A man can be a shooter and not be an outlaw. Look at Wild Bill Hickok."

"Didn't he die a long time ago?"

"Ten years, give or take."

"I was only six. I don't remember him."

"He was a shooter. One of the best. He once shot a man by the name of Tutt through the chest at seventy-five yards. He liked to gamble and he liked his whiskey but he never turned outlaw. Wore a badge now and again, in fact."

"I still don't understand why you say men like you."

Rondo sighed. He set down his bedroll and walked to the door. Hooking his thumbs in his gun belt, he gazed out over the farm and the valley. "Your folks have a nice place here, boy. Wouldn't you say?"

"I suppose," Andy said. "It's not the biggest farm ever but it's not the smallest, either."

"Forget the size. It's peaceable here, I bet. You can go the whole day without someone tryin' to kill you. And at night you can turn in without worryin' that someone will knife you in the back while you sleep."

Andy laughed. "Who would want to live like that?"

Rondo looked at him. "I do. Each and every day. I can't go anywhere but I have to watch out for those who want to do me in for no other reason than the uniform I wear. Or because they've heard of me and want to prove somethin' to themselves."

"Seems to me," Andy said, "that you could change that easy enough."

"Oh?"

"That old uniform," Andy said. "Why go on wearing it so long after the war? Wear clothes like everybody else wears and no one will know you were a Confederate."

"I want them to know," Rondo James said. "I want to remind them there are some of us who didn't bow to their will and never will."

"Remind who?" Andy said.

"Those who decided they had the God-given right to lord it over those who didn't think like they did."

"Are you talking about the war? I wasn't even born then. All I know is the North fought the South over freeing the slaves."

"That's what they want you to think but there was more to it. My family didn't own slaves. I might not have joined up at all except for that tyrant Lincoln sendin' troops to invade Virginia."

"Abraham Lincoln? My ma says he was the best president ever."

"To the Yankees he was. To those of us who had their kin killed and their homes burned and everything of value confiscated, he was a smooth-talkin' dictator. He denied the states their rights. He pitted brother against brother, cousin against cousin. And killed more Americans than the British ever did. The day I heard he was shot, I tipped a drink to his assassin."

Andy gnawed on his lower lip. "You'd be better off talking to Ma about all that. She knows more history than me."

"You asked about the uniform."

"So you wear it because you're proud of it?"

"I'm not just proud, I'm *damn* proud."

"I don't have much to be proud about," Andy remarked. "I'm too young yet."

"Your pa does." Rondo nodded at the farmhouse. "He's carved out a good life for you and the rest of your family. I don't mind admittin' I envy him."

"You do?"

"I can't ever have what he does. Don't get me wrong. I'm not whinin'. But I wouldn't do a woman any favors by marryin' her. Not when I could be bucked out in gore any day of the week."

"You could take a new name," Andy said. "Move where nobody ever heard of you."

"I tried, boy. I went all the way to Montana and that wasn't far enough. I suppose there's always Alaska but I'm not partial to cold and snow. As soon as General Lee is cured of his abscess, I'm headin' out. I don't rightly know where yet but I can't stay here."

"Darn. I was hopin' you'd stick around and help my folks. Ma is worried something awful about the killings."

"She should be. Somethin' bad is afoot."

"So will you or won't you?"

Rondo James didn't answer.

19

Roy had never heard his house so noisy.

They were all there.

The two ranchers, Olander and Buchanan, sat in straight-backed chairs off to one side. Whether they felt they had to sit apart from the rest, Roy didn't know.

With Aaron McWhirtle dead and Frank Jackson gone, that left seven farmers, including Roy. Tom Klinc and Moses Beard were on the settee. The other farmers were Haverman, Prost, Carson and Nettles.

The wives were out on the porch. There weren't enough chairs in the kitchen for all of them, and Martha had taken the tea outside.

The kids were upstairs.

Roy moved to the middle of the room and raised an arm and silence fell. "First of all, I want to thank all of you for coming on such short notice."

Nettles cleared his throat. He had a ruddy face and was much too fond of food but good with the soil. "Aaron dead and Frank gone? How could we not come? What in hell is going on, Roy?"

"That's what I'd like to know," Haverman said, and some of the others nodded.

"Don't forget my hogs," Tom said.

"Or the other animals that were killed," Moses mentioned.

Prost raised his hand as if he was in school. "Do you reckon all of it is related somehow?"

"Of course it's related," Carson said. He had coarse red hair and a lot of freckles. "It all happening at the same time can't be coincidence."

Several started talking at once but stopped when Olander rose out of his chair. Olander was short, the shortest man there, but carried himself as if he were the tallest. He also loved to hear himself talk. "I never thought I'd see the day that a murder was committed in Thunder Valley. It's been peaceful here. We all get along right fine. That isn't always the case between cattlemen and corn growers—"

"We grow a lot more than corn," Tom interrupted.

Olander blinked. "Why, yes, Tom, you do. I didn't mean that as a slight. I'm only saying we have a good thing here and I'd like to keep it that way."

"Hear, hear," Haverman said.

"Whoever is behind it might have already left," Olander talked on. "Outlaws and riffraff don't stay in one spot too long. But then again, it's damned peculiar that they started out by killin' a bunch of hogs and then came back and killed the McWhirtles and ran off the Jacksons."

"Damned peculiar," Carson said.

Buchanan, who rarely spoke, broke his silence. "That's why it ain't outlaws."

Olander looked down at him in confusion. "How's that again, Sam?"

"They didn't kill the Jacksons. They ran them off. Outlaws don't run people off. They rob them or they kill them. So it ain't outlaws."

"It could be dumb outlaws," Olander said.

"Even dumb outlaws wouldn't slaughter hogs for no reason," Buchanan said.

"Maybe they were drunk," Prost said.

"Drunk outlaws would be in town beddin' whores," Buchanan said. "They wouldn't be ridin' around lookin' for hogs to kill."

"He has a point," Carson said.

"I suppose," Olander said. "But I've seen people do a lot of strange things for no reason at all. The issue now is whether whoever is behind all this has moved on or hasn't. If they have, it's over. If they haven't, it's not."

"Come to that conclusion all by yourself, did you?" Buchanan said.

"Now, now, Sam, don't get irritable on us. We're only trying to get to the bottom of this."

"I'm from Texas," Buchanan said. "You're from New Jersey. We talk different. We dress different. And we get to the bottom of things different."

"How do you intend to get to the bottom of this?" Olander asked.

"I will shoot any son of a bitch who shows up on my spread and can't explain why he is there. I've given orders to my hands to do the same."

"You can't shoot people just because you don't know them," Olander said.

"Watch me."

"This isn't Texas. I'd like to think we're a little more civilized."

"Listen to you," Buchanan said. "And now you listen to me. Most Easterners are nitwits. They can't tell a steer from a heifer unless they get down on all fours and look underneath. But I'll hand it to you. You're not a bad rancher—"

"Thank you," Olander said.

"I ain't done. You're not a bad rancher, but you have the Eastern habit of thinkin' rings around things. When there's somethin' that needs doin', do it. Don't think it to death. And the thing to do with killers is to kill them."

"Hear, hear," Haverman said again.

"I'm postin' my land so it will be legal," Buchanan said. "Not that legal matters much way out here."

Roy had been listening as intently as the rest. "It matters to me. Mr. Buchanan. And I think that's a good idea. We should post Thunder Valley."

"Post the whole valley?" Tom said.

"Post it how?" Moses asked.

"We post signs," Roy said. "I can have my Andy and Sally make them. We'll tell of the killings, and warn that strangers must identify themselves or risk being shot."

"I don't know if I can shoot someone," Prost said. "I've never killed before."

"Who here has?" Nettles said.

"Me," Buchanan said.

Everyone looked at him.

"You did hear me say I'm from Texas?" Buchanan said.

"Speaking of killing," Olander said, and turned toward Roy. "What's this we hear about you taking in a boarder who has shot more men than there are in this room?"

Roy hid his surprise. Tom and Moses had given their word they wouldn't say anything. Then again, they had gone into Teton together, where a cowhand could have seen them and gotten word to Olander. "He's not a boarder. He's staying until his horse is healed."

"Maybe he's behind all this," Olander said. "The reputation he has."

"He's not."

"You can't be certain."

"He was with us when the McWhirtles were killed," Roy said. "It couldn't be him."

"He could have killed them the night before."

"Their blood hadn't dried," Roy said. "We got there soon after."

Buchanan stirred. "Who is this you're talkin' about, anyhow?"

"You haven't heard?" Olander said. "Mr. Sether, here, has seen fit to extend a helping hand to Rondo James."

"The hell you say," Buchanan said, and stood. "Where is he?"

Roy moved between the rancher and the hall. "I don't want you giving him trouble. I tell you, he's not to blame."

"Give Rondo James trouble?" Buchanan said, and for the first time ever, Roy heard him laugh. "Hell, I want to shake the man's hand."

"You know him?" Olander said.

"Never set eyes on the gent," Buchanan said. "I wore gray in the War of Northern Aggression."

"I've never heard it called that," Olander said.

"That's because you're a damned Yankee." Buchanan went to leave but Roy held out a hand.

"Hold on. Shouldn't we settle this business about the killings first?"

"I thought we had," Buchanan said.

"Posting Thunder Valley won't stop the killers if they're out to kill more of us," Roy said.

"Maybe we should patrol it," Tom suggested. "Like the army does."

"And who will work our farms while we're doing the patrolling?" Prost asked.

"In case you've forgotten," Haverman said, "it's planting season. I, for one, can't spare the time."

"Me either," Carson said.

The seven farmers looked at the two ranchers and Moses Beard said, "Both of you have punchers."

"Who I need to help run my ranch," Olander said. "I can't spare any for patrolling."

"I could spare one or two," Buchanan said. "But I've got a better idea."

Everyone waited.

"We hire Rondo James to hunt the killers down."

Olander smiled. "Hire a man-killer to kill a pack of killers? I like it."

Roy saw some of the others nod. "I don't know. He's not an assassin. He's a shootist."

"What the hell's the difference?" Nettles said.

"He might take it as an insult," Roy said. "And I happen to like him."

"It can't hurt to ask," Buchanan said. "And I'll do the askin'. One brother in gray to another." He started out and the rest fell into step in his wake.

Roy hesitated. He was sure Rondo would say no. Reluctantly, he caught up. The women all rose and a few asked where the men were going and all the women joined the exodus across the yard to the barn.

Buchanan stopped and called out, and in a few moments Rondo James strode into the sunlight, his pearl handles gleaming bright.

"What do we have here?"

Buchanan introduced himself to James, adding, "I fought for the South, same as you. Damn all blue-bellies to hell." He smiled and held out his hand.

Rondo James shook.

"I'll keep it short," the Texan said. "You know about the killin's. We'd like to hire you to find however many are to blame and—"

"There are four," Rondo said.

"You know this for a fact?"

"We found their tracks at the McWhirtles'. Roy and me went after them but a storm spoiled any chance we had of catching them."

Buchanan glanced at Roy. "No one tells me a damn thing."

"What's this about hirin'?" Rondo asked.

"We'd like to pay you to keep after them until they are dead," Buchanan said.

"I'm no assassin."

"I told them that," Roy said.

"He did," Buchanan confirmed. "But I saw no harm in askin'. One Confederate to another." He began to turn. "Sorry we bothered you."

"How much?" Rondo James said.

"Eh?"

"How much are you willin' to pay?"

"We hadn't gotten that far," Buchanan said. "I'll put up three hundred dollars."

"I'll match that," Olander offered.

Moses stepped forward. "I can spare a hundred."

"How about a hundred from each of the farmers?" Roy proposed. "That will bring the total to thirteen hundred dollars."

"Can't have that," Buchanan said. "It's unlucky. I'll add another hundred to make an even fourteen."

Rondo James became the focus of all eyes. "Gents— and ladies—you may consider me hired." And he patted his pearl Colts.

20

One Eye cackled and smacked the whore's naked fanny. "Not bad, darlin'," he complimented her. "All that fat makes you softer than the bed."

"Go to hell," the woman said sleepily.

One Eye smacked her again, harder, and slid off the bed and gathered up his clothes. He was having a fine time. Earlier, he'd downed half a bottle and let Myrtle talk him into forking over the price of a poke. Now that was done with, and the night was young yet.

"Yes, sir," One Eye prattled as he pulled on his pants. "I'll tell my pards about you. Any of them pays for a tumble, you give me a cut rate the next time, you hear?"

Myrtle mumbled something.

"That's all right, darlin'. You rest. Bein' with me always wears a gal out." One Eye tittered and was soon dressed with the Remington at his hip and his hat jammed low. Whistling, he sauntered down the hall and descended the stairs.

"Look at you, all smiles." Alice, the madam, was re-clining on a sofa fit for the queen of Persia. "I take it you got your money's worth?"

"Myrtle is a peach," One Eye said. "I may let her do me again the next time I'm in the mood."

"I thought men are always in the mood?"

"That's a rumor started by you females." One Eye strolled out into the cool night air. To the west reared the inky silhouettes of the Tetons. Stars speckled the dark vault of sky. He breathed deep and chuckled and ambled along Main Street until he came to the Grand Lady.

Brule and Axel were at the usual corner table.

"Where's Ritlin?" One Eye asked as he claimed a chair.

"Sleepin'," Brule said.

"This early?"

Brule shrugged. "You know how he is. He'll not get any for three or four days and then sleep the night away."

One Eye rubbed his hands together. "I'm so full of vinegar I could bust at the seams. We should head for Thunder Valley and put a scare into more farmers."

"There's no need to hurry," Brule said. "Rank gave us three months, remember?"

"The sooner we're done, the sooner we get the rest of our money," One Eye said.

"You rush things, you do it on your own," Brule said. "I am all for takin' our sweet time."

"As we all should be," Axel said. "Ritlin has spoiled it. I can't say I like what he's done."

"Don't let him hear you say that," One Eye said.

Brule said, "We'll give the farmers a few days to stew over the pair we shot. Then we'll hit them again."

"Fine," One Eye said. He chugged from their bottle

and smacked his lips. "I wish this was Denver. There'd be more things to do than we can shake a stick at."

"There's plenty here," Brule said. "Cards. Whiskey. Women."

"It's not Denver," One Eye persisted. He liked big cities. They were always so exciting. His favorite was Saint Louis. He'd been there once and had the time of his life.

"There's something I want to show you," Brule unexpectedly announced. Sliding a hand under his brown vest, he pulled out a large folded paper.

"What the hell is that?" One Eye asked.

"There's a surveyor's office here. I paid it a visit. At first he wouldn't give me what I wanted but ten dollars changed his mind."

"What's worth that much?"

Brule unfolded it. "The latest property map of Thunder Valley, with the farms and ranches marked."

One Eye leaned on his elbows. The lines and squares and rectangles were so much nonsense to him. "Why do we need it?"

Brule touched a cluster of squares and a circle. "This here is the Jackson farm. The pair who couldn't skedaddle fast enough after Ritlin was done with the wife." He touched a different cluster. "This is the McWhirtle farm. The pair we left for the buzzards."

"I get it," One Eye said. "We can tell who is where."

Brule nodded. "We'll pick who to hit in advance and know exactly where they are."

"I wouldn't have thought of it," One Eye said.

"Actually, it was Axel's idea. He comes up with some good ones."

"He's never shared any with me."

"You're not in charge," Brule said.

"Neither are you."

Brule was examining the map and didn't notice One Eye's expression. "I spoke for us with Charlton Rank. I set this job up."

"That doesn't give you the right to boss us around."

Brule looked up. "What the hell are you talkin' about? When have I ever bossed any of you? We agreed when we started ridin' together that each of us is our own man."

One Eye glued his mouth to the bottle. It seemed to him that he was being talked down to. "I'm always treated like the least of us."

"Are you drunk?" Brule said. "You have an equal say in everything and get an equal share of the money. Now stop your bellyachin'."

"There you go again," One Eye said in disgust. He pushed his chair back. "I need some fresh air." Sucking on the bug juice, he left the saloon. On an impulse he headed north. Since there was no law and no ordinance against public drunkenness, he went on sucking as he walked. About a third of the bottle was left when he turned west down a side street lined with cabins.

Windows glowed, and shapes moved across curtains.

One Eye placed his hand on his Remington. "I have half a mind to break some glass." He sniggered and drank and was about to turn and go back when his head exploded with pain and he was sucked into a black hole. Dimly, he was aware he had been struck from behind. He struggled to stay conscious and felt something being stuffed into his mouth. He tried to bite the fingers doing the stuffing but the man was too quick for him. He felt his wrists being bound and then his ankles. With a supreme effort he raised his head to try to shout through the gag but another blow sent him spinning into a void.

*   *   *

One Eye jolted awake. He was lying on his side. His head pounded and his wrists hurt from the tight rope. He tried to sit up and couldn't. He looked around and was stupefied to find he was no longer in town. He was in a clearing surrounded by woods.

A campfire crackled. Beside it, hunkered with a tin cup in his hands, was Axel. The aroma of freshly brewed coffee was in the air.

One Eye went to swallow, and froze. The gag was still in his mouth. If he swallowed he might dislodge it and suffocate. He held himself still and uttered a loud grunt.

Axel looked over. He took a sip of coffee. "I reckon your head must be splittin' something awful." He set down the tin cup and came over. "I'm goin' to pull the gag out. Try to bite me and I'll cut off your ears and maybe your nose besides." He hiked his pant leg and slid his fingers into a boot and pulled out a doubled-edged dagger. "Didn't know I had this, did you?"

One Eye felt the sharp tip pressed to his throat. He stayed still as Axel pried and pulled a wadded bandanna from his mouth. Axel tossed the bandanna onto the fire, replaced his hideout blade, and returned to his coffee.

One Eye wet his mouth a few times and swallowed to relieve his dry throat. Finally he croaked, "What the hell is this? Why'd you jump me?"

"You brought it on yourself."

"We're pards," One Eye said. "We've rode together on how many jobs now?"

"Eight in four years," Axel said.

"So I'm askin' you again," One Eye said, controlling his temper. "Why?"

Axel stared into the darkness and drank.

"Damn it to hell," One Eye growled. He tested the

rope but it was hopeless. To his considerable surprise, he realized his Remington was in his holster.

"We're about a mile up into the mountains," Axel said quietly. "You can cuss and shout if you want but no one will hear you."

"All I want is an answer, damn you, Axel."

"That's not my real name."

"What?"

"Sometimes you try a thing to see if it will work and if it doesn't you have to get rid of the loose ends, as my cousin would call them."

"What?" One Eye said again. He was too confused for words.

"You wanted to know why. I just explained."

Swiveling his legs under him, One Eye managed to make it to his knees. "You didn't explain nothin'. What does your name have to do with this?"

"Ask Rondo James. He knows about names. He can't go anywhere but his gives him away."

One Eye wished his head would stop hurting so he could think. "I don't savvy," he confessed.

Axel shrugged. "That's all right. It's not important that you do. Give me a minute to finish my coffee and we'll get to it."

"Get to what?"

"The end of you."

One Eye couldn't stand it anymore. Growing hot with anger, he bellowed, "Why me, you son of a bitch? Why turn on me like this?"

"You said it yourself at the saloon," Axel said. "You're the least."

One Eye cursed. Once he started, he couldn't stop. He swore using every cussword he knew, and then some. Axel wasn't fazed and showed no emotion whatsoever until in his rant One Eye spat, "Your ma was a whore and your sister, too."

"My mother is a sweet churchgoing lady," Axel said in a completely different voice than he ordinarily used. Gone was the twang and the inflections that marked him as a cowboy. Instead, he used impeccable English, with a hint of an accent. "She thinks I went off to sea with my cousin. I have two sisters and they're both happily married. I haven't seen them in years and I doubt I ever will. It would break their hearts to learn what I turned into."

"Wait," One Eye said. "How come you're talkin' so different?"

"I dropped the sham," Axel said. "It's part of the act. I know you and the others think I'm from Texas. But I was born and raised in Connecticut."

"God. I could sure use a drink."

Axel put down the cup and stood and walked around behind One Eye. "Hold still and I'll untie your hands. You can do your legs yourself. And then we'll get to it."

One Eye inwardly grinned. As soon as his arms were free he rubbed his wrists to restore the circulation. He undid the rope around his ankles and slowly stood and flexed his legs.

Axel had taken half a dozen steps back and stood watching him. "Whenever you're ready," he said, "go for your six-shooter."

"Givin' me a chance, are you?" One Eye said scornfully.

"No," Axel said. "Testing myself." His right thumb was wedged under his belt close to his holster.

"I think you're loco," One Eye said. "You pretend to be someone you're not. You turn on your pards. And now you want me to draw on you. Have you forgotten I'm almost as fast as Ritlin?"

"I told you before," Axel said. "I've seen quicker." And he smiled.

One Eye had had enough. Eagerly, he stabbed his hand for his Remington. The last sight he saw was smoke belching from the muzzle of Axel's Merwin Hulbert revolver and the last sensation he felt was a great searing pain as if he was being ripped asunder.

21

Roy started his day the same as he did most any other. The crow of the cock woke him. As dependable as the rising and setting of the sun, the rooster always crowed when the first rosy glow tinged the eastern horizon.

Roy sat up and stretched. Beside him, Martha rolled over but didn't wake up. Her hair hung loose, and he liked how a bang lay over her eyebrow and part of an eye. She was a lot older than when they met but he could see the young lines in her yet. It transported him back in his memory to that wonderful day when she took him for her husband.

He'd courted her for more than a year before she accepted his proposal. He'd wanted her so much, sometimes he would hurt inside.

Her parents had been dubious, saying they weren't sure he'd amount to much. He won them over by devoting himself to her, heart and soul. He was a hard worker and he'd done his best to provide for her, and now look. Their own farm, a big house, and three kids.

"What are you staring at?"

Roy smiled. "Didn't know you were awake." He tenderly brushed the hair from her eye.

"I have to get breakfast started." Martha slid back so she was braced by the headboard, and sat up. She tossed her head and yawned and said dreamily, "That was nice, last night."

Roy kissed her on the cheek. "I'll be glad when they move out so we don't have to be so quiet."

"By then we'll be too old to do it," Martha teased.

"Speak for yourself, woman. I'm a man. A man is never too old."

She grinned and kissed him. "All right. Enough lovemaking. They'll be up soon."

Roy dressed and went to the outhouse and then to the barn. He tried not to make too much noise as he lit the lantern and got the stool and the milk pail. He always started at the near end and worked his way down the line. Setting the stool next to the first cow, he perched and slid the pail under her. "Morning, Mary," he said. He had names for each.

The cow turned her head and looked at him and flicked an ear.

Roy bent and gripped a teat in each hand. He had done it so many times that the motion was mechanical. He squeezed and pulled and there was the thrum of the milk hitting the inside of the pail. He was well along when Mary looked past him. "I tried not to wake you."

Rondo James was fully dressed except for his slicker. His Colts jutted from his hips. "That's considerate but there's no need. I'm always up at the crack of day."

"Breakfast will be in about half an hour."

Rondo watched the milk spurt. "You sure you don't mind me eatin' with your family?"

"You're our guest," Roy said.

"Some folks would mind." Rondo walked down the aisle to General Lee's stall.

Roy moved to the next cow, and the next. When the pail was full, he emptied it in the milk can. He liked milking. It was one of his easier chores. Occasionally a cow was cranky and gave him trouble but usually they cooperated.

Rondo James returned, and he was smiling. "Another week or so and General Lee will be his old self."

"That's good," Roy said, continuing to squeeze and squirt.

"I don't want to wait that long to go after the killers," Rondo said. "I'd be obliged for the loan of a horse."

"Whatever you need," Roy said, and added, "It wasn't my idea, you know. Buchanan came up with it on his own."

"You sound as if you'd rather I didn't do it."

Roy stopped milking. "It's our problem. We should deal with it ourselves."

"You are. You hired me."

"You haven't said why you agreed."

"No, I haven't."

"Just so you're not hurt, or worse, on our account," Roy said. "It wouldn't be right."

Rondo turned to a pile of straw. A pitchfork was leaning against the wall. He grabbed hold and jabbed the pile several times, then leaned the pitchfork against the wall again. "Don't worry none about me. I can take care of myself."

"That's the closest to a brag I've heard out of you," Roy said. "Whoever these men are, they're clever and they're dangerous. If they find out you're after them, your life won't be worth a plugged nickel."

"It's not as if I'll be shoutin' it from the rooftops."

"How will you find them? Where will you start?"

"Where else but Teton?"

"Do you need the money? Is that why?"

"I don't appreciate folks pryin'," Rondo said, "but for you I'll say this much. Yes, the money is part of it. It will be my nest egg for somethin' I have in mind."

"What's the other part?"

"I haven't done much with my life since the war. Wandered, mostly. I take each day as it comes and try to stay alive. What money I've had, I made at playin' poker and odd jobs. I wouldn't mind havin' steady work but there's not many who will hire me." Rondo held up a hand when Roy went to interrupt. "Fourteen hundred dollars is more than I've ever paid for anything my whole life. And all I have to do to earn it is the one thing I'm good at."

"The four you are after might be good at it, too."

"There's only one way to find out," Rondo said.

"I don't know."

"It'd be no different than huntin' a bear or a buck. And my reputation would work for me. Those I go after might be disinclined to get into a shootin' scrape."

"I suppose it makes good sense when you put it that way," Roy said, "but the hard cases you'll be after would as soon shoot you in the back as the front."

"I've had to have eyes in the back of my head for so long, it comes natural."

Roy could see there was no talking him out of it. "How soon do you intend to leave?"

"Right after breakfast." Rondo touched his hat brim. "Now if you'll excuse me, I have to wash up."

It took half an hour for Roy to finish milking. As he emerged from the barn he met Sally coming from the chicken coop with an apron full of eggs. She had on a pretty green dress with a matching bonnet. "Morning."

"Good morning, Pa." Sally glanced at the house and bit her lip. "Can I ask you a question?"

"Since when do you need permission?"

"I asked Ma and she said I was being silly and not to bring it up again."

Roy stopped and so did she. "Not bring what up?"

"Mr. and Mrs. McWhirtle. What are the chances that whoever killed them will pay us a visit? Ma says no chance but I heard Mr. and Mrs. Kline talking and Mrs. Kline was worried it could happen to any of us. Which is it?"

Roy imagined that Martha was trying to spare Sally from too much worry but he didn't agree that telling a fib was the way to go about it. "There's a chance."

"I knew it!" Sally exclaimed. "Wait until I tell Andy and Matt I was right."

"You're not to say a word."

Her apron was sagging, and Sally firmed her grip. "They have a right to know."

"Andy has already figured it out, I suspect," Roy said. "Matt, well, he's too young."

"Shouldn't we move into town until the killers are caught?"

Roy laughed. He didn't mean to. It just spilled out. "And abandon our home?"

"At least we'd be alive."

"So long as we keep our eyes peeled, we should be all right," Roy said. "It's no different than keeping watch for hostiles."

"The Indians haven't killed anybody."

"We have two rifles and a shotgun," Roy reminded her. "I'll take a rifle with me when I'm out in the fields and your brother will have the other, and your mother will keep the shotgun with her."

"I'm scared," Sally said.

"That's natural." Roy placed his hand on her shoulder. "The important thing is not to let your fear get the better of you."

"How? I was hoping Ma would tell me but she won't even talk about it."

How indeed? Roy thought to himself. "The best way I can think of is not to think about it."

"How?" Sally said again.

Roy was at a loss. He was great at showing how to milk or hoe or how to help a new foal into the world, but he'd never been good at personal talks. He liked to leave that to Martha. And while this didn't exactly qualify as personal, he didn't know what to say other than, "You say to yourself, 'I won't think about it,' and then you don't."

Sally raised the apron. "I have to get these inside."

"Let me hold the door for you."

Martha was at the stove turning over slices of sizzling bacon.

Andy and Matt were already at the table.

So was Rondo James, his back to the wall. He always took the chair Roy usually sat in but Roy didn't say anything.

"Breakfast is about ready," Martha said.

Roy inhaled deep. He loved the smells. The coffee, the bacon, the eggs. He noticed a stack of pancakes on a plate, and maple syrup beside it. Ordinarily, they'd have eggs one meal, pancakes the next; Martha was showing off for their guest. "Can I help with anything?"

"You can sit down so you're ready to eat when the food is served."

It tickled Roy that the pearl handles of Rondo's Colts poked above the table.

"What are you grinning at, Pa?" Matt asked.

"I was just thinking."

Sally was setting out a plate stacked high with toast. "About not being afraid?" she said with more than a hint of sarcasm.

"Now, now."

Andy said, "Mr. James told us he's leaving right after breakfast."

"I know, son."

"He's going to Teton."

"I know that, too."

His adoration as obvious as his nose, Andy said to the Southerner, "How will you go about finding them, if you don't mind my asking?"

"It shouldn't be hard," Rondo answered. "We know there are four."

Andy's face went blank.

"How many times have you gone into town?" Rondo asked.

"I've never counted," Andy said. "Thirty or forty, I guess."

"And how many times did you see four men walkin' around together?"

"Most men are alone or maybe with a friend or a couple of friends."

"All I have to do is look for four men joined at the hip."

"What will you do when you find them?"

"There will be a reckoning," Rondo James said.

22

---·---

Federal Marshal Tyrell Gibson didn't resemble the dime-novel depictions of a marshal. He wasn't tall. He didn't have broad shoulders. He would never call himself handsome. If asked, he would say that thanks to his bulbous nose and cleft chin, he was downright ugly.

Tyrell wore an ordinary Colt in an ordinary holster. His clothes were ordinary and his hat was ordinary. There wasn't anything fancy or unusual about him except that he pinned his badge to the front of his belt near the buckle and not on his shirt as most marshals did.

It was the middle of the morning when Tyrell rode into Savage. He drew rein at the hitch post in front of the Tempest and wrapped the reins and went in. The few patrons looked at him but no one said anything. They couldn't see the badge under his coat.

Tyrell preferred it that way. He didn't like to draw attention to himself more than was usual. He found that he could accomplish more. Lawbreakers had a tendency to make themselves scarce when they knew a lawman was in the area.

Tyrell crossed to the bar and asked for a whiskey and, when the glass came, downed it in a gulp without batting an eye or coughing.

"Now, you are a drinker," the bartender good-naturedly complimented him.

"I should be," Tyrell said. "Been doin' it for pretty near forty years." He was one of the older marshals and he wasn't at all amused that some of the younger ones had taken to calling him "Gramps."

"Care for another?"

"What's your handle, friend?"

"Dorsey."

Tyrell rested an elbow on the bar. "I hear tell you had a shootin' in here not too long ago."

"That we did," Dorsey confirmed. "None other than Rondo James shot seven punchers."

"Seven is what I heard," Tyrell said. "I found it hard to believe."

"As God is my witness," Dorsey said. "I saw it with my own eyes, and I don't hardly believe it, myself."

"Tell me plain, is this true or hogwash? It's not a story you started to sell drinks?"

Dorsey wasn't offended. He chuckled and said, "You can go out back and count the graves. We don't have a boot hill so they were buried in last year's turnip patch."

"I'll be right back." Tyrell went out and around, and sure enough, seven fresh mounds testified to the truth of it. "I'll be damned," he said to himself, and ambled back in.

Dorsey was wiping the counter. "Satisfied?"

"I am," Tyrell said. "Now I'd like to hear the whole account from beginnin' to end."

"You're taking quite an interest."

Tyrell moved his coat so his badge was visible. "I have cause. Gibson is the name. Federal marshal."

"Well, I'll be," Dorsey said. "You're the first federal I've met in the flesh. And the first tin star of any kind with your kind of skin."

"There aren't all that many of us."

"Folks say that the few there are have uncommon grit. I guess you'd have to, the kind of work you do."

"It's the skin more than the work," Tyrell said. "Now, about the shootin'?"

Tyrell listened to the account and when Dorsey was done he said, "I can use another drink."

Dorsey laughed. "It does have that effect, don't it?"

"Seven, by God." Tyrell drank half and set the glass down. "All of them in the head, you say?"

"Smack in the face."

"There hasn't been a massacre like this since that Newton affair back in 'seventy-one," Tyrell marveled. "And there was more than one shooter involved in that."

"I seem to remember it," Dorsey said.

"Only four died at the O.K. Corral," Tyrell went on. "And four down to El Paso that time, with Stoudenmire. But again, there was more than one shooter."

"You keep up with your gun affrays."

Tyrell sheepishly smiled. "You might call it a hobby of mine. Some people have a memory for faces. I have a memory for shootin's."

"That's a new one on me," Dorsey said.

Tyrell nodded at the bloodstains on the floorboards. "This might be a record."

"It sure has brought in folks from miles around. If Rondo James ever shows up here again, he can have drinks on the house for all the business he's brought me."

Dorsey's eyes narrowed. "Say, are you fixing to go after him?"

"What for?" Tyrell said. "Sounds to me like a clear-cut case of self-defense." He considered a moment. "Tell me true. What was your impression of the man?"

"My impression?"

"There are so many stories, it's hard to tell the facts from the tall tales," Tyrell said. "You talked to him in person. What was your sense of how he is? What is he like?"

"I honestly haven't given it any thought," Dorsey said. "The best I can do is say that he looked tired."

"Tired?" Tyrell repeated. "As in he needed sleep?"

"No. As in he was tired deep down, if that makes sense. Haven't you ever met anyone like that?"

"Weary of the world," Tyrell said.

"Yes," Dorsey said. "That's it, exactly. Rondo James is a man who is weary of the world."

Tyrell finished his drink with another gulp. "Which direction did he head when he left?"

"I didn't see him ride off," Dorsey said, "but those who did told me he rode south."

"I haven't been out this way in a while but I recollect that Teton is the next town thataway."

"It is," Dorsey said.

"Then I reckon I'll mosey in the same direction. Wherever that man goes, there is bound to be more trouble."

"Who knows, Marshal. Maybe you'll get to meet him like I did."

"I doubt it," Tyrell said. "A man like him doesn't stay in one place too long." He turned to go, and stopped. "Damn. Where are my brains. I might as well ask about the gents I'm after while I'm here. There are four of them."

"What did they do?"

"One of them murdered a mixologist like yourself. His name was Hanks."

"The hell you say."

"Stabbed him and rode off. What they didn't know was that Hanks had a woman. A Shoshone he picked up somewhere. He always made her stay in the back. Probably for her own good. Drunks and red skin don't always mix."

"I'd imagine that drunks and your skin don't always mix, either. She saw who did it?"

"She heard voices and peeked out once and saw there were four of them but she didn't get a good look at their faces except for one. Whether he did it or not I can't say but when I find him I'll find out. He wore an eye patch and had a scar on his face."

"I haven't seen many men with eye patches, and none recently."

"His name is Charles Smith but he goes by One Eye. He's a backshooter who will do it for money." Tyrell touched his hat. "I'm obliged for the information. You ever get down to Cheyenne, look me up and I'll treat you to a drink."

"You're a damn fine gentleman, sir," Dorsey said. "And because you are, you might not want to go just yet."

"I generally don't have more than two drinks before noon."

"It's not about liquor," Dorsey said. "It's about the Bar H."

Tyrell stepped back to the counter. "I'm listenin'."

"They'll be mad if they find out I told you."

"They won't hear it from me."

"Your word? I wouldn't put it past them to wreck my place and string me up by my feet."

"When I say I will or I won't, I damn well do or don't," Tyrell said.

"Fair enough." Dorsey bent toward the lawman and lowered his voice. "Ike Hascomb didn't take kindly to havin' his punchers shot up. You might say he's mad as hell, and that wouldn't be the half of it."

"To be expected," Tyrell said.

"He doesn't care that his boys started it."

"Right and wrong don't count for much when someone is out for blood."

"Ike Hascomb sure is. He stood about where you're standing, and I can quote what he said." Dorsey paused. "'That no-good bastard Reb won't get away with this. He's wiped out half of my hands, and by God, he'll pay. He'll pay if it takes every dollar I have.'"

"Maybe it was whiskey and anger talk," Tyrell said. "Maybe it will come to nothin'."

"It already has."

"Him and the rest of his punchers have gone after Rondo James?"

"No. He's not stupid. He knows they wouldn't stand a snowball's chance in hell against a shooter like James. So he decided to fight fire with fire, as he put it."

"He sent for someone?" Tyrell guessed.

Dorsey nodded. "Two someones, in fact. Do the handles Shotgun Anderson and Kid Slade ring a bell?"

"God Almighty." Tyrell had heard of them, all right. So had most everyone else thanks to newspaper accounts of their shady doings. They hired out as assassins.

Everyone knew it, and every law officer west of the Mississippi River wanted to see them behind bars, or hanged. But they never killed where there were witnesses, and those who hired them weren't about to testify against them. The result: There wasn't a lick of evidence that would hold up in court. "I've changed my mind. I'll have another drink, after all."

Dorsey turned to the shelf and grabbed the bottle by the neck and poured. "I figured you ought to know."

"I'm obliged a second time." Tyrell sipped and pondered.

"Maybe it's not as serious as it sounds," he ruminated out loud. "It could take Hascomb weeks or months to track that pair down. By the time they show up, Rondo James will be long gone."

"That's good calculating but your numbers are off," Dorsey said.

"Don't tell me."

"I'm afraid so. A couple of Bar H punchers were in here last night. They were drinking and didn't pay much attention to me and I heard one of them say that Anderson and Slade are on their way to Teton, the same as you were about to do."

"So soon?"

"I'm only telling you what I heard. One of the punchers wasn't too pleased that Ike Hascomb is paying those two assassins a thousand dollars. Can you imagine?"

"I'm in the wrong line of work," Tyrell joked. "I don't make that much in a year."

"Well, anyway, the puncher allowed as how he'd do the job for half as much."

"If I can find Rondo James before they do, I can warn him," Tyrell said.

"You'd do that?"

"Why not? He's not wanted anywhere. And he wasn't to blame for the shoot-out here."

"But he wears gray. And you're, well, you."

Tyrell tapped his badge. "You see this? To the law, skin doesn't matter."

"What happens if Shotgun Anderson and Kid Slade find out?" Dorsey said.

"I imagine they'll try to kill me, too."

23

It felt good to be in the saddle again. Rondo James wished only that the saddle was on General Lee.

It also felt good to get away from the Sethers for a while. Rondo liked them. They were good people. But he could tell Martha was nervous about having him around, and the last thing he wanted was to cause the family unease.

Not that he could blame them. Rondo was all too aware of the effect he had on people. Not on all, but a lot. They acted as if he were a scorpion about to sting them with its tail.

Nor did it help that he was a mite on edge, himself. He couldn't shake the feeling that someone would come after him over the shootings in Savage. He'd had similar feelings before, and learned to his regret not to ignore them.

Rondo passed several riders along the way. Two were cowboys who worked for Buchanan. The third was Prost, who smiled and said, "A good day to you, sir."

There were four roads into Teton. A road for each point of the compass. Rather than ride in from the east, Rondo circled and rode in from the south so no one would associate him with the folks in Thunder Valley. There might be a few townsfolk who would remember him from the other day when he was with Roy, Moses and Tom, but he couldn't do anything about that.

Rondo pulled his hat brim low and kept his chin down so no one got a good look at his face. His white hair was a giveaway, but once again, he couldn't do anything about it except cut it short and he wasn't about to do that. He'd worn it long since the war. It was another way of telling the Yankees to go to hell.

He strolled into the Timberland with his saddlebags over one shoulder and his bedroll over another and asked for the cheapest room they had.

"How long will you be staying, sir?" the desk clerk inquired.

"I ain't rightly sure."

"We'll need at least one day in advance." The clerk turned the register toward him and held out a quill pen. "You have to sign your name. If you don't know how to write, an X will do."

Rondo wrote an X.

The clerk produced a key. "Here you go, Mr. . . . ?"

"Stonewall," Rondo said.

"Here's your key, sir. Your room is up the stairs and down the hall at the rear."

"I wonder," Rondo said, and gave his most pleasant smile, "if I could trouble you for a room on the third floor, at the front."

"They cost a few dollars more and you said you didn't care to spend a lot."

"I will for a room that looks out over the street,"

Rondo said. "I like to watch the people go by." He paid and climbed the stairs to the third floor and Room 301. Shutting the door, he threw his bedroll and saddlebags on the bed and dragged the chair to the window and sat.

From his vantage he had a clear view of most of Main Street. Stretching his legs, he spent the next several hours looking for sign of four men walking or talking together.

Once he did see four but two were townsmen.

Evening was falling when Rondo rose. He tucked his long white hair under his collar and made sure his slicker concealed his pearl-handled Colts, and went out. His first stop was the livery stable. The stableman said that no, he hadn't rented stalls to four men who showed up together, not in a year or so, anyway. His second stop was the general store. The proprietor couldn't remember four men coming in together and buying supplies, but then, he was usually so busy, he didn't pay a whole lot of attention to the comings and goings. His third, fourth and fifth stops were at saloons. Rondo asked each of the bartenders if they had seen four men keeping company together. They all said no.

By then Rondo was hungry. The aromas from Mother's Kitchen drew him in. It was the supper hour and most of the tables were in use. Fortunately, a corner table was being vacated and he claimed it and sat with his back to the wall.

At a table in the opposite corner sat two men, the tallest dressed in black, the other with a big belly and a rumbling laugh. At none of the tables were there three men, let alone four.

Rondo consulted the menu. *Fresh elk meat* had been scribbled at the bottom. His mouth watered. It had been a coon's age since he ate elk. It came with potatoes and whatever the vegetable of the day happened to be. He also ordered coffee.

Folding his hands, Rondo mulled his lack of success. He would have thought four men would be easy to spot. Apparently not. Or it could be the four had moved on and he was wasting his time. Regardless, he'd told Roy he would stay for a week and if he didn't find the four by then, he'd return to the farm. Roy had promised to look after General Lee.

Rondo's meal came. The menu hadn't lied. The elk meat was fresh, a slab two inches thick, so juicy it melted in his mouth. The baked potatoes were smothered in butter, the vegetables were chopped carrots. There was also thick gravy and several slices of corn bread to mop up the gravy.

Rondo ate with relish. He was about halfway done when a cowboy came in and joined the two at the other corner table.

The pair hadn't shown any interest in him and he hadn't paid much attention to them. But as the newcomer sat, he glanced over and seemed to give the slightest of starts. Rondo looked at him, but the man had turned away.

Jabbing his fork into the elk meat, Rondo sliced off another juicy piece. From under his hat brim he watched the three men to see if the cowboy said something to the other two but all three ignored him. They left well before he was done and he put them from his mind.

Rondo didn't usually have dessert but he treated himself to a slice of pie. He took his time, and by the clock on the wall it was past nine when he stepped out into the night air. He was feeling lethargic from the food, and he decided to take a stroll. He passed a saloon lively with music and a millinery, which was closed for the day. He came to an alley and glanced down it but didn't see anyone. He walked clear to the end of the street and turned back and he was passing the same alley when a voice whispered from its depths.

"Mr. James?"

Rondo went on walking. He took four more strides and stopped and placed his back to the window of a closed butcher shop. Sliding his hands under his slicker to his Colts, he waited. No one appeared.

Rondo moved on, his head twisted so he always had one eye behind him. The whisper had been a question. The whisperer wasn't sure it was him. Had he stopped, he might well have been blasted into eternity.

None of the people in the hotel lobby showed any interest in him as he crossed to the stairs. Once he was in his room with the door bolted, he let himself relax. He sat in the chair at the window.

Someone was out to get him. That was the only explanation he could think of. It disappointed him a little. He'd taken good care not to be recognized.

Rondo could see the alley. No one came out of it. No one was loitering near the hotel. With the patience of an Apache, he sat in the chair for more than two hours. Then, rising, he took it and wedged it against the door as an extra barrier, and turned in.

For a long time Rondo lay on his back, staring at the dark ceiling. Back at the Sether farm he'd fallen asleep easily. He liked that. Now he was in the real world again, and he was his old self, and for the first time ever, he didn't like that.

He'd briefly forgotten how it was to always be on his guard, to always live on the raw edge.

"Damn," Rondo said to the ceiling.

As so often happened when he couldn't sleep, memories washed over his mind—of his boyhood roaming the woods and the hollows; of his mother, teaching him to read and write; of his father, teaching him to be a man, to have pride in being a Virginian, to be a gentleman. They hadn't been rich but they weren't poor, either. He'd worn good clothes and had his own horse and some of the local girls were showing an interest when the war broke out. When the Yankees invaded Virginia, he'd been incensed. He enlisted to fight the invaders and never saw his father or his mother again.

When he was discharged and came home, it wasn't there. The house had burned to the ground. Their fields were weeds and their animals were gone.

Rondo had drifted, no purpose to his life, not feeling alive even though he was breathing. Then came the saloon and the four troopers who thought they could prod because of his uniform. Year by year the tally climbed, and now here he was, a notorious pistoleer.

Rondo closed his eyes. Life sure was peculiar. If anyone had told him when he was a boy how his would turn out, he'd have laughed and said they were loco.

He didn't realize he had drifted off until he awoke. The street outside was quiet. The window was gray and not black, which told him dawn was near. He stayed in bed. He felt no urge to get up, which was unusual.

The gray turned to a rosy hue and the rose to gold.

Rondo sat up. He didn't like the turn his thoughts were taking. It suggested he'd grown tired of the life he was living, and he could have no other. Not as well-known as he was.

He thought of Roy and Martha and their kids, and frowned.

Rondo had slept fully dressed except for his hat and his boots. He put them on and clomped down the stairs and was halfway to the entrance when the clerk called out.

"Excuse me. Mr. Stonewall?"

Rondo stopped.

"You have a letter, sir. I thought you might like to know."

"Me?" Rondo said.

"Yes, sir." The clerk turned and took a small envelope from the room slot. "Here it is. The night clerk told me about it when I came on."

Rondo went over. Someone had written in neat cursive, *For the gentleman in the gray slicker. At your earliest convenience.* "I'm obliged," he said.

"Just doing my job, sir."

"Did the night clerk say who dropped it off, or when?"

"No, sir, not the who, anyway. He did mention it was late last night but not how late."

Rondo went to a chair. He used his thumbnail to slit the envelope and unfolded the paper.

Mr. James,

   I wouldn't have shot. I had something to tell you. There are men out to kill you. Remember Mother's? And the two men who sat across from you? A tall man in black and a man with a gut? They are the ones. If you are smart you will kill them before they kill you.

                              A fellow Confederate

Rondo gazed about the empty lobby, and read it again. He was convinced of two things. No one from the South wrote it. The language wasn't right. And that whisper, brief as it was, had a Yankee tinge. The other thing was that whoever wrote it was educated. There wasn't a single misspelling, and the handwriting was almost elegant.

There was a third thing. If those two men were out to kill him, why hadn't they tried at the restaurant? They'd hardly looked at him the whole time. He doubted they knew who he was.

So the letter writer was a Yankee and a liar, and for some reason was using him to his own ends.

Rondo didn't like being used. He would find out what this was about. "Mister," he said to the paper, "whoever you are, there will be hell to pay."

24

"One Eye wouldn't just up and leave," Brule declared when they brought their horses to a halt in a belt of cottonwoods. "Not when there's money to be made. And not without tellin' us."

"It's strange he didn't meet us at the stable like he was supposed to," Axel said.

Ritlin pushed his black hat back on his head. "I don't care where he got to. I've never much liked him."

"We need him," Brule said.

"For what? Complainin'? It's all he knows how to do." Ritlin smothered a yawn. "We can do the job Rank hired us for without him if we have to."

"An extra gun is always nice," Axel said.

Brule said, "I've got a bad feelin' about it. It could mean someone is onto us."

"Who?" Ritlin said. "And how?"

"I don't know. I'm only sayin' it could be."

"You worry worse than my mother used to," Ritlin

said. "When we get back we'll turn the town upside down looking for him. Will that make you feel better?"

"You have no sympathy, Winifred," Brule said.

"Call me that again."

Axel smiled and held up a hand. "This bickerin' gets old. Let's get the job done, like Ritlin says."

"I'm obliged," Ritlin said.

Brule frowned and raised his reins. "All right. No more about One Eye. Let's go." He tapped his spurs to his mount.

They'd left Teton well before daylight in order that no one would see them leave. They'd swung to the south to fight shy of the farms, and for several hours they had been riding hard.

The land became more open, more flat, more grassy. It was prime cattle land, which was why the Olander and Buchanan ranches were at the east end of Thunder Valley.

It wasn't five minutes more that Brule pointed and said, "There."

Up ahead, twenty to thirty head were grazing peaceably. In the distance were more.

"How many punchers does he have working for him?" Ritlin asked.

"Ten to twelve, the word is," Brule said.

"Easy as pie."

"Don't get cocky, Winifred."

"Just one more goddamn time," Ritlin said.

They continued due east and hadn't gone half a mile when four riders galloped out of the morning haze. Their hats, their clothes, their boots marked them for what they were as clearly as if they wore signs on their chest.

"Some of the hands," Axel said. "Let me do the talkin'. They'll think I'm a puncher."

Brule said, with a pointed glance at Ritlin, "And no gunplay, you hear?"

"That'll depend on them," Ritlin said.

The quartet spread out and each man placed a hand on his six-shooter.

"Friendly bastards," Ritlin said.

"Not yet," Brule warned.

Axel kneed his mount past the two of them and raised a hand in greeting. "Howdy, gents."

The four cowhands drew rein. One had a well-worn white hat and a red bandanna and he did the talking. "This here is the Olander spread."

"So we were told," Axel said, smiling. He rested his hands on his saddle horn.

"I'm Carver," the cowboy said. "We're under orders to keep our eyes skinned for strangers."

"That would be you," another said threateningly.

"There have been killin's," Carver explained. "A man and his wife, and hogs."

"Hogs?" Axel said.

"And other critters. Done by four men."

"As you can see," Axel said, with a sweep of an arm at Brule and Ritlin, "there's only three of us. We've drifted up this way from the Green River country and we're hopin' to find work."

"You're cowhands?" The second cowboy sounded suspicious.

Axel patted his rope. "Don't I look like one?"

"You do," Carver said. He bobbed his chin at Brule. "And him, maybe." He bobbed his chin at Ritlin. "But if that hombre in black is a cow nurse, I'm a schoolmarm."

"He's new to the trade," Axel said. "But he's a hard worker."

"Our boss don't need more hands," a third cowboy spoke up.

"Shouldn't that be for him to decide?" Axel asked pleasantly, his smile a fixture.

"We could take you to him, I reckon," Carver said. "But you'll have to hand over your hardware."

"No one takes my six-shooter," Ritlin said.

The second cowboy straightened. "Then you don't get to see Mr. Olander. You can turn around and go back to the Green River country, for all we care."

"That's no way to be, Vern," Carver said.

"I don't like his looks," Vern said.

Axel twisted in the saddle. "What can it hurt?" he said to Ritlin. "It'll only be until we've talked to their big sugar. Either he hires us or he doesn't, and if he doesn't, we get our guns back and we go. That's fair."

"I like you," Carver said.

"Do as they want," Brule said to Ritlin. "Or we'll go without you."

"I don't like being naked," Ritlin said. But he palmed his Colt and held it out. "Take good care of it, or else."

"Tough hombre," Vern said. He brought his horse up and took the ivory-handled Colt. "Awful fancy six-gun for a cowpoke."

"I like fancy," Ritlin said.

"I can tell." Vern wedged the Colt under his belt and patted it. "Don't you worry, fancy-pants. I'll treat it like it was my own."

Axel drew his Merwin Hulbert and reversed his grip so he held it by the barrel. "Here you go, Carver."

Brule extended his Smith & Wesson. "Try not to breathe on it if you can help it," he joked, and laughed.

The four punchers moved around behind them and

Carver said, "Keep on the way you are. Half an hour and we'll be there."

"This a good outfit to work for?" Axel asked.

"As good as any," Carver answered. "Mr. Olander is from the East but he's cow-savvy and he treats those who ride for his brand decent. The bunkhouse is clean and free of lice, and he hired a bean-master who makes the best grub this side of anywhere."

"That he does," another puncher agreed.

"We hear tell there's another layout up this way somewhere," Axel said. "Run by a Texan."

"That would be Sam Buchanan," Carver said. "He owns all the range on the north side of the valley. Mr. Olander has the range on the south."

"They get along? I don't want no part of a gun crowd."

"I don't blame you," Carver said. "A cow prod should work with his rope, not his smoke wagon. Mr. Olander and Buchanan are right friendly. Not a hard word between them, ever."

"That's good to hear," Axel said. "I like outfits where everyone gets along."

"You won't find friendlier if the boss takes you on," Carver said.

They rode amid hundreds of cows, and now and then came on more cowhands. All Carver had to do was holler and wave and they were allowed to pass.

The ranch buildings were typical: a house, a barn, the bunkhouse and the cookhouse and sheds, an outhouse and a chicken coop. A few hands were busy at various tasks. The rest were out on the range.

"Mighty fine spread," Axel said.

"It still has that new look," Carver said. "Give it ten years and it'll look like any other."

"Can we have our guns back now?" Ritlin asked.

"Not until the boss says," Vern told him.

A man came out of the house and waited on the porch, his hands shoved in his pockets. "What do we have here?"

Carver came around and dismounted. "They say they're lookin' for work, Mr. Olander. The one in the cow riggin' talks like he knows cows but I'm not so sure about the other two."

"Why, thank you very much," Brule said.

Olander chuckled. "You can't blame us for being cautious. In case they didn't tell you, we have killers on the loose. We can't be too careful."

"Who would be dumb enough to try to kill you," Axel said, "with all the hands you have?"

"I tell you, mister," Olander said, "when it comes to stupid, I've learned to never take it for granted that other people have a brain. Which is why I gave the order to stop all strangers and bring them to me."

"And here we are," Brule said.

Olander studied them while rocking slowly on his boot heels. "Tell you what. Make yourselves comfortable over to the bunkhouse. You can eat with us this evening. By then I'll have talked to my foreman and made up my mind."

"Is he off on the range somewhere?" Axel asked.

Olander grinned. "No. He's standing about three feet from you." He pointed at Carver.

"We're obliged, sir," Axel said. He reined around and rode to the bunkhouse and climbed down. Putting a hand to the small of his back, he arched and said, "It would help if you two smiled more."

"I've smiled," Brule said.

Ritlin dismounted and glared at the ranch house. "I hate havin' my pistol took."

"Damn it," Brule said. "Play along a while yet and it will be over."

Axel nodded. "That's exactly what this is. Playactin'. We pretend until they think we can be trusted and then we show them we can't be."

"This is our boldest yet," Brule said. "We should have hit them at night like I wanted. But no. Someone had to do it in broad daylight." He glanced at Ritlin.

"I shoot better when I can see what I'm shooting at," Ritlin said.

"For once I agree with him but not for the same reason," Axel said. "At night all the hands are in their bunks. They'd rush out with guns blazin'."

Ritlin shrugged. "So?"

"So we do this smart. I want this job over with."

"You're gettin' worse than Ritlin," Brule said. "What's your hurry, anyhow?"

"I have plans," Axel replied.

"Hush, you lunkheads," Ritlin said. "Here comes one of the cow nurses."

The cowboy called Vern jingled up. "Mr. Olander says I'm to show you around. A tour, he called it."

"We don't need no—" Ritlin began, and stopped when Brule held up a hand.

"Don't listen to him, sonny. He's a grump by nature. We'd be happy to take a tour."

Vern sneered at Ritlin and beckoned. "Follow me. We'll start at the stable and make the rounds."

Axel followed him.

Brule shook his head at Ritlin and went to do the same but Ritlin put a hand on his arm.

"I tell you," the man in black said, "I can't wait to start killing."

25

It was unusual but not unheard of for Roy to take his rifle out into the fields. He did it whenever Indians were reported to be in the area. He did it that time a mountain lion took to killing livestock in Thunder Valley; eventually, one of Buchanan's punchers put lead in the big cat's head. He did it that time a black bear came out of the mountains at night to prowl around.

As he finished plowing the last section, Roy glanced at his Winchester, propped against a stump at the far end of the field.

He could reach it quickly if he had to. He was a pretty good runner.

Samson moved with ponderous might, his huge body bent.

As tireless as the year was long, he could work day after day and not show strain.

Of all Roy's animals, his ox was the most indispensable. They could get by without eggs for a while if disease should wipe out the chickens. They didn't eat that much ham and could live without the pigs. They liked the milk the cows gave, but he didn't raise them to sell, and if something happened to them, it wouldn't devastate him. His horses were for getting around, which they could do on foot if need be. But Samson—without the ox they couldn't till the soil, and if they couldn't till they couldn't plant and couldn't harvest the crops that were their lifeblood.

Roy came to the end of the last furrow and brought Samson to a stop. He walked up and patted him on the neck and said, "Good work."

Samson flicked an ear.

Roy gazed out over the acres of overturned sod and inhaled the dank odor into his lungs. He loved the smell of dirt. That might seem peculiar, but he was a farmer, and when you got down to it, dirt was his stock-in-trade. All that he had, he owed to the earth under his feet.

Like many farmers, Roy had a reverence for the land that was more than the pride of ownership. He thought of it as a stewardship. He took care of the land and the land took care of him. Dropping to a knee, he scooped a handful of the cool dirt into his hand and felt the texture with his fingers, and smiled.

"Thank you, Lord," Roy said softly.

Samson grunted and shook his head, his horns glistening in the sunlight.

Roy stood.

A rider was coming from the west.

"Thanks," Roy said. He started around the field at a run to get to the stump before the rider reached him. He went only a short way, and stopped. He recognized who it was.

Moses Beard smiled as he brought his roan to a stop.

He was riding bareback. The horse was a plow horse that doubled as his mount. "Afternoon, neighbor," he said cordially. "How goes things?"

"Can't complain," Roy said. "How's your new puppy?"

"He sure likes to pee," Moses said. "He's peed on the living room rug. He's peed on the bedroom rug. He's peed in the kitchen and he peed on the front porch. The only place he doesn't pee is in the yard."

"And how is your wife taking that?"

"Oh, Tilda is in love. She calls him her little darling. When I said we should rub his nose in the pee and spank him to get him to stop, she said if I so much as lay a finger on him, she'll take a rolling pin to my noggin."

Roy laughed. "Why, Moses, are you jealous of a pup?"

"It's too stupid for words," Moses said. "She treats that dog better than she ever treats me."

"Does it have a name yet?"

"Didn't I tell you? She's decided to name it after her father. We're calling it Aloysius."

"Has he taken your place in bed too?"

"That's not even a little funny," Moses said, and sighed. "If I live to be a hundred, I will never understand women. What I call logical she calls silly. What she calls logical I call crazy."

"Martha vexes me now and then," Roy admitted. "But to be fair, I vex her, too."

"Tilda told me once that if she had a double eagle for every time I've annoyed her, we'd be living in the lap of luxury."

"So you rode over to vent your spleen?"

Moses smiled. "No. I came to extend an invite. Tilda would like for you and yours to come over to supper this evening. She's making a special meal with all the trimmings."

"In the middle of the week?" Like most of the farmers, Roy reserved his socializing for the weekend.

"I know. But she would be delighted to have Martha and you over."

"What's going on?"

"She hasn't said but I suspect it's the killings and the Jacksons leaving," Moses said. "She's worried that something else awful will happen."

"Everyone is."

"I think she wants to get together and have a good time and forget the worry for a while."

Roy thought that a grand idea. Martha had been showing signs of frayed nerves and the kids went around as if they were walking on eggshells. "Tell your missus we'll be there."

"You don't want to ask Martha and make sure it's all right with her?"

"Go to hell. I'm not as browbeat as some men I could mention."

Moses chuckled. "I'm grateful. It'll do wonders for Tilda's disposition. If there was time, I'd ask Tom and Irene to join us." He paused. "Any word from Rondo James?"

"It's too soon."

"Tilda says it's Providence, him being here when we need someone like him to help us."

"Sometimes things just happen," Roy said.

"Don't ever say that to Tilda or you'll get her lecture about how there's a reason for everything."

"She really thinks God sent James to help us?"

"Tilda is a God-fearing woman," Moses said. "If they allowed lady ministers, it would fit her like a glove."

Roy thought about his friend's comments as he led Samson back. He wouldn't pretend to understand the outworkings of the Almighty, but it seemed to him that sometimes a coincidence was just that.

Andy and Matt were on the porch, keeping watch, and came to meet him. Roy imparted the good news. Matt raced to the house to tell Martha and Sally. Andy, for some reason, frowned.

"Anything happen while I was out plowing?" Roy asked as he brought Samson into the barn.

"Mr. Nettles stopped by."

"What did he want?" Of all the farmers in Thunder Valley, Roy liked Nettles the least. The man was always irritable, always griping. Being around Nettles was a test of his patience.

"To drop off his share of the money that you're paying Rondo James."

"He's the last to pay up," Roy said.

"And Matt saw some cowboys heading for town from the upstairs window."

Roy wondered if they were Olander's or Buchanan's punchers.

"Life goes on," he said.

"Pa?"

"We have to carry on, killings or no killings." Roy held the Winchester with the barrel on his shoulder and put his other hand on Andy's. "Let's go in. I need to wash up and change my shirt."

"The invite saved one of the chickens," Andy remarked, and grinned. "Ma was fixing to cook it for supper."

"It must have stopped laying," Roy guessed. His wife couldn't countenance a chicken that didn't earn its keep. If a hen stopped laying for any length of time, Martha marked it for the supper pot.

And that wasn't all.

Chickens had a lot of uses. After Martha chopped off the head, she always soaked the bird in a pail of hot water. It loosened the feathers to where they could be plucked out easy. Then Martha would shove the feathers into a flour sack. It took several chickens to fill the sack entirely. Martha would tie it off and slide a clean sack over the full sack and tie that off, too, and there it was: a homemade pillow. Sally complained that now and again the stems poked through and dug into her but Roy didn't mind.

Martha never plucked the wings. She always chopped the wings off, cleaned them, and used them as feather dusters.

There wasn't much left of the chicken after that except the bones, and Martha had a use for those, too. She crushed them into powder and fed the powder to the chickens.

It amused Roy no end, feeding chickens chicken feed made from chickens.

Martha was a marvel.

Roy leaned the Winchester near the front door and went down the hall to the kitchen. He'd heard voices, and a pot clang.

Martha and Sally were bustling about as if they had something important to do and no time to do it.

"Didn't Matt tell you about the Beards?" Roy asked. "You don't need to cook supper."

"We're baking a pie to take over," Martha said without looking up from her dough-making. "It'd be rude not to bring something."

"I'll wash up then."

"You might get the buckboard ready," Martha said. "So we don't have to at the last minute."

"You always think ahead."

"One of us has to," Martha said, and she looked at him and grinned and winked.

"Oh, Ma," Sally said.

Roy went out the back to the stand with the basin and pitcher. Martha didn't like for him to wash up inside after a day out in the fields because he was always so dirty and he made a mess. Stripping off his shirt, he hung it on a peg. He upended the pitcher over the basin. It was Sally's job to keep the pitcher full and she hardly ever forgot. The lye soap was on a small wooden tray. He lathered up plenty of suds and used a washcloth on his face and arms and chest. By the time he was done, the water was brown.

Putting his shirt back on, Roy went to the barn and brought out the horse he used for the buckboard. The other horses didn't take as well to the traces.

Andy came out to help and in no time it was ready.

Roy noticed that his oldest kept glancing at him. They walked around to the front and went up the porch steps and Andy cleared his throat.

"Pa, can I ask a favor?"

"You want to drive the buckboard?"

"No." Andy looked down and brushed a hand along the rail as if he were nervous. "I wanted to ask if I could take the bay over to Mr. Haverman's tomorrow evening to see Eb. I was going to ask to go tonight but now it will have to wait."

Eb Haverman was two years younger than Andy, Roy recalled. "Doesn't Haverman also have a daughter named Judith about your age?"

Andy blushed. "I don't rightly remember how old she is."

Roy would have laughed except he was his son's age once.

"I guess it would be all right so long as Mr. Haverman doesn't mind."

Andy brightened and said, "Thanks, Pa. I—" He stopped and blinked and pointed. "Who are they?"

Roy turned.

Two strangers were approaching from the road. Even at that distance Roy could tell that one was big and burly and had a long gun across his saddle. The other was younger, and wore two six-guns.

"I reckon you'd better fetch my rifle," Roy said.

26

Axel, Ritlin and Brule ate with the punchers in the cookhouse. They sat apart from the cowhands, who didn't act friendly except toward Axel.

"Only five," Brule said as he spooned his beans. "The rest are out on the range."

"We should do it now," Ritlin said.

"Olander would hear the shots," Axel pointed out.

"So?" Ritlin said. "He's a rancher. I can take him without half trying."

"Some ranchers are fine shots," Axel said.

"He's from the East. How fine could he be?"

Brule stopped chewing to say, "That's just dumb. You're from the East. Wild Bill Hickok was from the East. Kid Curry, too. Bein' from the East doesn't mean a damn thing when it comes to squeezin' a trigger."

"Call me dumb again," Ritlin said.

Axel set down his fork. "If you two infants are done, hush now. Here comes the foreman."

Carver had risen from the other table and came over

carrying a cup of coffee. "Thought I'd join you gents," he said as he pulled out a chair. "Get better acquainted."

"Fine by us," Axel said.

"The boss was impressed by you," Carver told him. "You have the look of a seasoned hand."

"A man is what he is," Axel said.

"Ain't that the truth." Carver moved the chair so he could stretch out his legs and sighed contentedly. "Next to breakfast, this is about my favorite time of the day. I can relax for a while."

"You must have a lot to do, being foreman and all," Brule said.

"The Circle O isn't as big as some of those Texas outfits but it keeps me hoppin'."

"What do you think of this killin' business?" Axel asked.

About to take a sip, Carver peered at him over the cup. "I don't know what to make of it. The farmer and his wife weren't robbed. They were gunned down and left lyin' in the dirt. And a lot of their critters were killed. That's plain loco."

"You would think so," Axel said.

"Could be whoever shot them will come here next," Ritlin said.

"I'd like to see them try," Carver replied. "You might have noticed we're all wearin' our hardware. Boss's orders. Until this is settled, we're a gun bunch."

"Wearing a gun and knowing how to use it are two different things," Ritlin said.

"No argument there," Carver conceded. "But more than a few of us are good shots, and Vern has killed a man."

Ritlin gazed at the punchers at the other table. "You don't say."

"Down to Kansas. It was a fight over cards. Vern caught a man cheatin' and words led to blows and the blows led to jerkin' their hoglegs and Vern was faster."

"Lucky for Vern," Brule said.

"Luck is for amateurs," Ritlin said. "A real shooter doesn't let luck enter into it. He practices until it's second nature. Until he can draw and shoot and hit what he aims at in the blink of an eye."

Carver said, "You sound as if you shoot for a livin'."

"I can think of worse ways to earn a dollar."

"Than goin' around killin' folks?"

"It wouldn't be dull, like being a clerk or a bank teller or an undertaker," Ritlin said.

"Wouldn't the killin' bother you?"

Ritlin sat back. "I've never understood that. We kill all the time. We kill bugs that get in our bedrolls. We kill spiders and scorpions and snakes. We kill deer and rabbits and squirrels for the cook pot. We kill chickens and turkeys. We kill cows and serve them up as beefsteaks. And no one thinks twice about it. But kill a person, and by God, everyone squawks."

"Killin' animals ain't the same as killin' people."

"Killin' is killin'," Ritlin said. "I've never seen a difference between bugs and people."

Brule coughed. "Pay no attention to my pard. He has some peculiar notions."

"I'll say," Carver said. He drained his cup and stood. "I've got to go see if the boss has made up his mind about hirin' you."

Brule drummed his fingers and when the foreman had walked out, he turned on Ritlin. "Wear a sign, why don't you, that says 'I'm a killer and proud of it.'"

"Don't start."

"He's right," Axel said. "That was careless."

"I won't put up with it from you, either," Ritlin said. "Him and his Vern."

"What the hell is the matter with you?" Brule said. "It's like you've thrown caution to the wind."

"Caution, hell," Ritlin said. "I'm tired of holding back. In fact, I'm not going to." He'd brought his saddlebags inside, and now he opened one and slid out a plain Colt. It was the first he'd ever owned, and he kept it for emergencies. Shoving it into his holster, he rose.

"Hold on," Brule said.

"No."

Axel rose, too. "At least give me a minute to get to the house." He didn't wait for an answer but wheeled and went out.

"I'm goin' with him," Brule announced, and did so.

Ritlin moved around the end of the table and stood where he could see the four punchers, and their hands, as they ate. "Vern," he said quietly.

Vern was at the end, dipping a buttered slice of bread into his beans. He looked up. "Did you just say my name?"

"That I did," Ritlin said.

"What do you want?"

"Your foreman was telling us how you're a regular man-killer."

"Carver wouldn't say any such thing," Vern said. "And it was only one."

"One is more than most but nowhere near as many as me."

"Oh?" Vern said, setting down the bread. "How many have you bucked out?" he scornfully asked.

"Seventeen."

Another cowboy snorted. "Sure you have, mister. And your real name is John Wesley Hardin."

The punchers had a laugh at that.

Ritlin turned so his left side was toward them. His

right hand brushed his holster. "I used to not let it bother me but it does these days."

"What?" Vern said.

"That men like Hardin and Rondo James become famous and I don't when I'm every bit the killer they are."

"Sure you are," said the cowhand who had snorted, and he and the others had another good laugh.

Vern didn't join in. "Damn me if you don't sound serious, mister."

"A man should always be serious about what he does for a living."

"This ain't funny," a puncher declared.

"Here's how it will be," Ritlin said. "I'll give you your chance. Whenever you're ready, start the dance."

They looked at one another. One cowboy set down his fork, and another placed his hand on the edge of the table above his holster.

"Are you drunk?" Vern said.

"I don't ever let myself be."

"Have I savvied this right?" said the man who had snorted. "You're threatenin' to gun us?"

"What's this about?" asked another.

Ritlin smiled. "That farmer and his missus? My pards and me shot them."

"And now you ride in here and kill all of us?" the snorter said.

"That's the idea," Ritlin said.

Vern shifted in his chair. "You haven't said why."

"I'll count to three," Ritlin said. "You can go for your six-shooters, or not. Whether you do or you don't, you're all dead."

"Bastard," a puncher snarled, and heaving out of his chair, he stabbed for a Smith & Wesson on his right hip.

Ritlin drew and fanned a shot from the hip. The slug

caught the puncher in the forehead and spun him half-around. The snorter was rising, his hand on a Colt. Ritlin fanned again and the lead smashed the snorter in the chest and flipped him back over his chair.

Vern and the last cowhand rose simultaneously, both unlimbering as they cleared the table. Vern was faster and almost had his revolver out when Ritlin fanned and the slug slammed into Vern's jaw.

The last cowboy froze, his eyes wide with sudden fear. "No," he said.

"Yes," Ritlin said, and fanned a shot into the center of the man's chest.

Brule had to run to catch up to Axel. "I hope he gives us time."

"With him there's no predictin'," Axel said.

Up ahead, Carver had just reached the house and was climbing the steps to the porch. He raised his fist to knock and happened to glance back and saw them. Lowering his arm, he came to the edge of the porch. "You gents decided to ask the boss yourselves?"

"Something like that," Axel said with a smile. He was still smiling as he reached the steps and thrust the dagger he had slipped from his boot into Carver's gut. Simultaneously, he snatched Carver's six-shooter from its holster.

Carver staggered, cried out, and gamely tried to grab his six-gun.

Axel shot him in the mouth. He bounded past the falling foreman, flung the front door wide, and was well into the hall when a shout came from the far end.

"What was that gunshot? Who's there?"

Olander appeared in the doorway. He wasn't armed, and on seeing Axel and Brule, he backpedaled and yelled at someone behind him, "Run! Get out of here!"

A woman said something.

Axel burst into the kitchen.

Olander was pushing a brown-haired woman in an apron toward the back door. Shielding her with his body, he thrust a hand at Axel. "Don't! Please!"

Axel shot him in the chest.

The woman screamed and clutched Olander as he started to fall. "Timothy! Timothy!"

Axel raised the revolver.

The woman looked up, her eyes brimming with tears, her lower lip quivering. "Why?" she bleated.

"It's what I do," Axel said, and shot her.

Brule came to his side and stared at the bodies. "Damn, you're quick."

"We have to fetch our own hardware. It's in the bunk-house."

Brule nudged Olander. "He ain't wearin' a revolver. Pretty stupid, if you ask me."

Axel looked around. "Do you see a rifle or a shotgun in here anywhere?"

Brule turned right and left and shook his head. "What do you want one for, anyhow? They're already dead."

"It would have made it easier." Axel stepped to the counter. A bowl of fresh-cooked corn and a platter of potatoes were next to an oval china plate heaped with thick slices of beef. Beside the plate was the butcher knife the woman had used to carve the beef. "They were about to sit down to supper."

Brule came over and hungrily licked his lips. "I might have some of that myself. I didn't get to finish my beans, thanks to Ritlin."

"Have this instead," Axel said, and whirling, he buried the butcher knife in Brule's throat.

27

———

Roy fingered his Winchester as the pair of strangers approached the farmhouse. He didn't like the looks of them. "Get inside," he said to Andy.

"I'm practically a grown man. I'll stay."

"Do as I say," Roy insisted. "Get your squirrel rifle and stand inside the door and be ready to cover me if need be."

Andy brightened. "You can count on me, Pa," he declared, and dashed inside.

Roy levered a cartridge into the chamber and stood so the porch post partially shielded him. He rested the Winchester's barrel on the rail. "That's close enough," he hollered when the riders were fifty feet out.

The pair drew rein. The burly one wore a bear-hide coat and a floppy hat. The gun across his saddle wasn't a rifle, as Roy thought; it was a shotgun. The younger one wasn't much older than Andy. He wore short-barreled Colts in holsters cut low so he could slide his fingers into the trigger guards as he drew. The young one wore a short-brimmed black hat, a green shirt, and checkered pants.

"You're not very neighborly," the man in the bear coat said.

"What do you want?" Roy demanded.

The young one had flinty features and eyes that glittered like shards of glass. "I don't like his tone," he said to the big one. "You want I should show him how useless that rifle of his is?"

"Simmer down." The burly man smiled at Roy but there was no warmth in it. "Folks call me Shotgun Anderson. This here is Kid Slade. Could be you've heard of us."

"Can't say I have," Roy said.

"We're bounty men, of a sort," Shotgun said. "We get paid to track people down."

A premonition wrenched at Roy's gut. "Once you've found them, then what?"

Kid Slade snickered. "Not too bright, is he?"

"Keep your trap shut," Shotgun Anderson said, and went on smiling at Roy. "We're lookin' for a gent by the name of Rondo James. We asked around in Teton last night and we were told he's stayin' with you."

Roy imagined the news was all over town. He didn't say anything.

"It won't do any good to lie to us," Shotgun Anderson said. "We'd like to get this over with, so where is he?"

"Answer him, dirt farmer," Kid Slade said. Suddenly he stiffened.

Out of the corner of his eye Roy saw Andy step into the doorway with his rifle. "Since when does Rondo James have a bounty on his head?"

"It's a private bounty," Shotgun Anderson said.

"Is that even legal?"

"That's neither here nor there," Anderson replied, and squared his wide shoulders. "I'll ask you again. Where's Rondo James?"

Roy saw no reason not to tell them. "He's not here and I don't know when he'll be back."

"You expect us to believe you, dirt farmer?" Kid Slade said.

"I won't tell you again," Shotgun Anderson snapped at him.

"You're too damn nice," Kid Slade said.

"I want the two of you off my property," Roy said.

Shotgun Anderson said, "I don't suppose you'd let us look in your barn before we go?"

"I will not," Roy said.

Shotgun Anderson nodded as if he expected Roy to say that. "I believe you that he's not here. So we'll go. But there's somethin' you should know. We've never once not gotten our man. We'll get Rondo James too. It might not be today. It might not be tomorrow. But we'll get him."

"Leave," Roy said.

The big man wasn't done. "So long as you and yours stay out of it, you won't come to harm. But get this through your head. I'll only bend so far. Then I'll let the Kid have his way, and trust me when I say you don't want that."

Roy did some taunting of his own. "What makes you think you two are a match for Rondo James?"

"All the men we've buried," Shotgun Anderson said without any trace of boast. He raised his reins. "Think about what I said. We'll be around."

"You can bet your ass we will," Kid Slade said.

Roy cradled the Winchester in the crook of his elbow and watched them depart. "This just keeps getting worse and worse."

Andy came to the rail. "I'd have shot that snot-nosed one if he'd pulled on you."

Only then did it hit Roy that his son could have killed a man, at his suggestion. "What was I thinking?" he said out loud.

"Pa?"

"Take the rifle in. They're leaving."

"They'll come back, though, won't they?"

"As surely as the sun rises and sets."

"You should have let me gun them," Kid Slade grumbled. "They wouldn't have got off a shot."

Holding his English-made double-barreled shotgun by its walnut stock, Shotgun Anderson slid it into his saddle scabbard.

"If your brain was half as quick as your hands, you'd be somethin' else."

"Just because we're pards doesn't give you the right to insult me."

"Damn it, Kid," Shotgun said. "When will you get it through that puny thinker of yours that you have to use it for more than a hat rack? With them dead, what reason would Rondo James have to come back?"

Some of Slade's anger faded. "Why didn't you say that before?"

"I shouldn't have to spell it out. We've been doin' this long enough, it should come to you."

"I pull my freight," Kid Slade said.

"In the killin' you do," Shotgun acknowledged. "But there's more to it than that." For him it was the thrill of the hunt. He'd always loved hunting. When he was a boy on his pappy's place in Arkansas, he'd spent every waking hour off in the woods hunting every critter that lived.

There wasn't an animal that he hadn't killed at one time or another. That included birds and reptiles, too.

He remembered the time he'd learned that Arkansas had its own coral snake. Well, sort of. The snake's territory bled into Texas. It was so rare, hardly anyone in Arkansas had ever seen one. Three and a half months of hunting, it took, until he found one and killed it. He was so proud, he'd skinned it and hung the skin on his wall.

Then there was the ivory-billed woodpecker. It'd taken him near half a year to hunt that one. It was a pretty bird, mostly black and white with a red crest and a long beak. After he'd shot it he'd admired it for a while and then tossed it on a garbage heap.

His hardest challenge had been a panther. Most had been killed off. He was eighteen when he journeyed to the southeast corner of the state after the newspaper gave an account of a panther that killed a few sheep. The local hunters were after it but didn't have any luck. They'd scoffed when he showed up. But he showed them how it was done, and the panther hide hung next to the snake skin.

Of course, neither had a head.

Anderson never used a rifle or a revolver. When he was eight his grandpa had given him an old shotgun. He'd loaded it with buckshot and shot a rabbit that was in his ma's vegetable patch, and he never forgot the sight. The rabbit exploded into bits and pieces. Buckshot didn't just put a hole in something, like a slug would do; it blew what you shot to bits.

Ever since, a shotgun was Anderson's weapon of choice. The one he had now cost more than most folks earned in a month of Sundays but it was worth it. When he shot a man in the chest with both barrels, it blew them in half.

Now that he thought about it, Anderson supposed it was inevitable that he'd go from blowing animals to hell to blowing men to hell. Hunting animals became too easy. It lost the thrill it used to have. He'd needed more of a challenge. So when he heard about a bounty placed on a robber's head, he hunted the robber down and blew it off.

Not long after, the incident happened that set him on his current course.

A gentleman came to see him. Someone he'd never met. The gentleman had heard about him killing the robber for the bounty and wondered if he'd do the same "unlegal-like," as the man put it. It seemed the gentleman had a cute heifer he was fond of and another gent was grazing on her pasture, so to speak. The gentleman had held out five hundred dollars and asked would he or wouldn't he?

Anderson would.

Now here he was, twenty years later, and he'd lost count of the heads he'd blown off and been paid to do it.

Only five years ago he'd taken up with Slade. He'd completed a job in Texas and gone into a saloon for a drink and there the Kid was, leaning against the bar and bragging about shooting someone in the next town over. The Kid dressed colorful, and he liked that. The Kid could kill, and he liked that. But most of all he liked how damn quick the Kid was. He'd never tell the Kid to his baby face but Slade might be the quickest alive.

That the Kid never seemed to age was peculiar. No one would guess to look at him that he was ten years older than he appeared to be.

Shotgun realized his partner was talking to him.

"—in blazes are we headin' west? Are you fixin' to spend the night in town?"

"I am," Shotgun confirmed.

"Shouldn't we keep an eye on the Sether farm?"

"We'll pick up some grub and head back in the mornin'. Only we'll swing wide and come in from the south so the Sethers ain't likely to see us."

"And then what? It's not as if Rondo James will ride up to us and say, 'Here I am.'"

"You say the stupidest damn things," Shotgun Anderson said.

"Didn't you hear me when I said I don't like it when you insult me?"

"I don't like your smart mouth."

Kid Slade's jaw muscles twitched. He glanced at his companion's shotgun, and said nothing.

After a while Anderson said cheerily, "This will be easy. It always is when we don't have to track them all over creation, and we don't have to track Rondo James."

"You're certain he'll come back?"

Shotgun glared. "You were standin' right next to me in that saloon when the barkeep said James is stayin' with the Sethers while his horse heals."

"How do we know it ain't already healed and Rondo James is gone?"

"From the way Sether was actin'. He was nervous. I saw it in his eyes." Shotgun Anderson chuckled. "All we have to do is keep watch on the Sether place, and when Rondo James shows up, blow him to hell."

"I reckon as how you'll want to do it in the back, him bein' so damn quick and all."

"At last you're usin' your noggin," Shotgun Anderson said.

"That Rebel is as good as dead and doesn't know it."

28

Rondo James was glad to leave Teton. He'd searched and searched and not seen any sign of four men who were always together and who may be the assassins. Either they weren't in town or there was some other explanation. He finally figured maybe they were roving Thunder Valley, looking for someone else to prey on. With that in mind, he bought supplies, saddled up, and began his own sweep, starting along the north side and working his way around to the south.

Rondo didn't push his horse. It wasn't General Lee, and its stamina left considerable to be desired. After a couple of miles of hard riding, it had to rest or it was worthless for the rest of the day.

Rondo fought shy of the farmhouses. Although the farmers hired him, he'd gotten the impression that more than a few weren't happy about it. Apparently they had a low opinion of shooters.

They weren't the only ones. While the newspapers

tended to glorify shootings, ordinary folks took a dim view of men who killed other men unless they wore a badge.

Rondo didn't think that entirely fair. It wasn't his fault he'd been forced to take lives to preserve his own. It wasn't as if he went round looking for people to shoot. Well, until now.

Staying alert for tracks, Rondo came across the hoofprints of cows and a few horses and once the boots of a farmer.

Not once did he come across a set of four shod horses riding together.

Toward sunset Rondo sought a spot to lay up for the night. A cluster of oaks was convenient. He moved to the center, where he was sheltered from the wind and his small fire was screened from prying eyes. He put coffee on to boil and spread out his bedroll.

His supper consisted of jerky and crackers. With the crackling flames and coyotes yipping in the distance, he chewed and toyed with the notion of riding to the Sether place in the morning to check on General Lee. He wasn't more than a couple of hours away.

Rondo stayed up late. He thought about the war and his wanderings and the people he'd met. Few were as nice to him as the Sethers. Most folks regarded him with suspicion if not downright dislike once they found out who he was.

"I never wanted this," Rondo said to the stars. He bit off a piece of jerky and slid a hand into his slicker and felt his poke. They'd paid him half in advance and would hand over the rest when the job was done.

Rondo would be the richest he'd ever been. He'd have enough to put down on a homestead, were he inclined to settle down.

Another idea he had was to head for South America. A man could lose himself down there. He could start over, make a whole new life. Leave the Civil War and all his uniform stood for behind.

Were he willing.

And the truth of it was, Rondo wasn't. He had never been a cheek-turner. He'd go to his grave resenting the North and all it stood for.

Sleep eventually claimed him. He woke only once, and thought he heard horses off in the night.

Daylight found him in the saddle. He didn't see a soul until he reached the road and spied a solitary rider to the west, heading for town.

Rondo was surprised to see two buckboards in front of the Sether farmhouse. They had visitors. Rather than disturb them, he rode around to the barn.

General Lee was in his stall, his hoof wrapped and dry, as it should be. The abscess was almost healed.

Rondo decided to give the Palomino a few more days before he threw a saddle on.

Figuring to slip off unnoticed, Rondo climbed back on and was riding around the rear of the farmhouse when the screen door smacked open and out came Martha Sether.

"Mr. James! Hold on, if you please. You need to have a word with my husband."

Rondo drew rein. "I don't want to intrude when you have company, ma'am."

"It's important," Martha said.

Wheeling his animal, Rondo rode over. "I don't have anything to report yet."

"We do."

Rondo climbed down. "Who else is here, if you don't mind my askin'?"

"The Klines and the Beards." Martha held the door

for him. "Thank goodness I happened to look out the window and saw you."

Voices drew Rondo to the parlor. The moment he appeared, silence fell. Their expressions troubled him. "I came to check on General Lee," he said.

Roy got up from the settee where he'd been sitting between Tom and Moses.

Tilda and Irene were in chairs.

"All of you look as if you've lost your best friend," Rondo said.

Roy winced. "Not our best but a good man, nonetheless. Tim Olander and his wife, Myrtle, were murdered yesterday."

"No," Rondo said.

"So were his foreman and four of his punchers and maybe someone else," Tom Kline said.

"Maybe?"

"They found blood in the kitchen that they can't account for," Moses said. "It didn't come from the Olanders."

"How did you find out?"

Roy said, "A cowboy brought the news to us this morning."

Rondo remembered the riders he heard in the middle of the night, and wondered.

"A terrible thing," Irene said. "To be slain in their own home. No one is safe anymore."

"We came over to talk about what to do," Tom said. "We have to take steps."

Roy hadn't taken his eyes off Rondo. "Have you found out anything? Anything at all?"

"I wish I had."

Roy didn't hide his disappointment. "You're our best hope. There's another meeting tonight of everyone in the valley. I'd be grateful if you could attend."

"I'll stay as long as you like," Rondo said.

Martha dabbed at the corners of her eyes. "Myrtle Olander was a dear. She liked to get together with us ladies. I can't hardly believe she's gone."

Tilda nodded. "I remember how much fun we had at her quilting bees."

"Was anything taken?" Rondo asked.

"Sorry?" Roy said.

"Did the killers steal money or take Mrs. Olander's jewelry or did they just kill?"

"Isn't the killing enough?" Moses Beard said.

"So far as we know," Roy said, "they didn't rob the Olanders of a cent."

"The same as the McWhirtles."

"Is that important?" Tom asked. "Does it give you a clue to what these outlaws are up to?"

"They aren't outlaws," Rondo said. "They're exterminators."

"They didn't exterminate the Jacksons," Roy said. "They drove them off."

"The Jacksons were the first place they struck."

"You're forgetting my hogs," Tom said.

Irene said, "Each place they hit, it gets worse. What will they do next? Hang women and children?"

"Don't talk like that," Tom said.

"I'm right, aren't I?" Irene said. "Whoever these men are, they won't stop until they've killed or driven everyone from Thunder Valley."

An atmosphere of dread filled the parlor. Martha sniffled. Irene and Tilda were pale. The men looked at one another in confusion.

Rondo James smiled and said, "I'd be obliged for a cup of coffee. I haven't eaten all mornin' and my stomach is complainin'."

Martha rose. "Where are my manners? I should have thought to offer you something when you came in."

"I'll go with you," Roy said.

As he went down the hall, Rondo noticed the three kids crouched at the top of the stairs. They had been eavesdropping. If the parents noticed, they didn't say anything. He walked to his usual chair and sat and tilted it back so his shoulders were against the wall. "Are you two all right?"

"I'm terribly upset," Martha admitted as she lifted the lid of the coffeepot. "I'm worried for my family."

"Olander and five of his punchers," Roy said, staring bleakly at the floor. "I wouldn't stand a prayer."

Rondo hated to see them so distraught. These people had been kind to him, and he never forgot a kindness. "I reckon I'll stick around here a spell."

"No," Roy said. "That wouldn't be fair. The other farmers don't have a shooter to protect them."

"The others didn't take me and my horse in."

"They would have, though."

"Maybe a few," Rondo said. "But not all of them. They're not you, Roy."

Martha turned. "I hope you stay. That's selfish, I suppose, but I have my children to think of, and they mean more to me than anything."

"Here's a notion," Rondo said. "How about the families move in together until this is over?"

"And leave their farms?" Roy said. "I can't see anyone doing that."

"Cows and chickens and dirt aren't worth dyin' over."

"To a farmer they are."

Martha stepped to the counter and took down the coffee. "What I don't get," she remarked, "is how the killers got into the Olander house. You'd think the punchers would have seen them."

"They must have struck in the dark," Roy said.

"No," Martha said. "A cowboy had come in from the range before the sun went down, remember? He was the one found the bodies."

Roy took a seat across from Rondo. "There's something else we need to talk to you about. You might not want to stay after you hear it, and I'd understand."

Martha nodded. "You have your own troubles. They come before ours."

"There's nothin' you could say that would make me desert you when you need help."

"How about the names Shotgun Anderson and Kid Slade?" Roy said. "I didn't know who they were when they paid us a visit so I asked Tom. He's heard of them."

So had Rondo. "They were here?"

"Looking for you."

"Hell," Rondo said.

"Anderson told me there's a bounty on your head but he wouldn't say who put it there."

"I can guess."

"They might be watching our house right this minute," Martha said.

"Maybe you should wait for dark and saddle General Lee and go for good," Roy suggested. "He's healed enough."

Rondo thought about the kindness the family had shown him.

"I'm stayin'."

"We don't want you dead on our account," Martha said.

Rondo James smiled. "I'll try not to inconvenience you."

29

Ritlin was fit to kill something. He sat with his body tense at a corner table in the Grand Lady saloon. His right hand was on the chair arm, above the ivory grips to his Colt. "Tell me again how it happened," he growled.

Axel sat across from him, sipping a beer. "I've told you ten times already."

"Tell me eleven," Ritlin said. He didn't like the little man's attitude.

Axel sighed. "We went into the kitchen. I was goin' to shoot them but you know how Brule was. He loved to hear himself talk. He told Olander how his foreman and his punchers were dead, and soon him and his wife would be."

"And the rancher didn't have a gun, you say?"

"Neither him nor his old woman," Axel said. "Maybe that's why Brule was careless. He went over to Olander, who was standin' by the counter. The next thing I knew,

Olander pulled a big knife from behind his back and stabbed Brule, and that was that."

Ritlin could see it happening that way but he still wasn't convinced. "Brule was quick and strong. I can't see Olander getting the better of him."

"It can happen to anyone."

"Not Brule," Ritlin stubbornly insisted.

Axel set down his glass. "What do you want me to say? You were on me about it the whole ride here. And since we got back it's all you talk about."

"Brule was my friend."

"I'm sorry for you," Axel said. "But if you need to be mad about it, be mad at yourself."

"Eh?"

"You were the one who started the ball rollin'," Axel said. "And us without our six-shooters."

"I had my spare—" Ritlin said, and stopped.

"Good for you," Axel said. "But what about the rest of us? I took the foreman's. Poor Brule didn't have one. If he had, maybe he would have shot the rancher before the rancher stabbed him."

"You're saying it's my fault?"

"Bingo."

Ritlin glowered.

"You should have waited for them to return our six-shooters."

"I didn't think—"

"No, you didn't. And now there's just the two of us. I grant you that we're not in a line of work that lends itself to us livin' to a ripe old age, but Brule might still be breathin' if not for you."

"Go to hell." Ritlin picked up his whiskey and swallowed. He'd been through half a bottle but it hadn't helped.

"I think we need some time to ourselves." Axel pushed back his chair. "See you later."

"Make sure you do," Ritlin said. "We still have a job to do."

"At twice the money," Axel said.

"Eh?"

"With One Eye and Brule gone, we're entitled to their shares. You can have Brule's and I'll take One Eye's."

"Charlton Rank might not see it that way," Ritlin said. "The agreement was for five thousand each."

"He'd better see it that way," Axel said. Wheeling on a heel, he jangled away.

Ritlin glumly refilled his glass. He hadn't been this upset about anyone dying since he was twelve and his grandmother passed on. She was the only human being who had ever truly been kind to him. Not his pa, who ran out on his drunk of a mother when he was seven. Not his mother, who liked to slap him around when she was mad, and she was always mad about something or other.

Ritlin drank and sulked and lost track of time. When a dove sashayed over and asked if he'd like company, he told her to get lost. He was in no mood for company. At least Axel got that right.

The truth be told, Ritlin never had liked the cowboy. Axel was the last to join them. One day when Brule, One Eye and he were in a saloon in Casper, Axel showed up out of the blue and said that seeing as how they all hired their guns out for a price, they should work together. He was against it but Brule said that four guns were better than three. One Eye went along with Brule.

Ritlin had demanded to know how Axel knew who they were, and Axel said a former client told him about them.

For five years now they'd been riding together, and

Ritlin never once warmed to him. He didn't get along all that well with One Eye, either, but then One Eye was an irritable cuss who didn't get along well with anyone.

Axel was different. He hardly talked. He kept to himself so much that sometimes Ritlin forgot he was there. And he hardly ever talked about his past.

Axel was part of them but he was apart from them.

Ritlin had mentioned it a few times to Brule. He said he didn't like how Axel stayed so aloof. Brule replied that Axel was a loner and that's how loners behaved.

The man was as cold a fish as Ritlin ever came across, and now he was the only partner he had left.

"Hell," Ritlin said, and tilted the bottle to his mouth.

He downed every drop, let the bottle clatter to the floor, and stood. He wasn't drunk but he wasn't sober, either, and he could feel the effects of the whiskey in him as he moved. His arms and legs were sluggish, and his brain, as well. It would slow his reflexes.

"Shouldn't have done that," Ritlin said. He hardly ever drank so much.

The night air helped some. He strolled down Main Street, his thumb wedged in his belt close to his Colt. He figured to walk a while, get the liquor out of his system, and be his usual self again. With his black clothes he blended into the dark so well that hardly anyone noticed him.

Ritlin drifted on tides of memory. He recollected the first man he'd killed, when he was fourteen. He did it for money. He was in Saint Louis, living in an abandoned shack, skin and bones from hardly ever eating, and one night he had to have food so he went out and snuck up behind an old coot and bashed him over the head with a rock. He got three dollars and twenty-seven cents.

He'd headed west, killing now and then, sometimes

with a knife but usually with a derringer he'd taken from a victim. He'd shove it into their sides and squeeze and delight in the surprised looks on their faces.

Then came the fateful day when he stabbed a man wearing a Colt. It was the spare he kept in his saddle-bags. He'd practiced with it and discovered a remarkable ability he would never have guessed he possessed. He was lightning quick, and got quicker, until there were few men alive who could match him. He thought so. Brule thought so. One Eye thought so.

Finally, Ritlin had been good at something. Finally, he could earn a better-than-most living. He'd met Brule in Kansas, in Topeka of all places, and the funny thing was, he wasn't there to kill anybody. He was passing through. So was Brule. They were standing at a bar and struck up a conversation, Brule doing most of the striking. And then a drunk had bumped into Brule and said it was Brule's fault and threatened to shoot him, and just like that, Ritlin drew and jammed his six-shooter into the drunk's cheek and told him to make himself scarce, or else. Brule had whistled and said he'd never seen anyone so fast, and since they were both heading west, would Ritlin mind if they rode together?

That was how it started, the best and only friendship Ritlin ever had.

Now here he was, alone again. All because of the damn rancher. If Olander wasn't already dead, he'd ride out there and take an ax to him and chop him to pieces while he screamed and pleaded.

Ritlin snapped back to the present. Somehow he'd drifted down a side street. It was nearly pitch black. Off a ways a dog was barking and in a cabin a child squalled.

Ritlin turned and saw the lights of Main Street and cursed himself for being so stupid.

"It's the liquor," he said. But it was more than that. He missed Brule. They'd argued now and again but generally they got along as well as two pards could.

Ritlin had half a mind to ride to the Olander spread and burn the ranch house to the ground. Hell, and the barn and the outhouse, too. He started to laugh, and doubled over slightly, and the night flared with fireflies and thunder boomed and he heard the sizzle of lead over his head.

Instantly, the Colt was in his hand. Ritlin fanned off three shots swifter than most men could blink, and then he moved, hurtling at a short fence and vaulting over it. He misjudged and hooked a stirrup, and crashed down hard on his elbows and his knees.

The dog and the child had gone quiet and the night was as still as death.

Ritlin reloaded. He could do it by feel, he'd practiced it so much. Sometimes he'd practice with his eyes closed in case he had to do it in the dark, like now.

His blood was pumping fast and furious and his brain began to clear.

He couldn't stay there. The shooter might have glimpsed him going over the fence. He ran in a crouch across a weed-choked yard to a pine. Slowly rising, he scanned the side street. He didn't spy movement. The shooter might be gone but his gut hunch was that the man was still there, waiting for him to give himself away.

Ritlin waited. He'd let the shooter come to him.

None of the cabin doors opened. No one called out, demanding to know what was going on.

Ritlin wasn't surprised. Most people cared more about their own hides than anyone else's and kept their noses out of business that didn't concern them.

There! A hint of motion. Ritlin fanned twice and was

answered by three shots as swift as his own. He heard the lead smack the trunk, and dropped into a crouch.

Again that terrible silence.

Ritlin replaced the spent cartridges. He had to get out of there. He wouldn't put it past the other shooter to circle around.

Like a racehorse out of a gate, Ritlin flew. He leaped the fence, cut around a woodshed, ran past a dark cabin, and made for Main Street. It occurred to him that he was silhouetted by the distant light, and he veered into the dark a fraction before a pistol cracked behind him. Again he heard the air sizzle to hot lead.

Ritlin stopped and turned and squatted. He thought the shooter might come after him but minutes went by, and nothing.

Keeping low and using every bit of cover, he reached Main Street. Darting around the corner of a feed store, he stood with his back to the wall.

Five minutes passed. Ten minutes. No one appeared. Ritlin moved to the recessed doorway of a haberdashery. After another wait he warily crossed the street and entered the first saloon he came to. It was called the Blue Spruce and catered mainly to the timber crowd.

Ritlin went to the bar and ordered a drink. Now that his head was clear, one more wouldn't hurt. And he needed it. He raised the glass and looked in the mirror and saw a familiar face staring back at him from a table.

Axel raised a glass, and beckoned.

Ritlin swallowed and went over and pulled out a chair.

"Did you come lookin' for me?" Axel asked. He had a bottle of his own, a third empty, and his face was flushed.

"I was takin' a stroll and stopped in," Ritlin said. "How long have you been here?"

Axel tapped the bottle. "Since I left you."

"Did you hear shots a while ago?"

"Some," Axel said. "I didn't pay much attention. Why?"

"Nothin'," Ritlin said. Now that he had a moment to think, it struck him that the shooter had been almost as good as he was. And in the entire territory, there weren't more than a handful who could make that claim.

One who could was sitting across from him.

30

It was about two in the afternoon when Marshal Tyrell Gibson rode into Teton. He drew a lot of stares, as he always did, and his badge wasn't even showing. He drew rein at the hitch rail in front of the Timberland, dismounted, and stretched. He slapped dust from his coat and his hat and went in and crossed to the front desk.

The clerk wore spectacles and a bow tie. The corners of his mouth curled down but he forced a smile and said, "May I help you, sir?"

"You can," Tyrell said.

"If you're looking for accommodations, there's a boardinghouse down the street."

"What's wrong with the rooms here?"

"We're full up."

Tyrell glanced at the two dozen slots, many with keys in them. "Looks to me as if more than half your rooms are empty."

"Be that as it may—"

"You don't want me to take one because of my color."

"That's not true, sir," the clerk said with shammed indignity.

Tyrell did something he rarely let himself do—he lost his temper. He moved his coat to show his badge. "Lie to me again, you peckerwood."

The clerk blanched. "I assure you that no offense was intended, Marshal."

"Does this town have its own tin star?"

"No, sir."

"A telegraph office?"

"No sir."

"A newspaper office?"

"No, sir."

"How in hell does it keep in touch with the rest of the world?"

"Well, there's the stage. It comes in three times a week. Due in today, in fact, and will head out again tomorrow morning."

"That doesn't help me much," Tyrell said.

As if to make amends for being a bigot, the clerk smiled and said, "However, there's the *Leader* man, sir."

"The what?"

"The correspondent for the *Cheyenne Daily Leader*. He has his own office, such as it is. He thinks it makes him important but all it means is he knows how to spell."

"You're a funny man," Tyrell said.

"Sir?"

"Who and where?"

"His name is Filbert. Adam Filbert. I can write down his address for you." The clerk produced a pad and a pen. "You can read, I would imagine, being a marshal and all?"

"Write the damn address."

"It's just down the street."

The best way to describe it was a breadbasket crammed between a bank and a billiard hall. A bell tinkled as Tyrell entered. At a small desk in a small chair sat a man big enough to be a tree. He was scribbling so intently, the tip of his tongue poked from his mouth.

"I take it back," Tyrell said to himself. "This is a funny town."

Filbert looked up. "Who are you and what do you want? I'm a busy man."

"I can see that." Tyrell revealed his badge. "It makes two of us." Much to Filbert's annoyance, he sat on the edge of the desk instead of the other chair. "So you work for the *Daily Leader*?"

"I do," Filbert said pompously.

"Then you must be nosy by nature," Tyrell said, "and know everything that goes on around here."

"A good correspondent keeps his eyes and ears open," Filbert intoned as if he were quoting it.

"What can your eyes and ears tell me?"

"Marshal?"

"I want to know everything that's been goin' on around here for, oh, the last month or so. And when I say everything, I mean everything."

"That could take a while," Filbert said, "and I have a report to get out on the stage."

"Which doesn't leave until tomorrow mornin'," Tyrell said. "We have plenty of time."

"Really, now, Marshal, this is a terrible imposition."

"I'm a fair man," Tyrell said. "I'll give you somethin' in return."

"Money?"

"No."

Filbert's features fell.

"Somethin' better. Somethin' that will make your bosses in Cheyenne as pleased as punch with you."

"Really?" Filbert leaned on his elbows, all interest.

"What is it?"

"You first."

Tyrell had to hand it to him. The man had a memory like a trapdoor. For half an hour Filbert related every piddling detail of any consequence involving everyone from a bank president who liked to take hot baths two times a day to an unwed scrub woman who was pregnant with a married tailor's child. He learned that Charlton Rank of the Wyoming Overland Railroad had paid Teton a visit. That the tree operations were doing booming business.

"Then there are the murders," Filbert said.

Tyrell had been half bored but now he wasn't. "How's that again?"

"I assumed that's why you're here."

"This is the first I've heard of them. What all can you tell me?"

Filbert could tell a lot. He consulted his notes. "There have been nine so far—" he began.

Tyrell listened in amazement. He pulled out his pencil to write down the names. Aaron and Maude McWhirtle. Timothy and Myrtle Olander. George Carver. Four cowhands. "Good God," he said when Filbert was done.

"And then there's the hogs."

"The what?"

"Tom Kline, a farmer, had all his hogs killed. Their throats were slit."

"What the hell?" Tyrell said.

"I know. We've got a massacre going on of people and animals and no one knows why."

In all his years wearing a badge, Tyrell had never

heard the like. He stared at the long list. "I reckon I'll be stickin' around this area for a while." He would have to get a report off. It could go out on the next stage.

"If you're not here about the murders, why are you?" Filbert asked.

"Ever hear of Shotgun Anderson and Kid Slade?"

"Who hasn't?" Filbert's brow crinkled. "Are you saying they're in Teton?"

"They are around somewhere."

"It can't be them responsible for our murders. None of ours had their heads blown off."

"No, they couldn't have got here much more than two or three days ago," Tyrell said.

"I thank you for the tip," Filbert said. He opened a drawer and took out a new sheet of paper. "My boss at the *Leader* will wet himself when he sees all of this."

"There's more," Tyrell said. "I have reason to believe that Anderson and Slade have been hired to kill someone and I know who that someone is."

"I'm all ears," Filbert said.

"They're after Rondo James."

"The hell you say," Filbert exclaimed, and grinned in delight. "I bet the *Leader* will hire me full-time now instead of part-time, like I've wanted for so long."

"Will they print the James story? He's probably long gone, but it's worth a mention."

About to write, Filbert looked up. "Then you haven't heard?"

"How would I hear except from you?"

"Rondo James isn't long gone. He's staying out to the Sether place. His horse came up lame and they put him up. Everyone knows it."

"Hell," Tyrell said.

Filbert sat back in his small chair and it made sounds

as if it were about to collapse. "Hold on. I'm puzzled, Marshal. You looked me up specifically about James and those two assassins?"

"I did."

"You want everyone to know that they are looking for him?"

"I want him to know," Tyrell said.

"To warn him? Now I'm more puzzled than ever. Why in the world would you, of all people, want to help Rondo James?"

"Why wouldn't I?"

"Marshal," Filbert said, with the air of someone explaining to a ten-year-old, "James is an unrepentant Rebel. The last of his breed. He still wears his Confederate uniform. And the Confederacy, you might remember, went to war over their right to keep people like you as slaves."

"That was settled twenty years ago. And I come from a long line of free men."

"Even so."

Tyrell stood. "I'm obliged for the information. If I can do you a favor, I will."

"Keep me informed, that's all I ask."

Tyrell touched his hat brim and turned to go.

"If you need a place to stay, there's a boardinghouse down the street. You can't miss it. Has a sign out front."

"You're the second person to tell me about it," Tyrell said.

"You might want to take a look," Filbert said, with an odd smile and a wink.

Tyrell had no intention of doing so. He returned to the hotel hitch rail for his horse and headed out of Teton. He passed Filbert's office and saw the sign on a picket fence.

A woman in a green dress was on her knees in a flower bed, prying with a trowel. She wore a yellow shawl that accented her black curls and complexion.

Tyrell drew rein. "My God," he blurted. "There are two of us in the territory."

The woman raised as fine a face as he had ever seen and smiled a smile that made him tingle. "Look at you on your fine horse," she said.

Tyrell coughed and placed his hands on his saddle horn and nodded at the sign. "Is it you lets the rooms?"

"I do," she said. "I'm Bessie Mae Cyrus. I run this establishment."

Tyrell tried to remember the last time he heard anyone use the word "establishment."

"Who might you be?"

"I'm a United States marshal," Tyrell said with more pride than he had in a long time.

"You don't say."

Tyrell told her his name.

Bessie put down the trowel and rose and came over to the fence. "That's a distinguished job you have."

Tyrell tried to remember the last time he heard anyone use the word "distinguished." "Thank you, Miss Cyrus," he replied, his voice unusually raspy.

"None of that. Call me Bessie." She bestowed another dazzling smile. "Are you going to be in town for any length of time?"

"I hadn't thought I was, but now yes," Tyrell said.

"I'm very pleased to hear that," Bessie Mae Cyrus said.

Tyrell thought his ears would burn off.

31

Charlton Rank's mansion wasn't the biggest in Cheyenne but he was still adding on. The workers were under orders not to begin each day until he finished
breakfast. The hammering and pounding annoyed him
no end. He liked his breakfasts quiet and peaceful.

On this particular morning, Rank sat gazing out the
wide kitchen window at the mountains. He had a cloth
napkin in his lap and was holding his fork and knife. "I'm
hungry," he declared in mild annoyance.

The cook hustled over with his plate and carefully set
it down. "Here you are, sir."

"You're running late, Esmeralda," Rank chastised her.
"I like my meals to be punctual."

"It was the eggs, sir. The boy dropped the basket on
his way in and then he had to go fetch more and—" Esmeralda stopped.

Rank arched an eyebrow. "How many eggs did he
break?"

"All of them, sir," Esmeralda answered. "But it wasn't his fault. He tripped over some boards the workers left out back of the house."

"I see." Rank sniffed. The boy she referred to was a ragamuffin who had shown up one day begging for work. "He didn't see the boards lying there, I suppose."

"He was in a hurry to get the basket to me."

Rank decided not to let it spoil his morning. "Inform the simpleton I'll overlook it this time. But if it happens again, he'll be fired."

"Yes, sir."

"And Esmeralda?"

"Sir?"

"My coffee and my toast, if you please. And don't forget the jam this time."

Rank grinned as she bustled to obey. He liked cracking the whip. Not just with her, with everyone. Or to be more precise, he liked having power. He liked lording it over others. He liked snapping his fingers and having people jump.

The eggs were done to a turn, the bacon was thick and juicy with fat. Rank would never tell her, but Esmeralda was the best cook he'd ever retained. Her meals were one of the highlights of his day.

He ate, and washed his food down with coffee laced with sugar, and admired the mountains and the vista of the growing city, and was pleased.

Rank pricked his ears at the clomp of boots and was mildly surprised when Bisby came into the kitchen, followed by Bannister and Tate. "Gentlemen," he said. "To what do I owe this intrusion?"

Bisby fidgeted as he often did when he was nervous. "We're sorry to disturb you, sir, but I thought you would want to know right away."

"Know what?" Rank said.

"Bannister and Tate were on their way here when—" Bisby looked at Bannister. "Perhaps you should tell it."

"There's not much to tell," the former Pinkerton man said. "There was a kid hawking papers, and when I heard what he was yelling, I bought a paper in case you hadn't seen it yet."

"That was very thoughtful of you, Mr. Bannister," Bisby said.

"I was the one heard the boy yellin'," Tate said in his Texas drawl.

"And it was thoughtful of you, too," Bisby said.

Rank set down his fork on the plate with a loud *thwack*.

"All this thoughtfulness is giving me indigestion. One of you had better get to the point, and quickly."

Bisby held out a folded newspaper he had been holding at his side. "This says all there is to say, sir."

Rank snatched the paper and snapped it open and went rigid at the headline.

MURDER AND MAYHEM NEAR TETON!

"Surely not," he said. "You've read this?"

Bisby gulped, and nodded.

"How bad is it?"

"Brace yourself, sir."

Rank closed his eyes and took a deep breath and mentally counted to ten. It was a trick he used so he wouldn't fly into one of his rages. It didn't always help. He opened his eyes, pushed the plate out of the way, and laid the newspaper flat.

The account took up half the front page.

MURDER MOST FOUL IN THUNDER VALLEY

Our correspondent in Teton reports that the entire countryside is in an uproar. Nine murders have been committed, two people have disappeared, notorious assassins are on the loose, and the infamous shootist Rondo James has been sighted. The situation has become so critical that United States Marshal Tyrell Gibson is on the scene to restore order.

Rank stopped reading. He looked at Bisby and his two Enforcers and at the newspaper again. "Jesus God Almighty. What have those idiots done?"

The bloodletting started with the strange deaths of all the hogs belonging to farmer Thomas Kline.

Rank looked up again. "Did I read this right? Did it just say hogs?"

But that was as nothing compared to the brutal killings of farmer Aaron McWhirtle and his wife, Maude. Their bodies were found riddled with bullets. Their horses, cows and chickens were also slain.

"Chickens?" Rank said. "Who the hell kills fucking chickens?"
Neither Bisby nor the Enforcers offered an answer.

The worst was yet to come, though. Rancher Timothy Olander, his wife Myrtle, their foreman, George Carver, and four of Olander's hands were found ruthlessly gunned down.

There appears to be no rhyme or reason to the murders. The mystery is compounded by the disappearance of rancher Frank Jackson and his wife, Elizabeth. It's reported that two of their cows had their throats slit.

"I could just scream," Rank said.

As if all this were not enough, Shotgun Anderson and his partner Kid Slade are said to be in the area. Our correspondent reports that it is believed they are after the man some say is the new Prince of Pistoleers—a mantle once worn by Wild Bill Hickok—none other than Rondo James. Should James and the assassins clash, there is bound to be more bloodletting. What connection, if any, there exists between the murders and the presence of the three man-killers is unknown at this time. The homesteaders in Thunder Valley are rightfully alarmed. They have armed themselves and are patrolling their valley and say they are determined to prevent any more murders. The *Leader* will continue to follow this story as we are sure it is of great interest to our readers.

Rank stopped reading. He gazed out the window and then bowed his head and closed his eyes. "They came so highly recommended. I thought I was hiring professionals."

Bisby coughed.

"I told them to be discreet. You heard me tell them to be discreet."

"I did, sir," Bisby said.

"I did, too, sir," Bannister said.

Tate coughed. "In Texas we have a sayin', Mr. Rank. If you want somethin' done right—"

"Do it yourself," Rank finished for him. "Yes, I'm well aware of the wisdom of that proverb. But some things a man in my position can't always do himself." He folded the newspaper and sighed. "Very well. They've turned a simple job into a debacle. I can't allow them to make things worse than they already are. I must take a direct hand." He smiled. "Discreetly, of course." He turned in his chair. "Mr. Bisby, we leave tomorrow for Thunder Valley. Make the usual preparations. Mr. Bannister—"

"Sir?"

"I would like you and Mr. Tate to go into Cheyenne and find four more men to hire as Enforcers. Make it clear these are temporary positions but might become full-time if they impress me."

"May I ask why you feel you need them?" Bannister said. "The six of us have always been enough."

"I don't mean to belittle your abilities," Rank said, "but with what I have in mind, the extra guns might come in handy."

It was Bisby who said, "Might we inquire about the specifics of your plan, sir?"

"You may not. Suffice it to say that I intend to clean up this mess to my advantage."

They waited.

"Mr. Bannister."

"Sir?"

"I also want you to purchase half a dozen shotguns. I believe Buckshot Anderson uses a .12-gauge so ours must be the same. You are to conceal them on one of the packhorses. And don't forget to purchase plenty of shells."

"Our men prefer rifles, sir," Bannister remarked.

"Do as I say."

"As always, sir. It just seems strange, sir, that you'd want us to use shotguns when we never have before."

"They will be useful in spreading the blame."

"Sir?"

"You're dismissed. All of you."

The three men began to file out.

"Wait," Rank said. "I almost forgot. Those suits and bowlers of yours stand out like sore thumbs. Buy a set of ordinary clothes for every Enforcer."

"Ordinary, sir?"

"The kind a farmer would wear, or a rancher."

Bannister nodded and they departed.

Rank stared at the newspaper and then pounded it and swore.

Rising, he stepped to the window and stood with his hands clasped behind his back. He'd planned so carefully. To have everything unravel thanks to four incompetents filled him with fury. Their bungling threatened to delay the laying of the new line. That would cost the Wyoming Overland Railroad money. A great deal of money. He couldn't have that. He couldn't have that at all.

There was only one thing to do, Rank reflected. And unlike the four incompetents he'd hired, he would do it smartly. He would go to Thunder Valley and solve the problem by doing what he always did. When an obstacle stood in his way, he eliminated it.

The solution, therefore, was simple.

He would kill the four incompetents and drive the people in Thunder Valley out—or kill them.

He didn't care which.

32

Roy Sether was up before dawn, as he always was. He milked the cows, as he always did. He returned to the house and had breakfast with his family, as usual. But it wasn't usual for them to be so quiet. They hardly spoke the whole meal. Even Matt was subdued. They were tense and uneasy. Roy didn't need to ask why.

Martha prepared a plate for Rondo James and Roy took it out to the barn. At that early hour the interior was cool and quiet. He went to the ladder to the hayloft and looked up.

"You could have ate with us, you know."

There was the rustle of hay and small bits rained down as the Southerner poked his head over the edge. "Not and keep my eyes skinned, I couldn't."

"I have your breakfast," Roy said, indicating the plate.

"Bring it on up."

Careful not to tip the plate, Roy climbed. The loft smelled of the hay and of dust. The loft door was open and Rondo James was cross-legged in front of it, peering out. Roy sat next to him. "Here you go."

"I'm obliged."

Roy gazed out the door. From their vantage he could see the house and most of the yard and as far as the road. "It's been days since they were here. Maybe they've changed their mind."

"You know better." Rondo balanced the plate on his lap and picked up the fork. He sniffed the eggs and bacon and buttered toast and smiled. "Makes my mouth water. Your missus is a fine cook."

"Why are they waiting so long?" Roy asked.

"So that we'll think what you were thinkin'," Rondo said, "that they're not comin' back. Then we let down our guard and make it easy for them."

"I hadn't thought of that."

"They're assassins," Rondo said. "Assassins like an edge." He forked a piece of scrambled egg into his mouth and chewed.

"Andy might have seen someone watching the house yesterday," Roy mentioned.

Rondo stopped chewing. "Oh?"

"He was taking a turn at an upstairs window so Matt could do his schoolwork and he thought he got a glimpse of a man in the trees to the southwest."

"He's not sure?"

"It could have been a deer," Roy said.

Rondo James resumed eating. "I'm sorry I brought this down on you and yours."

"It's not your fault. Blame whoever hired despicable characters like Shotgun Anderson and Kid Slade."

"Some folks would say *I'm* despicable."

"They're wrong. They don't know you like I do."

Rondo bit off the fatty end of a strip of bacon. "You're the first friend I've had in a coon's age."

"I'm honored."

"If anything happens to any of you, I'll never have another."

Roy coughed and looked out the loft door. "I've heard that Buchanan is taking over the Olander spread and has hired on the punchers who were left."

"How are the other farmers holdin' up?"

"Prost's wife is after him to pack up and leave but he says he's sticking."

Rondo chose a second strip and said, "If there is anything I like more than bacon, I have yet to make its acquaintance."

"You're taking all this calmly. I don't see how you do it." Roy plucked a blade of straw and stuck it in his mouth.

"When you've lived with death as long as I have, it doesn't rattle you as much."

Roy saw a buckboard out on the road. Haverman, he thought, and Haverman's wife, on their way to town. "I could never get used to it. Not in a thousand years."

"You'd be surprised," Rondo said.

"All I ever wanted was to live in peace," Roy said. "But the outside world won't leave us be."

"Life does that." Rondo put a piece of egg on a slice of toast and folded the slice. He licked his lips and took a bite and chewed.

Roy gazed at his house, awash in the bright morning sunlight. He gazed at the road—the buckboard was gone. He gazed in the other direction, out across his tilled fields, and blurted, "I'll be damned."

A rider was coming up the track that Roy used when

he went back and forth. The man wore a light coat and the coat was swept back so his holster was clear.

"You'll be damned what?" Rondo asked. He was intent on his food.

"Look for yourself."

Rondo stretched his neck out. "I'll be damned." His gray eyes narrowed. "And black, by God."

"Do you think he's with Anderson and Slade?"

"They work alone." Rondo James set down the plate and moved to the ladder. "Come on. Let's go introduce ourselves to the gent and find out what he's doin' on your property."

Roy spit out the blade of straw and scrambled to catch up. By the time he hurried from the barn, the rider had come around the corral and drawn rein and he and Rondo James were staring at one another. "I'm Roy Sether," he announced. "This is my farm."

"I know," the man said. He didn't take his dark eyes off Rondo James.

"Who are you and what are you doing here?"

The rider tapped a metal circle on his belt.

Roy moved nearer and received a shock. "A marshal! I didn't know there was a lawman within two hundred miles."

"You must not read the newspapers." Still eyeing the Southerner, the lawman dismounted. "Tyrell Gibson is my name. I've been watchin' your house for four days now, Mr. Sether."

"You have?" Roy realized that it must have been Gibson that Andy saw out in the trees.

"I was hopin' to catch Shotgun Anderson and Kid Slade in the act of tryin' to kill your friend, here."

"I declare," Rondo James said. "Ain't you the clever fox."

"Clever enough to get you and the rest of these folks mentioned in the newspapers," Tyrell Gibson said.

"That's twice you've mentioned the newspapers," Roy said. "What are you talking about?"

Without taking his gaze off Rondo, Tyrell Gibson turned to his saddlebags. One-handed, he opened one and slid a hand in and pulled out a folded newspaper. Without looking at Roy, Gibson tossed it at him.

Roy almost dropped it.

"Read that to your friend," the lawman directed.

"What part?" Roy asked as he unfolded it. He saw the name of the paper, and the headline. "It's the *Leader*. Out of Cheyenne, no less. And it's about us." He read the headline aloud and then the rest of the account, not stopping until he was done. He looked up quizzically. "You say this was your doing?"

"The mention of him was," Tyrell said, with a nod at Rondo. "I figured it might scare Anderson and Slade off."

"Knowing that you're around?" Roy said.

"And everyone knowin' that they're after your friend."

"His friend has a name," Rondo James said. "You can use it if you want."

"What I want," Tyrell Gibson said, and began to slowly walk in a circle around the Southerner, who turned so they always faced one another, "is to know where I stand with you."

"How's that again, lawdog?"

"Have you looked in a mirror lately?"

Rondo James glanced down at himself, and grinned. "I wear gray and your skin is black. Is that it?"

"You're a clever fox yourself," the marshal said, and chuckled. He completed his circle and hooked his thumb in his belt so that his hand touched his revolver.

"I'm not one of them," Rondo James said.

"Them who?"

"Those who hankered to keep your kind in chains. I fought to protect my home and my kin and my state, and that's all."

"Then why keep wearin' that uniform?"

"I get asked that a lot."

"What do you say when people do?"

"That I won't be trod on. The North might have broke the South but the Yankees didn't break me." He placed a hand on his gray slicker. "I wear this to rub their noses in it."

"Were you good at holdin' grudges when you were a boy, too?"

"Grudge, nothin'," Rondo said. "I call it pride. I call it dignity. I call it bein' a man."

Tyrell Gibson started walking in another circle. "I call it askin' for a slug between the shoulder blades."

"Are you one of those back-shootin' lawmen?" Rondo said, turning as the marshal turned.

"I always go at my man straight up."

"Straight up with me is the same as bein' buried."

"Modest cuss."

"Still-breathin' cuss. And I aim to stay that way."

"You're a puzzlement."

"How so?"

"I've been here more than a few minutes and you haven't called me a nigger."

"I'm still waitin' for you to call me a cracker."

Tyrell Gibson grinned and said, "Cracker trash."

Rondo James grinned and held out his hand. "I'll let you call me that and go on livin' since I find myself takin' a shine to you."

"For a gent in gray you are damned decent," Tyrell said, shaking. "Where are you from, anyhow?"

"Virginia. You?"

"Cheyenne, by way of Georgia."

Roy looked from one to the other and shook his head. "Are all Southerners as peculiar as you two?"

"Says the Yankee," Tyrell Gibson said, and laughed.

"He's got a Southern heart when it comes to hospitality," Rondo James said.

Roy snorted. "Northerners don't have hearts?"

Rondo and Tyrell said at the same time, "No."

The screen door banged and Andy came out and cupped a hand to his mouth. "Ma saw that man ride up. She says if we have company, you should invite him in for coffee. Mr. James, too, if he's so inclined."

"Can you stay a while?" Roy asked the lawman.

"As long as I like."

They headed for the house, Rondo and Tyrell walking side by side.

"It was a good idea you had," the pistoleer said, "but it won't work."

"Why not?" the lawman asked.

"I've heard tell that once Shotgun Anderson and Kid Slade take a job, they see it through."

"Over my dead body," Tyrell declared.

"For a man you hardly know?" Rondo said.

"You're forgettin' this," Tyrell said, and tapped his badge. "This tin means that south of the Mason-Dixon and north of the Mason-Dixon are one and the same."

"Not to me they're not," Rondo declared. "And they never will be."

"Like I said," Tyrell said. "Stubborn."

"Like I said," Rondo said. "Breathin'."

Roy had been waiting for a chance to join in, and said, "Here's hoping you stay that way."

33

Ritlin had been doing a lot of thinking. As a general rule he tried not to think too much but now it couldn't be helped. He'd nearly been shot the other night and he'd like to find out who was out to kill him before they put lead in his skull.

The more thinking he did, the more suspicious he became. One Eye up and disappearing like that could only mean One Eye was dead. The runt had liked money as much as he liked anything and would never quit in the middle of a job.

Then there was Brule. Ritlin had accepted Axel's story that the rancher, Olander, was to blame. But all he had to go on was Axel's word, and when he got down to it, he knew less about Axel than any of the others and not enough to trust him as completely as he had trusted Brule.

And now that Ritlin was doing some thinking, he remembered a lot of little things that singly didn't amount to much but taken together added to his suspicion.

For starters, Axel claimed he was a cowboy from Texas. But there was that time they hired out to kill a well-to-do gent who was dipping his wick into another gent's wife. The man they killed had a painting in his parlor. Ritlin had come out of the bedroom and saw Axel staring up at it with a smile on his face. Since Axel so rarely smiled, he asked if he liked the painting.

"It shows a sailboat off the coast back east," Axel had answered in a voice that didn't sound like his own. "It reminds me—" And he'd stopped and turned and said in his Texas drawl, "It's a nice paintin'."

Then there was that other incident.

They were in Dodge City. Ritlin came around a corner and saw Axel talking to another man. The other man wore city clothes and a round-topped hat with a short brim. The man had the top two buttons of his jacket buttoned but not the rest. A bulge on his hip suggested why. The pair were smiling and Ritlin distinctly saw the other man clap Axel on the arm. Then Axel noticed him and said something to the other man, who wheeled and melted into the shadows. Ritlin had gone over and asked, "Who was your friend?"

"Never saw him before," Axel had answered. "He was askin' if I had tobacco to spare."

Later, Ritlin spotted the same man again, at a bar in a saloon. He'd asked a poker player across from him if he knew who the man was.

The player had looked, and paled. Bending and dropping his voice, he'd said, "What are you asking about him for? Do you have a death wish?"

"Who the hell is he?"

"Why, that's Dave Mather, himself. Mysterious Dave, folks call him. He's a man-killer through and through."

Ritlin had never heard of him. "Why do they call him Mysterious Dave?"

"Because no one knows anything about him or his past. He keeps it a secret. Never talks about himself, they say. Never tells where he's from. Which is pretty smart, if you ask me."

"Why smart?" Ritlin had asked.

"If people don't know who he is or where he's been, he's less likely to end up behind bars for things he's done."

Ritlin thought it silly, being so secretive. He'd gone on playing cards and forgotten about it.

Until now.

Ritlin was at a corner table in the Grand Lady nursing a bottle when Axel pushed through the batwings, scanned the room and saw him. Axel came over and pulled out a chair and nodded in greeting.

"Here you are."

"Here I am," Ritlin said.

"I've been lookin' all over for you the past few days. Where have you been?"

Ritlin mentioned that he'd taken a room in a boardinghouse run by a colored woman.

"We've sat around long enough," Axel said. "We need to get on with the job."

"With Brule gone I don't much care whether we do it or don't," Ritlin said.

"We took money in advance," Axel reminded him. "We have to finish it."

"Brule did most of the plannin'," Ritlin said.

"We can do it without him. We start with the farmers and save the other rancher for last."

"You have a particular farmer in mind or do we stick a pin in that map of yours?"

Axel didn't seem to notice Ritlin's sarcasm. "As a matter of fact, I do. We start with Roy Sether."

"Why him?"

"From what I can gather, the others look up to him. He's had meetin's at his house. He's the closest thing to a leader they have." Axel paused. "And he's the one Rondo James is stayin' with."

Despite himself, Ritlin was suddenly interested. "Rondo James?"

"You remember when we were being chased?" Axel said. "We waited in the woods to ambush two riders who were after us?"

Ritlin nodded. "The storm spoiled our little surprise."

"I thought one of the riders was a cowboy and the other was a farmer. But now I think it was Sether and Rondo James. We get them out of the way and the rest of the farmers will be so scared, they'll skedaddle."

"I would sure like a chance at that Reb," Ritlin said.

"Think of it," Axel said. "You shoot him, you'll be as famous as Hickok or Hardin or anyone."

"Do you think I'm stupid?" Ritlin said. "There would have to be witnesses or no one would know, and there can't be witnesses."

"If we do it at the Sether farm. But what if you shoot him here in town?"

"How would we get him here?" Ritlin sneered. "I send him an invite?"

Axel smiled. "In a manner of speakin'. I have it all worked out."

"Do you, now?"

"We snatch one of Sether's kids or his wife. I'll leave a note sayin' that if Sether wants to see them again, Rondo James is to come into Teton, alone."

"What makes you think James will do it?"

"Word is that they're friends. When James shows up, you gun him and you'll have all the witnesses you need."

"And you're sure this will work?"

Axel's smile widened. "Trust me."

"The lawdog is leavin'," Kid Slade announced from his perch in the fork of an oak.

Shotgun Anderson was leaning with his back to the oak, his shotgun propped against the trunk. "About damn time." It was close to sunset and the shadows were lengthening.

The tree shook slightly as Kid Slade descended. On reaching the bottom limb, he slid his legs over and swung lithely to the ground. "About damn time is right. James has been there for days. Why didn't we hit him sooner?"

"Patience, cub," Shotgun Anderson said. "By now he's half convinced we gave up and went elsewhere."

"So that's why you waited."

"You shoot a bear when it's hibernatin' and you're less likely to be bit than when it's awake. You tromp on a snake when it's sunnin' itself and you're less likely to get bit than when it's coiled to strike."

"I don't need no lecture," Kid Slade said.

Shotgun sighed and picked up his prized hand-cannon and moved through the trees to a small clearing and their camp. Their horses were saddled and ready. A small fire crackled, barely giving off smoke, and a coffeepot sat on a flat rock. He sat and filled a tin cup. "Might as well make yourself comfortable. It'll be a spell. We'll wait until they turn in."

Instead of sitting, Kid Slade commenced to pace, his hands on his short-barreled Colts. "Rondo James, by God," he said with glee. "I can't hardly wait."

"What have I told you?" Shotgun said. "What have I told you a thousand times?"

Kid Slade stopped and scowled. "God, I am tired of you treatin' me as if I'm dumb."

"Let me hear you say it."

"Damn it."

"Show me you remember."

Kid Slade stamped a boot like a petulant child and growled, "Keep a cool head. No matter what, keep a cool head. Don't let myself get worked up."

"And why?"

"So I'll think straight and shoot straight." Kid Slade threw in, "Happy now?"

"No. The way you're behavin', it went in one ear and bounced out again." Shotgun fingered the cup. "You get mad at me for tryin' to keep you alive?"

"That's not it, at all. It's you actin' like I'm no-account."

"Would I have taken you for my partner if I thought that?" Shotgun said.

Kid Slade turned and sank down. He rested his elbows on his knees and his chin in his hands. "There. I'm sittin' and I'm calm."

"Not calm enough."

"What will we take back as proof?" Kid Slade asked. "We always take somethin'."

Shotgun wasn't fooled by the Kid's clumsy attempt to change the subject but he went along with it. "With him it's easy. His hat or his coat or his pistols."

"There might not be much left of the hat if you do as you usually do and blow his head clean off."

"His coat, then. Or his pistols."

"I might like them for myself."

"I can tell by his holsters they have six-inch barrels or better. You like four-inchers."

"I'm not sayin' I'd use them," Kid Slade said. "But they'd be fine keepsakes."

"You've never wanted anything from anyone else."

"It's Rondo James."

"There's that," Shotgun acknowledged. "Fair enough. We'll give Ike Hascomb the coat and any Reb doodads that James has on him."

"Doodads?" Kid Slade said, and snickered.

"Medals or buttons and such."

Half the sun was gone. Vivid red and orange streaked the western horizon. An early owl hooted.

Kid Slade breathed deep and said, "I'll want to remember this day the rest of my life." He pushed a log that was sticking half out of the fire into the flames. "Which ones do you remember best?"

"I don't."

"All the men you've splattered and you don't remember any?" Kid Slade said skeptically.

"I don't try to," Shotgun Anderson said. "Once they're dead I forget about them."

"Not me. I like to remember. That one who got on his knees and blubbered like a baby. That one who put his hands over his face and you blew his hands and his face off, both. That one who was runnin' and I shot his knees out and stuck my six-shooter in his ear to finish him." Kid Slade grinned. "At night I like to think about them before I fall asleep."

"I had no idea."

"I remember the blood, the bullet holes, their brains oozin' out. All of it."

"Now that's damned peculiar," Shotgun said.

They both laughed.

34

Roy Sether liked to read the *The Farmer's Almanac*. It was all he liked to read. Often after the kids had been tucked in, he'd sit in the parlor reading the almanac while Martha knitted in her rocking chair.

Tonight Roy was paging through the articles on everything from gardening to fishing tips and came to a section on recipes. Since he knew Martha was always interested in trying new ones, he cleared his throat and said, "The almanac has a recipe here for corn muffins. Not that yours need improving."

"Read it to me," Martha requested without looking up from her needles.

"Pour one quart of boiling water over one pint of fine cornmeal. While the mixture is still hot, add one tablespoon of butter and a little salt, stirring the butter thoroughly. Let it stand until cool. Then add a small cup of wheat flour and two well-beaten eggs. When mixed sufficiently, put the batter into well-greased shallow tins or, better yet, into gem pans, and bake in a brick oven for one-half hour, or until richly browned. Serve hot."

"It's not much different than my own recipe," Martha commented. "I add two tablespoons of butter and three eggs. As for using a brick oven, a stove is perfectly fine."

"They have some other recipes," Roy said. "Do you want me to read them?"

Martha stopped clacking the needles. "What I want is to talk about Rondo James."

Her tone warned Roy that she was upset about something. Setting the almanac in his lap, he said, "I thought you liked him."

"I do. He's a perfect gentleman. I meant it when I said he was welcome to stay."

"But?" Roy prompted when she stopped.

"That was before this assassin business," Martha said. "From what the marshal told me, this is serious."

"I never took it any other way," Roy assured her.

"Yet Rondo is still here."

Roy was taken aback. "You want me to ask him to leave? Is that what this is about?"

"It's about Andy, Sally and Matt," Martha said. "His being here puts them in harm's way."

Roy had thought of that, too, but he didn't say so.

"If there is any shooting, they could be caught in the cross fire. Or take a stray bullet," Martha continued. "We can't allow that."

"Then you do want me to ask him to leave?"

"I want what is best for our family. You should, too."

Roy felt a surge of indignation. "I care for them as much as you do. No one can say I don't."

"I know, dear. You'll have a talk with Mr. James, then? You'll convince him it's best for all of us if he moves on?" Martha smiled. "He told me today his horse is healed, so there's no reason he can't."

Roy hid his disappointment. He had gotten used to having the Southerner around. And he liked him, a lot. "What about our own problem?"

"The killings?"

"The killings. I feel safer going off into the fields when he's here to watch over you."

"There haven't been any since the Olanders," Martha said. "I was talking to Irene and Tilda and they both agree that whoever was to blame has moved on."

Roy tried to think of some other argument and all he could come up with was, "I'd still like to give it a day or two."

"And I think—" Martha stopped and her eyes widened and her mouth formed an O. She was looking toward the window.

Roy did the same.

Earlier Martha had opened the window to let in the night breeze, as she often did in the summer, and tied the curtains back.

Shotgun Anderson was leaning in the window, his double-barreled shotgun trained on them, a smile on his face. "How do you do, folks?" he said pleasantly.

Roy started to rise and heard the clicks of the twin hammers.

"I wouldn't, Mr. Sether," Shotgun Anderson said. "I cut loose at this range, you're sitting so close to your missus, I'll blow you and her apart."

Roy's mouth went dry. He'd never had a gun pointed at him before. "What do you want?" he demanded.

"You already know," Shotgun Anderson said.

"How dare you," Martha said. "This is our home."

"You'd be surprised at what I'll dare, lady," Shotgun

Anderson said. "I want you to set your knittin' on the floor and go open the front door for my pard."

"I will not," Martha declared.

"Mrs. Sether," the assassin said, "I'm bein' polite. But if you don't do as I ask, I'll stop bein' polite and splatter your husband's brains all over that wall."

"You're a hideous brute."

"I've been called worse." Anderson wagged the shotgun. "On your feet. Go throw the bolt like I asked."

"How do I know you won't shoot us anyway?"

"We're here for Rondo James. No one else need be hurt if you'll do as we say."

"I don't trust you."

"You're stallin'. If you're still stallin' by the time I count to five, you'll need to buy widow's black for the funeral." Shotgun Anderson trained the shotgun squarely on Roy. "One," he said.

"You pull those triggers and Rondo James will hear."

"Two."

"You won't have surprise on your side."

"Three."

Martha let her knitting fall and stood. "If I only had a gun."

"You'd be dead. Now do as I damn well told you. And no hollerin' to warn the Reb, you hear?"

"Despicable," Martha said, and walked from the parlor with her spine as stiff as a ramrod.

Shotgun Anderson chuckled. "That's some firebrand you've got there, Sether."

"Please," Roy said. "Don't do this."

"Not much for gumption, are you?"

"Rondo James is my friend."

"Ain't that nice?"

"My children are upstairs."

"I'm not here for them. We're only paid for James."

It hit Roy, then, that the assassin was lying. He and his family were witnesses and Anderson and Slade couldn't leave witnesses. A chill ran through him. He almost leaped up to try for his Winchester but he knew he wouldn't take two steps before he'd be blown to kingdom come.

There were voices, and a chuckle, and Martha came back into the parlor with Kid Slade behind her. The Kid had his Colts in his hands and was smirking.

"Go over by your husband, and no more insults."

"What did you say to him?" Roy asked.

"That he's a worthless cur."

The Kid covered them and said, "You can come in now, pard. They so much as twitch wrong and I'll blow out their wicks."

Anderson eased out of the window and in a few moments came down the hall. He gazed up the stairs and turned an ear as if listening, and nodded to himself. "I reckon all your sprouts are asleep."

"We tucked them in over an hour ago," Martha said.

"We know," Kid Slade said. "We've been spyin' on you for days now. So we'd know what my pard likes to call your routine."

"Find a weak spot in a person's habits and they're as good as dead," Shotgun Anderson said.

"Do you think I care, you horrible brute?" Martha said. "There is nothing lower than a man who kills his fellow man. 'Thou shalt not kill,' remember?"

Kid Slade laughed. "That's the Bible, ain't it? My pa was always goin' on about it."

"It's a shame none of his instruction took root," Martha said.

"Not a shame to me. I like what I do. I wouldn't do anything else."

"The Devil has hold of you," Martha said. "Your soul is doomed to perdition."

"God Almighty," Kid Slade said. "We have us a female parson here, pard."

"I'm a good Christian woman," Martha said indignantly. "Or so I like to think."

"Get off your high horse, lady. That hogwash didn't take with me when I was ten. It sure as hell won't take now."

"Thou shalt not kill," Martha said again.

"Who are you tryin' to fool?" Kid Slade snapped, growing angry. "I told you my pa quoted all that stuff. And as I recollect, a lot of it was about killin'. Cain and Abel. The walls of Jericho. Samson and the thousand whoever-it-was. There's more killin' in that Bible of yours than you can shake a stick at."

Shotgun Anderson glared at his partner.

"What?" Kid Slade said.

"What the hell do you use for brains? We're on a job and you're arguin' religion?"

"She started it," the Kid said.

Roy was worried about his children. They might hear and come down to investigate.

Shotgun Anderson faced them. "Here's what we're goin' to do. You two are goin' to walk to the barn. You'll stop just outside and call for Rondo James to come out. Try anything, shout to warn him, and you die where you stand."

"Don't think we won't, either," Kid Slade said.

"He's probably asleep by now," Martha said.

"You sure say stupid shit," the Kid said.

Martha folded her hands in front of her, and sniffed.

Roy decided to intervene before she made the young gun shark even madder. "What if he asks what we want? It's not usual for us to wake him at this hour."

Shotgun Anderson gave it some thought. "You'll say that you thought you saw someone skulkin' about the place. That ought to bring him out quick."

"And then we gun him," Kid Slade said.

"You expect us to betray his trust?" Martha said. "What if I refuse?"

Roy marveled at her courage. She was the one who had grown uneasy having the Southerner stay with them, yet here she was, refusing to be a party in his murder.

"If you refuse," Kid Slade said, "I march upstairs and snuff your kittens. How would that be, bitch?"

Before Roy could stop himself, he took a step with his hands clenched. "Don't talk to her like that."

Quick as thought, Kid Slade's short-barreled Colts swung toward him. "Or what? Fists against six-shooters, six-shooters win every time."

"Enough," Shotgun Anderson declared. "This ain't a goddamned debatin' society. Walk in front of us, you two. Sether, put your arm around your wife. Mrs. Sether, remember what my pard just told you about your kids. They're dead if you don't cooperate."

Roy was convinced they were dead anyway. He needed to do something, but for the life of him, and his family, he couldn't think of what. A sense of helplessness came over him such as he had never known.

Shotgun Anderson moved aside so they could go down the hall to the front door. "Let's get to it."

35

Ritlin came out of the boardinghouse and crossed the street. He walked north until he came to the Grand Lady and paused at the batwings.

Axel was at the end of the bar, nursing a drink.

Shoving on in, Ritlin strolled over. He plastered a smile on his face even as he placed his right hand on his gun belt close to his ivory-handled Colt. "Are you ready?" he asked.

Axel frowned. "I've been ready for days," he said irritably. "You're the one who kept puttin' it off."

"I said tonight would be the night and I'm as good as my word," Ritlin said.

Draining the rest of his glass, Axel said, "About damn time. I was set to go out to the Sether place myself. We agreed that he would be next."

"We did," Ritlin said. "Let's go."

They walked out. At that hour the saloons were jammed, and music and laughter tinkled on the breeze. A half-moon added its pale glow to the few streetlights.

Axel went to the hitch rail and unwrapped the reins to his horse. He was about to mount when he saw Ritlin still standing there. "Where's yours?"

"At the boardinghouse."

"Why the hell didn't you bring it with you?"

"I can get it on our way out." Ritlin wheeled on a boot heel and headed back down the street. He whistled to himself and gave the impression he didn't have a care in the world.

Axel followed, leading his mount. "I still think we should have done this sooner," he complained.

"With that lawdog sniffing around?" Ritlin shook his head. "It was smart to wait. I saw him ride into town about an hour ago. He's at the boardinghouse now, talking to Bessie Mae, the woman who runs it."

"It was risky of you to take a room there."

"I did it so I could keep an eye on him," Ritlin said. "I've already told you that three or four times." He grinned. "You're turning into more of a grump than One Eye ever was."

That shut Axel up.

When he was directly across from the boardinghouse, Ritlin crossed to the hitch rail. He had tied his sorrel at the far end, where it was darkest.

Axel led his zebra dun up and stared uneasily at the boardinghouse. "Let's light a shuck."

"I'm for that," Ritlin said. He checked the street to be sure no one was near them, and turned and opened a saddlebag. "Care for some jerky? I bought some today at the general store."

"Hell," Axel said. "Can't that wait until we're out of town?"

"Grumpy as hell," Ritlin said, and his hand closed on what he had really bought. He slid the hammer out and spun and struck Axel on the side of the head. Axel staggered, and clawed for his Merwin Hulbert. Ritlin slammed the hammer against his head a second time. Axel's hat went flying and Axel crumpled into a bow, his body twitching briefly before it went still.

Ritlin looked around. Satisfied he had gone unseen, he stooped, relieved Axel of the six-shooter, got hold of him around the waist, and slung Axel over the zebra dun, belly down.

Quickly climbing on the sorrel, he snagged the zebra dun's reins and hurried out of Teton. When he was well past the last of the buildings, he drew rein. From his saddlebag he took two short lengths of rope and proceeded to tie Axel's wrists behind his back, and to bind his ankles.

"Soon, you son of a bitch," Ritlin said to the unconscious form.

Climbing back on, Ritlin rode another half a mile, to a well-marked trail that led up to a timber camp. He climbed for about fifteen minutes, to the edge of a meadow. Veering across, he entered the trees at the far end, and once again stopped. Dismounting, Ritlin dumped Axel to the ground. The firewood he had gathered earlier that day was still there, and he soon had a fire going. He put coffee on and sat on a small log he had dragged over for a seat. He was humming to himself when he sensed eyes on him and said, "Surprised?"

Axel shifted so he was on his side facing the fire. "What the hell is this?"

"I reckon you already know."

"You about bashed in my head, damn you."

"Oh, I wouldn't do that." Ritlin looked at him, and grinned. "Not until we have our little talk."

"Talk?" Axel said.

"The biggest mistake of your life was taking me for a fool," Ritlin said.

"You've gone loco."

Ritlin leaned back. "I want to know why. You rode with us for five years."

"Why what?"

Ritlin sighed. He got up and went to the sorrel and reached into his saddlebags and brought back the hammer. "See this?" He wagged it. "I could have shot you but I wanted answers."

"I don't know what you're talkin' about."

"I knew if I went for my six-shooter you'd likely go for yours and I'd be forced to kill you." Ritlin stood over Axel's legs. "I'll start with your knees. After I break them, I'll do the ankles."

Axel strained against the ropes, to no avail, and said, "You son of a bitch."

"I'm not the one who killed Brule," Ritlin said. "I'm not the one who killed One Eye."

"I didn't either."

"Your mistake," Ritlin said, "was in trying to gun me the other night. It set me to thinking, and that set me on to you."

"You're loco, I tell you."

"I'll ask one more time," Ritlin said. "Then the hurting begins." He smacked the hammer again his left palm. "We trusted you and you turned on us. I want to know why."

"I didn't kill them, I tell you," Axel insisted.

"You shouldn't ought to call my bluff," Ritlin said, and raised the hammer over his head. "Say good-bye to your right knee."

"Wait."

Ritlin slowly lowered the hammer. "If this is a trick, you'll regret it."

"No trick," Axel said. "You have the better of me. It would be stupid to hold out. I'll tell you everything."

Ritlin noticed that Axel's drawl was gone, and that he spoke fine English with an accent. He moved to the log and sat. "We'll start with where you're from."

"Connecticut."

"The hell you say," Ritlin said. "Everyone says you're from Texas. Even Charlton Rank thought you were."

"Who do you think started that story?"

Ritlin mulled that while he poured steaming hot coffee into his cup. "Is Axel your real handle?"

"No."

"Damn. What is it, then?"

"Jim Mather."

"How long have you been calling yourself Axel?"

"Since my cousin and I took to cattle rustling down in Arkansas with Dave Rudabaugh and Milt Yarbarry. The sheriff there was called Axel and I used his name to make him mad."

Ritlin almost gave a start. Rudabaugh's name was familiar; he was a notorious gun hand and train robber involved with the Billy the Kid fracas that made headlines across the country. "Who's your cousin?"

"Dave Mather," Jim Mather said. "He's more generally known as Mysterious Dave."

"The gent you were talking to in Kansas," Ritlin remembered.

"After Arkansas we drifted into Texas," Jim Mather said. "That's when I took to speaking with a drawl and telling everyone I was a Texan."

"You lie like there is no tomorrow," Ritlin said.

"Every lie is to a purpose," Jim Mather said. "I learned that from my cousin."

Ritlin sipped and said, "I'm listening."

Grunting, Jim Mather rose onto an elbow. "I've lived on the wrong side of the law for a good long while now. The less people know about me, the less chance I'll wind up behind bars, or hung."

"So you lie to throw them off the scent."

"I do more than lie. I dress like a puncher when I'm no such thing. I talk like a Texan when I'm from New England. I use a different name."

"Even with those you ride with."

"Especially those I ride with," Jim Mather said. "They're liable to be caught and the law might make them talk."

Ritlin held his tin cup in both hands and shook his head in bewilderment. "All this time, we took you at your word."

"Anyone who would take the word of an outlaw—" Jim Mather said, and didn't finish.

"None of this explains Brule and One Eye and why you tried to kill me."

"I'd rather not," Jim Mather said.

Ritlin reached down and touched the hammer on the ground by his boot. "I pick this up, I won't stop until every bone in your body is broke."

"It's your fault they're dead."

Straightening, Ritlin sneered, "This should be good. You kill them and blame me?"

Jim Mather nodded. "You were the one who wouldn't go slow. You were the one who acted as if we had to wipe out everyone in Thunder Valley when Rank wanted us to *scare* them off."

"I figured killin' a few would scare off the rest."

"Or it might make them stand and fight," Jim Mather said, "which is what they're doing."

"So you didn't like how I was handlin' things," Ritlin said. "How was that cause to kill Brule and One Eye?"

"You were too reckless. The law was bound to take notice. And if the law got its hands on One Eye or Brule, they might strike a deal and give the rest of us up."

"Brule would never do that."

"Not to you. You were his pard. But he might have turned me in."

"So? What could he tell them? What could One Eye tell them? Neither knew your real name or where you're really from."

"They could give a description."

"You backstabbing prick."

"Don't take it personal," Jim Mather said.

"What is it, then?"

"Self-preservation. I've lasted as long as I have because I always cover my tracks. That's why my cousin and I parted company. I wanted to kill Rudabaugh and Yarbarry so they couldn't identify us but he was against it."

"I'd like to have seen you kill Dave Rudabaugh. They say he was the meanest son of a bitch alive."

"I think I could outdraw him if I had to. But a bullet to the back of the head would have worked as well."

"God, you're a bastard."

"A careful bastard," Jim Mather said, "who always has a dagger in his boot and a derringer up his sleeve."

"What?" Ritlin said. He streaked his hand to his holster and was wrapping his fingers around the ivory handles of his Colt when Mather's hand flashed up holding a derringer. He saw the muzzle spurt smoke and felt a jolt to his forehead and then there was nothing, nothing at all.

36

Roy Sether was filled with dread. Dread for his wife and dread for Rondo James and dread for his own life. He held Martha's arm as they moved down the hall and out the front door to the porch.

Behind them came Shotgun Anderson with his double-barreled shotgun leveled at their backs and Kid Slade with his twin Colts pointed.

One wrong move, Roy knew, and he and the woman he loved would be blasted to ribbons.

"We'll be right behind you, so don't try anything," Shotgun Anderson warned.

"That goes double for you, bitch," Kid Slade said. "With that mouth of yours."

Roy boiled with anger. Ordinarily, he'd never let anyone talk to his wife like that.

Thunder Valley lay deceptively peaceful under the stars. The night was clear, the breeze still, the animals on the farm were quiet.

"I can't get either of you to reconsider?" Martha said. "To murder someone is wrong."

"Quit preachin' to us," Kid Slade snapped.

"I'll go him one better, lady," Shotgun Anderson said. "Not another damn word out of you, you hear?" He poked her in the back with his shotgun.

Roy almost turned and slugged him.

"Another couple of minutes and this will be over with," Anderson went on. "The Reb will be dead and we'll ride off and you and your kids will be fine."

Roy doubted that. He doubted it very much. The pair would kill them. He had to do something but he couldn't think of anything that wouldn't get him instantly shot.

"Let's go," Kid Slade said.

Roy went down the steps and started for the barn. He walked as slowly as he dared, hoping they would attribute it to fear.

"I can't wait to be shed of this place," Kid Slade remarked.

"Hush," Shotgun Anderson said.

"We should go to Denver after we get paid. They have more whores than just about anywhere."

"I said hush, damn it. Don't put the cart before the horse."

The assassins fell quiet.

The barn door was open. Roy stared at the wide black hole, aghast. Rondo James was sleeping in the loft, as he usually did. The loft door itself was shut, and Rondo wouldn't hear them approach.

Roy felt Martha's nails dig into his arm. She was in turmoil, too. He smiled encouragement but in the dark he didn't know if she could see.

They were within ten feet of the barn when Shotgun Anderson hissed, "That's close enough."

Roy stopped.

"Now holler to him. Tell him what I told you to."

Roy glanced over his shoulder. Both Anderson and Slade had crouched so they wouldn't be seen.

"Get to it, damn you," Kid Slade whispered.

Clearing his throat, Roy called out, "Rondo! Rondo James, it's me, Roy."

There was no answer.

"Mr. James, we think we saw someone skulking about the house. You might want to come out. Did you hear me, Mr. James?"

Again there was no reply.

Roy waited, every nerve raw, Martha's nails digging so deep, she drew blood.

"Call him again," Shotgun Anderson whispered.

"Mr. James!" Roy yelled. "Where are you, Mr. James?"

A minute passed. Then two. Nothing happened. The silence was unbroken.

"What the hell?" Kid Slade snarled. "Where is he?"

"I don't like it," Shotgun Anderson said.

Suddenly the pair were on either side of Roy and Martha. Anderson pointed his shotgun at Roy's head and Kid Slade jammed a Colt against Martha's temple.

"Rondo James!" Shotgun Anderson bellowed. "You hear me in there? If you don't come out right quick, these friends of yours will be blown to hell and back."

It took every ounce of self-control Roy had not to grab the shotgun and try to wrest it from Anderson's grasp.

"We won't wait all damn night," Kid Slade hollered. "Show yourself, Reb, or this lady gets a new ear hole."

Once again, silence, save for a few clucks from the chicken coop.

"What the hell?" Kid Slade said to his partner.

"Somethin' ain't right. Keep them covered." Wedging the shotgun's stock to his shoulder, Shotgun Anderson cautiously entered the barn and was swallowed by the darkness.

"Nothin' better happen to him," Kid Slade said, "or I'll drop you two where you stand."

"It's not too late to change your minds," Martha said. "It's not too late to go."

"Lady, I'm going to enjoy killin' you," Kid Slade said. "You don't know when to shut the hell up."

Roy's skin prickled. He thought for sure he'd hear shots. More minutes went by, and a bulk emerged from the shadows.

"He ain't in there," Shotgun Anderson announced.

"Where did he get to?" Kid Slade wondered. "The last we saw, he went in right before dark."

"We'll take them back into the house and tie them," Shotgun Anderson proposed, "and have a look around."

"Don't you dare disturb my children," Martha said.

Kid Slade shoved her. "I am sick of you. You hear me? Open your mouth again and see what happens."

Roy hit him. Before he could stop himself, his fist was up and around and he caught Slade flush on the jaw and sent him tottering. He was about to say that Slade should keep his hands off his wife when the side of his head seemed to cave in, and the next he knew, he was on his knees and his head was throbbing with agony and Martha was holding both his hands and saying his name.

Roy blinked and looked up into the muzzles of Anderson's shotgun.

"You two are startin' to rile me."

"Don't you dare strike him again," Martha said, throwing an arm in front of Roy's face. "He was only protecting me."

"Get him up," Shotgun Anderson barked.

Roy's legs were mush. He had to try three times to stand. Wobbling unsteadily, he let Martha steer him toward the house.

Kid Slade came up and jammed a Colt against his ribs. "That hurt, mister. But nowhere near as much as I'm fixin' to hurt you."

"Leave him be," Martha said.

They climbed the steps and the Kid opened the door. Anderson stayed behind him, his shotgun inches from their heads.

"Into the parlor."

Roy's strength was returning. He couldn't let them tie them or it was all over. He'd have to fight even though it would get him killed. "I'm sorry," he said softly to Martha.

"For what?"

"Shut up," Kid Slade snarled.

They were almost to the parlor. Roy steeled himself for what he must do.

"As soon as we tie them—" Shotgun Anderson began.

Rondo James came out of the parlor. He was around the corner in a swift stride, a Colt Navy in each hand. He thrust the pistols between Roy and Martha and simultaneously shot Shotgun Anderson and Kid Slade both in the face.

Both assassins staggered. A look of bewilderment came over Shotgun Anderson, and his legs gave out. Kid Slade's mouth moved but didn't utter a sound as he followed his bearish pard to the floor.

Rondo James pointed his Colts at them until they stopped convulsing. "I reckon that's the end of them," he said.

Roy's right ear was ringing and the acrid odor of

gunpowder was strong in his nose. He pulled Martha to him and they embraced.

"Thank God," she breathed.

Roy caressed her hair and gave silent thanks, and looked at the man in gray. "Thank you," he said.

"Thank yourself," Rondo replied, slowly lowering his Colts." It was all that 'Mr. James' business you were yellin'. You never call me Mr. James so I knew somethin' wasn't right."

"You saved us," Martha said.

"I cat-footed out the back of the barn and ran like Hades around to the house," Rondo related. "I came in the back door and peeked out the front window and saw all of you comin' this way, and I decided to spring a little surprise."

Roy stared at the bodies and the spreading pools of blood.

"That was slick as could be."

"I took an awful chance," Rondo James said. "They might have got off a shot."

Martha went to him, and to Roy's amazement, she kissed the Southerner on the cheek. "We are forever in your debt."

Rondo smiled and shrugged. "What are friends for?" he said.

A commotion upstairs preceded a flurry of footsteps. Andy, Sally and Matt were halfway down the stairs when Roy thought to turn and raise a hand. "Stop where you are!"

Out of habit they obeyed. They were confused, and Sally and Matt were scared.

"What's going on, Pa?" Andy said, and spied the still forms. "Who are they?"

"Go back upstairs," Roy directed. "You shouldn't see this."

"No, you shouldn't," Martha said, and bustled over. "I'll tuck you in." She winked at Roy and went up, herding them before her.

"That's some lady you have there," Rondo James said.

"Don't I know it."

"I'm awful sorry about these two," Rondo said, with a nod at the assassins. "I didn't mean to bring this down on your heads."

"How were you to know that rancher hired them?" Roy said. "Come to think of it, it's Marshal Gibson we should thank, for warning us."

"I owe him," Rondo said. He began to replace the spent cartridges.

Roy's head was hurting worse. He had a goose egg above his ear.

"I'll be headin' into town tomorrow to tell the lawdog," Rondo James said. "And then I'll be on my way."

"What?"

"General Lee is healed."

"Stick around another day. For the kids. They'll be sorry you're leaving, and so am I."

"I reckon one more day can't hurt." Rondo twirled the right Colt into its holster and did the same with the left, and patted them. Stepping to the bodies, he went through their pockets. "What have we here?"

Roy glanced up the stairs. Martha had the kids in their rooms and he could hear her saying goodnight to Matt. When he turned back to Rondo James, the Southerner was holding out two leather pokes. "What's this?"

"As near as I can tell, their life savin's." Rondo tossed one to him and Roy caught it. "Must be a couple of thousand in each."

"Martha wouldn't let me take this," Roy said. "It's blood money."

"She doesn't have to know." Rondo slid the other poke into his slicker.

Roy hefted it and coins jingled. He opened the drawstring and saw a thick wad of folded bills. Pulling the string tight, he shoved the poke into his pants pocket. "God forgive me," he said.

"It's a good thing I'm leavin'," Rondo James said, and grinned. "I'm a bad influence."

"No," Roy said sincerely. "You're not."

37

"Oh my," Marshal Tyrell Gibson said.

The table had been set with china plates and silverware and glasses that sparkled. Folded napkins were by the plates. A heaping platter of venison was at the center, along with bowls of hominy and collard greens.

Tyrell's mouth watered. "You did all this for me, Miss Cyrus?"

"I told you to call me Bessie," she said as she came out of the kitchen with two candles in silver holders. She placed them on the table, one toward his end and the other toward her end, and set to lighting them.

"Candles, ma'am?" Tyrell said in some amazement.

"Don't call me that, neither." Bessie smiled sweetly and moved to her chair and stood there.

It took a few seconds for Tyrell to realize what he was supposed to do. Scooting around, he pulled her chair out and she eased into it and bestowed another smile.

"Thank you, kind sir."

Tyrell went around and sat. He saw her looking at him and snatched off his hat and hung it over the chair. "It's been a spell since I ate this elegant." Actually, he couldn't recollect ever being served so fine a meal.

"I'm happy to do it," Bessie said.

"I didn't mean to put you to all this bother. I got in so late, I figured I'd missed supper and would get by until mornin'."

"Nonsense. It's the least I can do."

Tyrell glanced at the six empty chairs. "It'll just be the two of us?"

"The other boarders have already ate. Most are abed, I'd imagine." Bessie picked up a bowl. "Care for some collard greens?"

"I surely would." Tyrell had to stretch to reach it. He spooned out a helping and did the same with the hominy and speared a slab of deer meat.

"I pay a local hunter to bring me fresh venison," Bessie mentioned. "It's less costly than buying beef from the butcher and my boarders don't seem to mind."

"Venison is fine," Tyrell said. "We used to eat it to home, too."

"In Georgia."

"Yes, ma—" Tyrell caught himself. "Yes, Bessie Mae. Down Atlanta way."

"I'm from South Carolina, myself."

"A Southern gal, by God," Tyrell blurted, and coughed to cover his embarrassment.

"And you're a Southern gentleman," Bessie said. "That we should meet is quite a coincidence, don't you think?"

"If you say it is," Tyrell responded. He wasn't quite sure what she meant.

"So tell me," Bessie said. "How was your stay at the Sethers'?"

Tyrell usually didn't like to talk about his work but with her he couldn't talk enough. He expressed his disappointment that the assassins hadn't showed and concluded with, "It's just as well, though. The Sethers might have been hurt and they're good people. And Rondo James has been through enough."

"You sound as if you like him," Bessie observed.

"I reckon I do. He's not at all as he's painted to be." Thinking that she might not approve of him being fond of a notorious shootist, Tyrell mentioned, "He's from the South, too."

"So I've heard." Bessie stared at him as if she were thinking and finally she said, "You take your job very seriously, don't you, Tyrell?"

Tyrell's ears burned again. "How else would I take it? It's serious work."

"I like that in a man. It shows he has a sense of responsibility. He's not frivolous."

For the life of him, Tyrell couldn't recall ever hearing that word before. Her vocabulary scared him sometimes. "I took an oath and I live by it."

"To uphold the law."

"Yes, ma—"

Bessie laughed. "That's all right. If you call me ma'am now and again I won't throw a fit."

"Thank you," Tyrell said. He forked some greens and remarked, "I can't tell you the last time I had hominy and collard greens."

"You could have them every day if you had a wife."

Tyrell nearly choked. He coughed and swallowed and clutched the glass of water. After he drank, he said quietly, "I hardly ever think of marryin'."

"Why not, a fine figure of a man like you?"

Tyrell was too stupefied to respond.

"Cat got your tongue?"

"No, ma'am," Tyrell said. "I mean, well, law work is dangerous, and I have to do a lot of travelin', and it wouldn't be fair to leave a woman at home worryin' over whether she'd see me again."

"That should be for the woman to decide."

"I suppose." Tyrell concentrated on his meal. The talk was disturbing him.

After a while Bessie said, "I'm almost past marrying age, myself."

"That's not true," Tyrell said. "You can't be much over twenty-five."

"Why, Marshall Gibson, you fibber," Bessie said. "I'm thirty-three, Tyrell. How old are you?"

"Thirty-nine."

"There you go."

Tyrell tried to figure out what that meant and couldn't. "There I go what?"

"We are both of us almost past our prime. We don't find someone soon, I'm liable to end up a spinster and you'll be a grumpy old man."

"I'm hardly ever grumpy," Tyrell said.

"I know. It's another thing I like about—"

Tyrell looked up to see why she had stopped and saw that she was gazing past him at the hall. Shifting in his chair, he was startled to discover a man standing in the shadowed doorway.

"Who's there?" he demanded.

The man came into the light. He was dressed in typical puncher clothes. "Howdy." He smiled and took off his hat. "Sorry to disturb your meal."

"I'm Miss Cyrus," Bessie said. "I run the boarding-house. Are you looking to take a room, Mr. . . . ?"

"Axel," the cowboy said. "Axel Jones. And, no, ma'am.

I'm here on account of Ritlin. He already has a room. He got a job with the Buchanan spread, and he asked me to stop by and make sure he didn't leave anything here."

"Oh. So he won't be back?" Bessie rose. "I'll show you which one it is."

"I'm obliged, ma'am," the cowboy said in his pronounced drawl.

Tyrell said, "Hold on. Why didn't he come for his things himself?"

"Like I said," Axel replied, "he just got a job at the Buchanan ranch and can't come into town for a spell. I was on my way in and he asked me if I'd do it for him."

"Nice of you," Tyrell said.

Axel chuckled. "He paid me a dollar."

Bessie moved to the hall and the cowboy stepped out of her way. "Follow me."

Tyrell watched them walk off. It was an ordinary enough request, and the puncher seemed harmless enough, but something about the man bothered him. He couldn't say what. He almost got up to follow them but figured Bessie might not like him acting as if he was her nursemaid. Besides, he had that marriage talk to consider. It had sounded to him as if she was about to suggest that he and she should be man and wife.

"Surely not," Tyrell said to himself. A fine lady like Bessie could have most any man she set her sights on. "Or could she?" he reflected. A lot of whites wouldn't want anything to do with her because her skin wasn't. And now that he thought about it, he hadn't seen another black man anywhere in Teton.

Tyrell ate, and after a while he wondered what was taking them so long. He was about to get up and go find her when he heard her laugh and they came back down the hall, the puncher's spurs jangling. He wondered how it was that the spurs hadn't made a sound when the cowboy first appeared.

Bessie was saying, " — too bad he had you go to all this trouble for nothing."

"It was no trouble, ma'am," Axel said. "And I could use the dollar."

Bessie came to her chair, remarking as she passed Tyrell, "Mr. Ritlin had cleaned his room out. He must have forgot."

"He was probably just bein' sure, ma'am," Axel said. He looked at Tyrell. "She tells me you're a federal lawdog."

Tyrell moved his cost and showed his badge. "I am."

"Are you passin' through? Or are you here after some outlaw?"

"I'm lookin' for a man called One Eye Smith," Tyrell revealed. "Short fella. Wears an eye patch. Could be you've seen him around?"

"No, sir," Axel said. "I haven't seen a man wearin' an eye patch since I can't recollect when." He paused. "Is he the only one you're after?"

"Smith rides with three others," Tyrell said. "Or so I was told."

"Know who they are?"

Tyrell shook his head. "I don't even know what they look like. But when I find him, I'll find them."

"I take it you don't even know their names?"

"Wish I did," Tyrell said.

"Good luck with your hunt." Axel put his hat on. "Well, I'd best be goin'. Pleasure meetin' you folks." He turned and jingled away.

"What a nice man," Bessie said.

"If you say so." Tyrell was still bothered and couldn't account for it.

"Now, then. Where were we." Bessie smiled. "Oh yes. We were talking about being compatible."

"We were?"

"It would be worth finding out if we are," Bessie said. "We're not getting any younger."

"That's for sure." Tyrell was trying to remember what compatible meant. "You must read a lot."

"Why, as a matter of fact, I do. Why did you bring that up?"

"You talk like a book," Tyrell said.

Bessie laughed. "And you? Do you do much reading?"

"I can wrestle with a menu and a circular," Tyrell said. "But generally, ma'am, no."

"There you go again. Try my name. It's not hard to pronounce."

"You are a tease, Bessie," Tyrell said.

"I have my playful moments."

Their eyes met, and it wasn't just Tyrell's ears that burned. He drank some water.

"How long will you be around?" she asked.

"I wasn't plannin' to stay much longer," Tyrell said. There was no sign of One Eye, and he had done his good deed for the month and warned Rondo James about the assassins.

"But now?"

"I reckon I might," Tyrell said.

"You can have Mr. Ritlin's room. At no charge."

"I couldn't."

"Do you have another woman somewhere?"

"I don't have a woman anywhere," Tyrell said.

"You do now."

"Oh my," Tyrell said.

38

Charlton Rank arrived in Teton shortly after eight in the morning. He went straight to the Timberland and took the same suite as before. Bisby, his secretary, was with him. So was Floyd, his manservant. As well as Bannister and Tate and eight other Enforcers.

No sooner had Rank made himself comfortable than there was a knock at the door. Rank nodded at Tate and the former Texas Ranger went over and opened it.

To say Rank was surprised was an understatement. His visitor was one of the four incompetents he had come to kill.

"If it isn't Mr. Axel," he said coldly.

Axel didn't seem to notice. He entered and crossed to the divan. "I saw you ride in."

"Did you, now?" Rank responded. "And where are your friends?"

"Dead."

"What?"

"I killed them."

Rank and everyone else stared. "What are you saying?"

"I just said it," Axel said. "You told us how you wanted the job done and they weren't doing it the way you wanted. Ritlin went kill-crazy. And the others went along with him."

"So *you* killed *them*?"

"When I take money to do a job," Axel drawled, "I do it the way the man who is payin' me wants me to do it."

"Well, now," Rank said. "This is a most welcome turn of events."

"You're not mad?"

"On the contrary." Rank smiled. "You've spared me from having to eliminate them. I am, as the saying goes, pleased as punch."

"Pleased enough to pay me their shares?"

Rank blinked, and laughed. "Why, Mr. Axel. I do believe you're a man after my own heart. You are one greedy son of a bitch."

"I'm worth it," Axel said. "I know how you can make the rest of the homesteaders stampede out of Thunder Valley."

"I'm listening," Rank said.

"There's a farmer by the name of Roy Sether. The rest all look up to him. He's the closest thing they have to a leader. Take care of him and the rest will skedaddle."

"And by take care you mean kill."

"What else?"

"And you want to do it?"

"Who else?"

Rank sat back and spread his arms along the back of the divan. "I like how you think. But it won't be just you."

Axel frowned. "Why not?"

"Let's just say that while I'm pleased you took the initiative and disposed of your friends, you should have eliminated them *before* the *Daily Leader* got wind of the situation." Rank leaned toward Axel, his face twisted with barely contained rage. "Thanks to their stupidity and you taking your goddamn sweet time about stopping them, I have to take a direct hand. And I don't like that. I don't like it even a little bit."

"I'd rather work alone," Axel said.

"Be my guest. Go off and find work somewhere else. Alone." Rank smiled an icy smile. "But if you hope to receive more money from me, you'll do things my way, and my way is this." He paused. "Mr. Bannister and Mr. Tate and the rest of my Enforcers are going with you. They'll change into ordinary clothes and you'll lead them to the Sether place. Once you're there, you will wait until dark and then follow your own suggestion and eliminate the entire family."

"You like that word, don't you?"

"Don't be petty," Rank said. "Now, do we have an agreement or not?"

"I get the five thousand you were goin' to pay Ritlin, Brule and One Eye, plus my cut?"

Rank snorted. "Twenty thousand dollars for botching the job? I don't think so."

"How much, then? It should be more than five. I did you a favor."

"I'll concede that much," Rank said. "So I'll tell you what I'll do. If this Sether business goes smoothly, I'll pay you another five. Which will bring your total to ten thousand dollars. More than most people earn in ten years."

"That's not bad. That's not bad at all. We have a new deal."

Rank grinned and rubbed his hands together. "Now that that's settled, how about a bite to eat? I'll have Floyd prepare a meal and we'll eat while the others get ready."

"It doesn't spoil your appetite, talkin' about wipin' out an innocent family?"

"Does it spoil yours?"

"No, but I've been killin' for a livin' for a good long while. What's your excuse?"

"I'm a cold-hearted bastard," Rank said, and laughed.

Marshal Tyrell Gibson was whistling to himself as he walked down Main Street toward Bessie's boardinghouse.

Tyrell was having a wonderful day. It had started with breakfast with Bessie. Just the two of them. He'd looked at her across the table and wanted to pinch himself to be sure he wasn't dreaming.

Tyrell had had all night to think about her proposition and he'd come to a decision. Bessie Mae Cyrus was the best thing that ever happened to him. A woman like her, interested in a man like him. It was a miracle. He'd be all kinds of a fool to turn her down, and he liked to think he wasn't a fool.

He'd lost all track of time talking to her. Her voice, her face, he was lost in her charm and beauty. At one point she said something and he realized she was waiting for an answer, and he blurted, "What was that?"

"You're not even listening to me, are you?"

"Every word," he had assured her.

"Then what did I just say?"

"I don't know," he'd admitted. "I was looking in your eyes."

Bessie had bowed her head and said quietly, "That was about the nicest compliment anyone has ever paid me."

"I'll try not to look in them so much so I hear you better."

She'd glanced up and said huskily, "You may look in them as often as you like."

Tyrell thought his body would explode.

It was the middle of the morning before he could tear himself away to pay the *Daily Leader* correspondent a visit. He figured that if anyone had heard about any more goings-on in Thunder Valley, it would be Filbert.

To his relief, Filbert hadn't heard a thing. So now he was free to spend more time with Bessie and become better acquainted.

Tyrell had gone a block from Filbert's small office and was nearing the Timberland hotel when who should come out the front door but the cowboy called Axel. Tyrell stopped. As he watched, Axel went up to a porch post and leaned against the post and hooked his thumbs in his gun belt, apparently waiting for someone.

Tyrell retreated into the shadows. He was curious what the man was up to. He still couldn't get over how the puncher had snuck up on him at Bessie's without making a sound.

Men were coming out of the hotel. Five, six, seven, Tyrell counted. Eight, nine, ten. All of them were dressed in new store-bought clothes. Even their hats were new. Axel said something and led them down the steps to the hitch rails. Every last man had a revolver strapped to his waist and some carried bundles.

Long guns, Tyrell suspected, wrapped in blankets. "Now, why would they hide them?" he asked himself.

Axel motioned, and the whole group rode to the next junction and reined to the east, toward Thunder Valley.

An awful premonition came over Tyrell. He broke into a sprint. People stared as he raced down Main Street to the hitch rail in front of the boardinghouse. Within moments he was in the saddle and heading east.

Tyrell tried to tell himself that he must be mistaken. There could be a perfectly ordinary explanation for what Axel and the others were up to. But it was suspicious as hell, them hiding their long guns.

Tyrell had been a lawman for too long to take anything for granted. He would find out what they were up to and if there was an explanation, no harm done.

They raised enough dust that he was able to stay well back and not lose them.

The day was warm, the sun bright, the birds were singing. It was the kind of day made for going for a stroll with Bessie. He hoped she would forgive him for disappearing on her.

Teton fell far behind. So did the last of the forest.

The grassland of Thunder Valley spread ahead, and the dust changed direction.

Tyrell used his spurs. Soon he saw the riders, bunched close together. They were no longer on the road. Instead they'd swung to the south and were cutting across the tilled fields.

Tyrell drew rein. It was more and more obvious that Axel and the other men were up to something, but what? He stayed put until they were out of sight, then followed their tracks at a walk.

Presently, the signs bore to the east again. The country was much too open for Tyrell's liking, and he dismounted and led his horse by the reins.

The sun was well up in the afternoon sky when Tyrell came to a stand of oaks. He tied the reins and crept to the opposite side. A quarter of a mile farther east was a belt of trees. He could see figures moving among them—Axel's bunch.

To the north, about a mile, stood a farmhouse and barn. With a start, he realized it was the Sether place.

Tyrell took off his hat and scratched his head. He was at a loss what to do. He couldn't go riding up to that many armed men and demand they tell him what they were up to. And he couldn't reach Roy Sether's house without being seen. His only recourse was to sit and wait.

Sinking down, Tyrell plucked a blade of grass and stuck it between his teeth. He'd rather be back with Bessie. He imagined the two of them on her settee, imagined him being bold enough to take her hand, imagined . . .

"Move and you're dead," said a voice behind him, and a hard object touched the back of his head.

Tyrell froze.

The man who called himself Axel Jones came around in front of him, a revolver cocked and steady in his hand. "Fancy meetin' you again," he said.

Since the hard object was still pressed to the back of Tyrell's head, he knew there was someone else behind him. "What is this?"

"You shouldn't have stuck your big nose in," Axel said.

"How did you spot me?"

"I'm good at what I do."

"And what is it you do, exactly?"

"You haven't guessed yet?"

The man behind Tyrell said, "We can't just kill him. He's a lawman."

"So?" Axel said.

"Discreet, remember?" the other man said.

"Discreet hell," Axel said. "He can identify me." And with that, he bent and drew a dagger from his boot and plunged it into Tyrell's chest.

39

It was Martha who came up with the idea. Along about the middle of the afternoon she'd turned to Roy and said, "I don't want Rondo to go yet. To show him how grateful we are we should hold a farewell gathering. Invite the Klines and the Beards. Andy can ride over and invite them."

Roy had stared at her. This was the same woman who'd wanted him to force the Southerner to leave.

"Well?" Martha prompted when he didn't respond. "What do you think?"

"I think it's a wonderful idea, dear," Roy tactfully told her.

Now it was close to evening. The sun was low on the horizon and would soon set. Two buckboards were parked out front. The women were in the kitchen seeing to refreshments and chatting up a storm. Roy sat in the parlor with Tom and Moses, drinking beer.

"You're lucky you're still alive," Tom was saying, and

sipped. "You say you hauled the bodies out and buried them and you're not going to tell anyone?"

"Not even the marshal?" Moses asked.

"I was going to, yes," Roy said, "but Rondo pointed out they could have friends who might come after us. He says he's seen it happen before."

"He should know," Moses said.

Tom nodded. "Where is the guest of honor, anyhow? Shouldn't he be here?"

"He should," Roy said, and rose. "I'll go see what's keeping him." He set his glass on the table and went out and over to the barn. He stopped when he heard voices, and peeked in.

General Lee was out of his stall and saddled. Rondo James was standing next to the Palomino with his arms folded, smiling.

Matt was petting it. "One day I want a horse like yours. He's awful fine."

"He's the best friend I have," Rondo said.

"A horse?" Matt laughed. "I thought only people can be friends."

"Anything can be. A horse, a dog, a cat. Some critters are just pets but some are friends."

"I wish you weren't going," Matt said. "I'll miss our talks."

"You have your pa and ma to talk to," Rondo said. "You don't need me."

"You're my friend," Matt said. "And you're Pa's, too, aren't you?"

"I think highly of him," Rondo said. "More than of most men."

"He likes you." Matt patted General Lee's neck. "My ma will miss you, too. I heard her say so."

"You have a good family, Matthew. Always be there for them and they'll always be there for you."

"Sir?"

Rondo straightened. "We should go in. They're prob-ably waitin'."

Roy smiled and entered. "So here you are," he said. "The party has started and you two are nowhere around."

"I came out to say so long," Matt said sadly.

"Plenty of time for that later." Roy clapped him on the shoulder. "Your mother baked a pie for the occasion and I've never known you to pass up pie."

Matt beamed and scooted off.

"That's a good boy you have there," Rondo James said.

They strolled out into the waning light. A robin was warbling. Over in the coop, the chickens were clucking and settling in for the night.

"I'm obliged for all you've done for me," Rondo said. "I can never repay the debt I owe."

"What debt? Friends help friends for free."

The parlor was bustling. The women had come out of the kitchen and Andy and Sally had come downstairs and everyone was talking and laughing and having a fine time.

Roy reclaimed his beer and drank and mostly listened until an elbow nudged him.

"You're quiet tonight," Martha said.

Roy shrugged.

"You're sorry to see him go."

"He's a good man. All those stories they tell aren't true."

"People don't care about the truth," Martha said. "They hear what they want to hear." She looked around. "I'd better light the lamps. It's getting dark out."

"I'll get the one in the kitchen," Roy offered. "I need more beer, anyway." It was a nightly ritual to light all the lamps at the same time and get it over with. He walked down the hall. The matches were in a box in a drawer under the counter. He lit the lamp and blew the match out. He was near the window, and went over and parted the curtains and gazed out over his farm. Night was on the cusp of falling. A few early stars sparkled. He was about to close the curtains when he thought he glimpsed movement, far off. A deer, maybe, although he couldn't be sure.

Roy refilled his glass and rejoined the others. For an hour or so they made small talk, the women gay, the men doing more drinking. At one point Moses leaned toward Roy and said quietly, "This weak bladder of mine. I need to use the outhouse."

"Can you find it or do you need help?" Roy joked.

"I haven't had that much, thank you very much." Moses headed down the hall to go out the back door.

Roy became involved in a conversation with Tom about planting and forgot about Moses until he was nudged a second time. Only now it was Tilda.

"Where did my husband get to?"

"Nature called," Roy said.

"He's been gone a good while," Tilda mentioned. "What did he do, fall in?"

Both Roy and Tom laughed.

"I'll go see," Roy said. He went to the kitchen and opened the back door. A half-moon gave light to see by. He was about to step outside and call to Moses when he saw two men, crouched low, over near the outhouse, holding long guns in their hands.

For a few heartbeats Roy was riveted in astonishment. Recovering his wits, he bounded back inside. He shut the door and threw the bolt. He was about to run to the parlor when it occurred to him to douse the lamp. As he did so he saw silhouettes move across the curtains.

Roy raced down the hall to the parlor. Everyone was talking and didn't notice him and he was about to shout a warning when he saw that the front door was opening. Without hesitation he hurtled toward it, thinking to slam it shut and bolt it, but it swung wide before he could reach it.

Moses Beard ducked in and closed it again, saying, "There are men with guns out there."

"I know," Roy said.

"I was coming out of the outhouse and saw them and snuck around before they spotted me," Moses said.

Roy reached past him and threw the bolt. "Into the parlor," he directed, and went to follow.

The clomp of a boot on the porch warned him that more intruders were out front.

Roy ran down the hall. The conversations had ceased.

Moses was telling about the men.

"I saw them, too," Roy confirmed.

Suddenly Rondo James was in motion. He darted to the first lamp and blew it out and sprang to the other lamp and blew it out, as well.

"What in the world?" Irene Kline blurted.

"Everyone get down," the Southerner said. His Colt Navies glinted in the near darkness as he moved to the front window.

Careful to stand to one side, he used the barrel of a Colt to move the curtain.

Shock and disbelief had rooted most of the others.

"Do as he says," Roy said. Turning, he took the stairs three at a stride and raced into his bedroom. He'd left his Winchester propped in a corner. Grabbing it, he moved to the window and peered out.

Below were more men with guns.

Dear God, Roy thought, how many are out there? He

hurried back down. Everyone was low to the floor, Martha with her arms over Sally and Matt.

Rondo James was still at the front window.

"What's going on?" Martha said. "Why are those men out there?"

"I intend to find out," Roy said, and joined Rondo James.

"What do you make of it?"

"They must be after me," the Southerner said. "I've brought more trouble down on your heads."

"Maybe not," Roy said. "Remember the McWhirtles and the Olanders? Maybe these men were to blame."

"There are more than four," Rondo said.

Tom Kline came over, crabbing on his hands and feet. "What do you want me to do? I didn't think to bring a gun. I thought all this was over."

"Listen," Rondo said.

There was more clomping on the porch, and other sounds Roy couldn't quite make out.

"What are they up to?" Tom whispered.

Roy was wondering the same thing. "I think they have the house surrounded."

"One of us should go out and demand to know what they're up to," Tom suggested.

"They'd shoot you dead," Rondo James said.

"You don't know that," Tom replied.

"We don't need to go out," Roy said, and raising his head, he hollered, "You on my porch! Who are you and what are you doing here?"

The noises stopped, but only for a few moments. No one answered him.

"I have half a mind to march out there and confront them," Tom said.

"We stay put. Make them come to us," Rondo said.

"Pa?" Sally said anxiously.

"Be still," Martha said. "So far they haven't done anything."

Roy had a thought. "You women should go upstairs. Take the kids. If shooting breaks out, you'll be safer."

It was plain Martha didn't want to go but she said, "Come along, children."

A scraping noise prompted Roy to move to the other window. It looked out on the barn. He saw men going back and forth between it and the house.

Moses and Andy crept over, and Moses remarked, "It's strange they don't say anything."

Roy glanced at his son. "You should be upstairs with your mother."

"I'm not a kid," Andy said.

Moses put an eye to the crack between the curtains. "Will you look at that. What are they carrying?"

Two men were coming from the barn with their arms filled.

Roy was filled with sudden dread. "Why, that's hay or straw."

The pair dumped it at the side of the house and went back for more.

"Oh God," Roy said.

Over at the front window Rondo James gave voice to Roy's fear. "Whoever these gents are, they're fixin' to set your house on fire."

40

"Surely not," Roy said, but there was the evidence right before his eyes: another man dropped an armful and hurried back to the barn for more.

"I don't believe this," Tom echoed his sentiments. "Who *are* they? Why would they try to burn you out?"

"Roasting people alive," Moses said in horror. "I couldn't ever be so cruel."

Roy moved to the front door and pressed his ear to it. He heard footsteps, and rustling. "You out there!" he yelled. "Someone had better talk to me or we'll start shooting."

The sounds stopped. There was muffled talk, and after a minute someone came to the other side of the door.

"Roy Sether, I take it? I hear you threatened to start shootin'," said a man with a drawl.

"Who are you?" Roy said.

"You don't need to know my name," the man said. "It wouldn't mean anything to you if you did."

"How many men are with you?"

The man on the other side of the door laughed.

"You can't mean to burn my house down," Roy said. "Not with us in it."

"What good would it do to burn it down with you not in it?" the man said, and laughed.

"What have we done? Why are you doing this? Are you the same ones who killed the McWhirtles and the Olanders?"

"Questions, questions," the man said.

"I want answers, damn you."

"You should have left when you had the chance."

"What are you talking about?"

Someone else out there made a comment and the man on the other side of the door said gruffly, "I wouldn't talk to me like that again, were I you. I'm not an idiot. He has no idea what this is about."

Roy said, "There are women and children in here."

"So?"

"So you can't mean to kill them, too."

"Why not?"

Anger burst in Roy like a cannonball. He stepped back and pointed the Winchester at the door—and then lowered it. The men outside might riddle the house in retaliation. "Please," he said. "I'm sure we can talk this out."

"I'm sure we can't," the man said.

"I won't let you burn my house down."

"Listen, farmer," the man said. "We have the doors covered. We have every window covered. You try to bust out and you'll be shot in your tracks."

"*Why?*" Roy cried.

"Because you're a flea on a mean dog and the dog is about to scratch you off."

"That makes no sense."

"Not to you," the man said, and his drawl disappeared. "You have it so cozy, you have blinders on."

"Are you drunk?" Roy said.

"Listen. This valley of yours, Thunder Valley, is a nice place to live. Everyone is kind and polite and looks out for their neighbor. Isn't that how it is?"

"More or less," Roy said, puzzled as to what the man was getting at.

"Outside this valley life isn't cozy. Life is dog-eat-dog, Sether. The big dogs eat the little dogs and you are a little dog."

"People aren't dogs," was all Roy could think of to say.

The man laughed. "Anything else you want to know?"

"You haven't told me anything."

"Yes, I have," the man said. "You haven't listened."

Moses had come up behind Roy and cleared his throat, "I have a question, mister."

"Who might you be?"

"Moses Beard. I have a farm down the road. My wife and I came over to visit."

"The wrong place at the wrong time," the man said. "You should have picked another night. What's your question, Mr. Beard?"

"How do you plan to get away with this? A federal marshal is in Teton. He'll hear about it and call up a posse and track you down."

"Wishful thinking."

"How so?"

"He's dead."

"No!" Moses exclaimed.

Roy smothered a growing sense of despair. "You're just saying that."

"I stabbed him myself," the man bragged.

"I'd like to stab you," Roy bristled.

"Now you're learnin'," the man said, his drawl back.

Roy had more to say but a hand tapped him on the shoulder.

It was Rondo James. The Southerner put a finger to his lips and motioned for Roy and Moses to move away from the door. When they were out of earshot, the pistoleer whispered, "You know what he's doin', don't you?"

"What?" Roy said.

"Stallin' so those others can pile as much as they want around your house."

Roy hadn't thought of that. "We have to stop them."

"There's only one thing we can do," Rondo James said. "A whole lot of people are about to die."

The pain brought Tyrell back. He was adrift in a black abyss, floating as if on air, when a sharp pang made him open his eyes and gasp for breath. His vision swam, and he blinked to clear it. His chest felt wet, and his arms and legs were tingling.

Tyrell was on his back under the trees. He tried to rise onto his elbows but he was too weak. Around him the night was still and quiet. He remembered the men who jumped him, remembered the burning sensation when the dagger plunged into his chest.

"I'm still breathin'?" Tyrell marveled. The only explanation was that the blade had missed his heart. He looked down at himself. Even in the dark he could see a stain. He managed to move his right hand to his chest and groped his shirt. It was wet but he hadn't bled nearly as much as he'd expect. He pried at the buttons and slipped two fingers underneath. As best he could tell, the knife had glanced off his sternum.

"I'm lucky as can be," Tyrell said. He braced himself

and got his elbows under him. From there it wasn't too difficult to prop himself against an oak and slowly sit up. His strength was returning.

Tyrell's elation at being alive evaporated. He'd been careless. Axel Jones and the others should never have caught on that he was trailing them.

Axel. If it was the last thing he ever did, Tyrell would bring him to justice. He gazed at the distant lights of the farmhouse. The Sether place. Roy Sether must be warned. Or was it Rondo James they were after? They hadn't said.

Tyrell checked his holster. Jones hadn't taken his revolver. He turned his head but couldn't see his horse. Gritting his teeth, he used the tree to make it to his feet. A light-headed sensation came over him, and he had to stand there until it went away.

Tyrell slowly moved toward where his horse should be. Wonder of wonders, it was still there. He gripped the saddle horn in both hands and put his brow to the saddle. He needed to take it slow. One step at a time. As much as he wanted to get to Roy and Rondo, he couldn't do them any good if he passed out.

Tyrell had to lift his leg three times before he hooked the stirrup. His chest hammering, he pulled himself up. More dizziness caused him to sway. He clutched the saddle horn until it passed.

"Damn," Tyrell said. His stomach was churning. "Don't let me be sick," he said. He clucked and tapped his spurs and rode out of the stand.

The house was a long way off.

Tyrell hoped he would make it. Another wave of weakness made him bow his head. When he looked up again he couldn't see the farmhouse.

"What the . . . ?" Tyrell said, and realized the lights

had been extinguished and the windows were dark. That wasn't a good sign. It was too early for Roy and Martha to be turning in.

Tyrell rode faster. The pain in his chest was almost unbearable. He needed a sawbones but his duty came first.

Tyrell grew hot and his skin prickled as if he had a rash. His mouth was dry and he broke out in a sweat. He was in a bad way. He should stop and rest but he pushed on.

Tyrell kept thinking he'd hear shots but he didn't. It suggested the Sethers were still alive. Or maybe Axel and his friends had killed the Sethers quietly. Even so, there was Rondo James to deal with. Tyrell could see them taking the Sethers by surprise but not that ornery Rebel. They'd have a fight on their hands with him.

Tyrell chuckled. Here he was, hurrying to help a man who once fought for an army that, among other things, was defending the right of white folks to keep people with his skin color against their will. Life was plumb silly sometimes.

More nausea brought him to a stop. Sweat poured from his pores and bile rose in his gorge and he was almost sick to his stomach.

"You can do this, Tyrell," he rallied, and gigged his mount. Lives were at stake. He must do what he must do, and his wound be damned.

Out of nowhere he came on a whole lot of horses. Axel and his bunch had left them about two hundred yards from the farmhouse and gone ahead on foot.

Tyrell drew rein and dismounted. The effort cost him, and he clung to the saddle until his head stopped spinning. He tried to pull his Winchester from the scabbard and gave it up as a lost cause.

That was all right. He had his six-shooter. He drew it
and shuffled toward the house, taking small steps so as
not to trip and fall. If he did, he may not be able to get
back up.

It seemed an eternity before something hove in his
path. The odor told him what it was. He moved around
to the side and leaned against the outhouse.

Over at the farmhouse, figures moved. A lot of them,
coming and going from the barn.

Tyrell tried to fathom what they were up to. They appeared to be carrying something. He was about to move
into the open when he spied a man who wasn't taking
part. The man was at the rear of the house, covering it
with a rifle.

His back was to Tyrell.

Gripping his revolver tighter, Tyrell crept forward.
His vision swam and he feared he'd collapse. Not now, he
chided himself. He needed to hold out, for the Sethers'
sake.

From the front of the house came muffled voices.

The man with the rifle had the stock resting on his
thigh and was holding the rifle by the barrel. His other
hand was on a six-gun on his hip.

Tyrell extended his arm. He'd forgotten to cock the
hammer and now he didn't dare; the man would hear it.
He had to get right up to him.

Twenty feet more. That was all. Without warning the
pain in his chest became twice as bad. Waves of agony
washed over him and he stopped. He must have groaned
because the man with the rifle glanced back and saw
him.

The next instant the night crashed to gunfire.

41

The man on the porch had made a mistake. While he kept Roy Sether talking so the others could pile hay and straw around the house, Rondo James was on the move. He went from the window at the front to a window on the east side and then a window on the west side.

Only then did Rondo inform Roy that there was only one thing they could do.

"What do you have in mind?" Roy asked.

"We have to take the fight to them before they can light the fire."

"You want us to go out there and start shooting?"

"Not us," Rondo said. "Me." It was against his nature to stay cooped up. He was an ex–Confederate raider. He'd learned the art of war from guerrillas who lived by the code of strike fast and strike hard. "You stay here and shoot anyone who breaks in."

"Just you alone against all of them?" Roy said. "That's

not right. This is my house. My home. I can't stand by and do nothing while you risk your life for me and mine."

Rondo looked at the front door and smiled a cold smile. "They aim to kill me too. I have as much at stake as you do." He nodded at the stairs to the second floor. "Well, almost as much."

"I should help you."

"Listen to Mr. James," Moses Beard said. "He's right. You have Martha and the kids to think of."

Tom Kline nodded. "Your family comes first."

"Stay with Roy," Rondo said to them. "And whatever you do, don't any of you go outside." He turned and hastened along the hall to the kitchen. Quietly throwing the bolt, he opened the back door a crack. A lone assassin with a rifle stood about fifteen feet off, watching the house. He was about to burst out when he spied someone behind the assassin, shambling toward him. It was so dark that Rondo couldn't see the second man's face. But then he realized, no, it was the man's face that was dark, and he realized who it must be even as the assassin glanced over his shoulder.

Rondo flung the door wide and bounded out. The man with the rifle had started to turn, and saw him. For an instant the man was riveted with indecision—should he shoot at Rondo or should he shoot at the man coming up behind him?

Rondo drew and shot him in the face and didn't give the falling body another look as he ran past it. "Tyrell?" he said.

The lawman swayed and said thickly, "Thanks for savin' me. I can't hardly think straight."

Rondo saw a plate-sized dark circle on Gibson's shirt and said, "You were shot?"

"Stabbed." Tyrell's knees began to give.

"Here," Rondo said, and gripping him by the arm, he

quickly propelled the lawdog into the kitchen. "Stay inside. Roy and the others are at the front."

"Wait," Tyrell said.

But Rondo had already turned and was racing back out. The other assassins had heard the shot and some of them were coming on the run. He ran to the west corner, and stopped.

Boots pounded, and another rifleman rushed around the corner.

Rondo shot him in the face.

Shouts broke out on all sides. More boots drummed.

Taking a deep breath, Rondo hurtled toward the barn. He had a plan, such as it was: he would draw the assassins away from the farmhouse and the people inside. He snapped two shots at moving shadows. Fireflies flared, and the night boomed to multiple thunders. He felt a tug at his shoulder.

A man came hurrying out of the barn, his arms filled with hay. "What the hell?" he shouted, looking around in confusion. "Who's doing all the shooting?"

"Me," Rondo said, and shot him in the face. Then he was in the barn and moving down the aisle, replacing cartridges as he went.

The firing outside stopped.

Rondo swung onto his saddle, reined General Lee around, and stuck the reins between his teeth. With a pistol in each hand, he jabbed his spurs.

A fierce cry tore from his throat, the Rebel yell he had voiced in countless battles and skirmishes. It was both a savage challenge and an exultation. It was rage at the Yankee machine that had destroyed his homeland and fury at the nameless assassins who were out to destroy his friends. It was the very essence of what made him who and what he was.

General Lee exploded out of the barn. Some of the assassins were caught flat-footed and Rondo shot one on the right in the face and shot another in the face on the left.

On the front porch a six-gun cracked and Rondo felt a pain in his leg. He swept past the porch and reined around to the side of the house and shot a man in the face. Hauling on the reins, he wheeled General Lee. He charged around the front again, into a pair of men who were rushing after him. Both had shotguns. He swept his pearl-handled Navies out and up and shot both in the face.

Rondo didn't know how many were left but it didn't matter. He let out with another Rebel yell. He fired and a shotgun boomed but it missed and he shot a tall man in the face and a bearded man in the face.

There was another shot, just one, but not from Rondo's pistols.

Roy Sether was in the front doorway; it was his rifle that blasted.

A man dressed as a cowboy was struck in the back and knocked off the porch onto his hands and knees. He straightened and shifted and aimed a revolver at Roy, and Rondo shot him in the arm and the leg, both. The man cried out and dropped the six-shooter and clutched himself.

Rondo slid down and limped over, his Navies leveled. He kicked the revolver out of the man's reach.

"He was about to shoot you in the back," Roy said. "I didn't know what else to do."

"You did right fine." Rondo began to reload.

The cowboy inched a hand into a sleeve.

"No, you don't," Rondo said, and stomped on the hand. Finger bones cracked, and the man swore. Bending, Rondo discovered a derringer hideout. He tossed it and finished reloading. "Now, then. I've seen you in town. What's your name?"

The man grunted and said, "I didn't think it would be like this."

"Your name?" Rondo repeated.

"Today it's Axel Jones."

Rondo shot him in the other arm. When the thrashing and cursing stopped, he said, "Your real name."

The man grinned and said, "Abraham Lincoln."

Rondo shot him in the knee. The man bucked and howled and rolled back and forth, spittle flecking his lips. "Your real name or the next one is between your legs."

"Mather," the man said. "Jim Mather."

"Who hired you and these others?"

Covered with blood and shot to pieces, Mather was nonetheless still defiant. "How do you know they weren't working for me?"

"I warned you," Rondo said, and pointed a Navy at the man's private parts.

"Charlton Rank," Mather said.

"Now the big question. Why?"

"The railroad wants this land."

"Where do I find Rank?"

Mather told him.

"I reckon that's all I need from you," Rondo said, and put a slug from both pistols into his face.

Bodies littered the yards and tendrils and clouds of gun smoke hung in the air.

Rondo reloaded. He twirled the right Colt into its holster and twirled the left Colt into its holster, and looked up.

They were all on the porch. Roy and Martha and the kids, the Klines, and the Beards. Even Marshal Tyrell

Gibson, sagging against the wall. Their expressions were mixed.

Sally's look of horror struck Rondo to his marrow. He turned and limped to General Lee.

"Wait," Roy said, coming down the steps. "What are you doing?"

"What I should have done long ago." Rondo winced as he mounted. The hole in his leg was bleeding, but not much; the lead had gone clean through.

"You're not leaving?"

Rondo surveyed the carnage. "I've got somethin' that needs doin'."

Martha came to the rail. "Your leg. You've been shot. Get down and I'll bandage you."

Rondo glanced at Sally, and smiled. "No need." He went to rein around but Roy put a hand on his boot.

"Not like this. Come back in and stay until morning."

"You're a good man, Roy Sether," Rondo said. "Take good care of this family of yours." He jabbed with his good leg and held to a trot until he had put more than a mile behind him and he no longer had a lump in his throat. He coughed, and breathed deep, and settled down for the long ride.

Dawn had yet to break when Rondo reached Teton. Hardly anyone was abroad. He drew rein at the hitch rail in front of the Timberland and limped inside.

The lobby was empty. A desk clerk dozed at the front desk, chin in hand.

Rondo smacked the counter and the clerk gave a start and smoothed his jacket.

"May I help you?"

"Charlton Rank."

"What about him?"

"Which room?"

The climb to the third floor didn't do Rondo's leg any favors. He knocked, and when there was no answer, he knocked louder.

A balding man in a heavy robe opened the door. Stifling a yawn, he said sleepily, "What can I do for you, sir?"

"Are you Rank?"

"No. I'm Floyd, his manservant." He nodded at the closed door to what must be a bedroom. "Mr. Rank is asleep. He won't be up for a couple of hours yet."

Rondo brushed past.

"Hold on, sir," Floyd said, catching up. "I'll inform Mr. Rank that you're here."

Rondo stopped. "Make yourself scarce."

"Sir?"

Rondo swept his slicker aside, revealing the Colts. "I won't tell you twice."

Shaking his head, Floyd backed away. "You won't have to."

A hotel as fine as the Timberland, the door hinges were well oiled. The door opened silently.

A man snored loudly on a four-poster bed.

Rondo went up to it. Drawing his pistols, he tapped the sleeper on the nose. "Rank. Charlton Rank."

The man sputtered and muttered and opened his eyes. "What is it?" he demanded. "Who's there?"

"Are you Rank?"

"Who wants to know?" the man demanded. He saw the Colts, and stiffened. "What is this? Who are you and how did you get in here?" He didn't wait for an answer. "If you know who I am, you know I'm a very important man. Harm me and you'll be a fugitive for however long you live."

"You must reckon you're a mighty big man."

"Damn right I am," Charlton Rank said. "I have the ear of the governor. I have a senator and a congressman in my pocket. I will ask you one more time. Who the hell are you and what the hell do you think you're doing?"

"This," Rondo said, and pointed the pistols at his face.

42

The cool of a summer's evening brought relief from the heat. Cornstalks and wheat and oats had turned the brown of the tilled fields green with growing life.

Roy and Martha sat in their rocking chairs on the front porch. Roy had brought chairs from the parlor out for their guests and all four of them were sipping the delicious raspberry tea Martha made.

"I wonder where he got to?" Martha was saying. "I still think of him a lot."

"So do I," Roy said.

Tyrell nodded, and smiled. "He was quite a man, that Rondo James."

"The way you all talk, I wish I had met him," Bessie lamented.

"A sheriff saw him in Denver," Tyrell said. "I know that for a fact. Later there was word of him bein' spotted in Kansas City and Saint Louis. The last report I got, a man claimed to have talked to him in Lexington, Kentucky."

"Denver, Kansas City, Saint Louis, Lexington," Roy recited. "He was heading east."

"To where?" Martha said.

Roy pondered. "I suspect he was going home to Virginia."

"After all this time?"

Tyrell nodded. "I think Roy is right, ma'am. Maybe Rondo James got tired of all the killin'. Maybe he finally accepted that the war was over."

"How about you?" Roy said. "How's your chest?"

Thunking it with his fist, Tyrell said, "Fine as can be. The doc says I'm healed."

"He also said you were the luckiest man ever born," Bessie said. "You could have died."

"Look at the bright side," Tyrell said. "It made me rethink things." He glanced down at the spot on his belt where his badge used to be. "I don't miss it as much as I thought I would."

Bessie's eyes twinkled mischievously. "Runnin' a boardinghouse has its advantages, Mr. Gibson."

"That it does, Mrs. Gibson," Tyrell said, and laughed.

Martha drank tea and slowly rocked. "I hear tell the Jacksons are back. And someone bought the McWhirtle place."

"Life goes on." Roy stood and moved to the rail and gazed out over his fields. "Life always goes on."

"Thank God," Martha said.